T0130181

THE GARDEN OF DECEIT

Another Luke Tremayne
Adventure. A Daughter
Sacrificed England Early 1657

Geoff Quaife

Order this book online at www.trafford.com
or email orders@trafford.com

Most Trafford titles are also available at major online book retailers.

© Copyright 2016 Geoff Quaife.
All rights reserved. No part of this publication may be reproduced, stored in a
retrieval system, or transmitted, in any form or by any means, electronic, mechanical,
photocopying, recording, or otherwise, without the written prior permission of the author.

Print information available on the last page.

ISBN: 978-1-4907-7197-7 (sc)
ISBN: 978-1-4907-7198-4 (hc)
ISBN: 978-1-4907-7199-1 (e)

Library of Congress Control Number: 2016906586

Because of the dynamic nature of the Internet, any web addresses or links contained in
this book may have changed since publication and may no longer be valid. The views
expressed in this work are solely those of the author and do not necessarily reflect the
views of the publisher, and the publisher hereby disclaims any responsibility for them.

Any people depicted in stock imagery provided by Thinkstock are models,
and such images are being used for illustrative purposes only.
Certain stock imagery © Thinkstock.

Trafford rev.   04/26/2016

www.trafford.com
North America & international
toll-free: 1 888 232 4444 (USA & Canada)
fax: 812 355 4082

THE LUKE TREMAYNE ADVENTURES

(In chronological order of the events portrayed)

CHARACTERS

Cromwell's Men

Luke Tremayne (Colonel)	Cromwell's special agent
Sir Evan Williams (Captain)	Luke's deputy
John Martin (Lieutenant)	Luke's third in command
Bevan "Strad" Stradling	Luke's sergeant

The Conspirators

Miles "Yarrow" Thornton	Hired radical assassin
Tom Archer	Lifeguard
Belladonna, Foxglove, Thrift	Code names of the Royalist
Woodruff, Woad, and Weld	conspirators

The Army for Flanders

Christopher, Lord Liffey (General)	Former colonial governor
Sir Peter Marlowe (Colonel)	Liffey's deputy
Richard Grey (Colonel)	Infantry commander
David Halliburton (Lieutenant Colonel)	Cavalry commander
Robert Peebles (Major)	Shipwreck survivor
Anthony, Viscount Audley (Major)	Artillery expert
Timothy Redmond (Lieutenant)	Young officer
John Blair (Captain)	A spy?

The Female Suspects

Lady Isadore Liffey	Sister of Christopher
Lady Penelope Marlowe	Wife of Sir Peter Marlowe
Lady Evadne Rede	Wife of Richard Grey
Lady Ursula Audley	Daughter of Viscount Audley
Lady Lydia Veldor	Potential wife of Lord Liffey
Sophia, Baroness Veldor	Mother of Lydia
Lady Felicity Harrison	Betrothed of Audley
Lady Grace Harrison, also	Sister of Felicity
Grace, Countess of Merrick	
Rose Grant	Friend of Colonel Halliburton
Veronica Grant	Cousin of Rose
Jane Castle	Wife of Jared

Others

John Garrett, Wally Coyfe	Petty thieves
Harry Haybittle	
William Acton	Thurloe's agent
John Greenwich	Thurloe's agent
Jared Castle (Captain)	Thurloe's agent
Asa Glover (Captain, later Colonel)	Commander, Cromwell's Lifeguard
Simon Cobb (Colonel, later General)	Experienced soldier/ administrator
Barnaby Brett	Sophia's steward

Referred To

Baldwin, Earl of Merrick   Grace's husband

John, Baron Veldor   Sophia's husband

Earl of Liffey   Christopher and Isadore's
                             father

Alphonse Dupont   Lydia's valet

Real Historical Personages

Oliver Cromwell   Lord Protector

John Thurloe   Cromwell's intelligence head

John Desborough   Senior general

Charles Fleetwood   Senior general

John Lambert   Senior general

George Monk (General)   Military governor of Scotland

Charles Stuart (Charles II) Exiled king

Historical Prologue

At the beginning of 1657, conspiracies escalated among Royalists, Republicans, religious radicals, and disaffected senior officers of the army. Discontent was fueled by Parliament's decisions to offer Oliver Cromwell the Crown, abolish the rule of the major generals, and increase taxation to continue the unpopular war with Spain. Royalists prepared for an invasion, awaiting only Spanish money and troops to launch the attack and an English port able to accommodate the invasion forces. Many former supporters of Parliament and the Protector viewed the attempted recreation of monarchy as a betrayal of the principles that had driven them to remove Charles Stuart. Senior army officers, in particular, resented their loss of power in an increasingly civilian-dominated regime.

Elements within these opposition groups plotted to destabilize the government by assassinating Cromwell.

Government agents had a simple task: uncover and abort these attempts and ensure that the disparate opposition did not combine.

The task was complicated by the potential conflict between the military and civilian arms of the administration.

It was made even more difficult as alleged public plots and assassination attempts, and the countermeasures adopted to thwart them, were often a cover for personal ambition, vendettas, and murder.

In this complex and confused environment, Cromwell turned to his top investigator: Luke Tremayne.

1

Whitehall, London, January 1657

Luke, his deputy Evan, and sergeant Strad waited in an antechamber off the Banqueting House within Whitehall, where Oliver Cromwell—Lord Protector of the Commonwealth of England, Scotland, and Ireland—received officials and visitors.

As he waited for an audience, Luke thought of earlier times.

He had been stationed in Whitehall when it was an army base immediately following the defeat of the king.

As soon as the troops left, the republican government allowed the old palace to disintegrate.

During more than five years of official neglect, the precinct became a small city as its dozens of buildings and some fifteen hundred rooms attracted a variety of unauthorized inhabitants.

Now it housed Cromwell's court, Council of State, and his domestic quarters.

Surprisingly, when once more it became the center of power, not all the squatters were removed.

Luke, who in the past had guarded the person of Oliver Cromwell, shuddered as he assessed the difficulties of securing the Protector's safety in this sprawling warren.

Their wait ended when a black-and-gold liveried retainer told them that Cromwell would not receive them in the Banqueting House but in a more private location.

They were to follow him.

After a short walk, the servant led them into a building at the back of the Banqueting House that overlooked a neatly manicured garden.

Evan and Strad remained in its small entrance hall as the servant led Luke deeper into the edifice to an imposing door, which was guarded by two well-armed bodyguards, splendidly arrayed in red jackets with an excess of gold braid, shining breast plates, and plumed helmets—a display of pomp that irritated the veteran soldier.

The door opened from within, and Cromwell emerged.

He embraced his longtime comrade and then guided him into the room to a cushioned bench under one of the large windows.

Cromwell was effusive as he sat beside his old friend. "It's good to talk to you alone. It is like old times. It is almost ten years since I sent you on your first adventure—to Ireland."

The moment of nostalgia was short-lived.

The window under which they sat suddenly shattered, showering them with shards of glass.

Cromwell lurched forward, clutching his head, and fell to the floor.

Before Luke could move to help, there was a massive explosion.

Luke was hit by flying masonry and rendered semi-conscious.

The remaining windows were blown in, and a collection of glass and ceramic ornaments that had rested on several tables were pulverized.

The furniture itself disintegrated into various-sized planks and dangerous splinters.

Clouds of dust and smoke rose through the badly holed floorboards.

Luke's first vision on recovering his faculties was of the Lord Protector with blood streaming from his face, lying inertly beside him.

Luke was distraught. Cromwell had been assassinated in his presence.

Before Luke's distress escalated, Cromwell opened his eyes, winked, and jumped to his feet. "Years of experience taught me that when confronted by gunfire and you are in no position to retaliate, hit the floor. The initial interruption was a musket shot, which missed me, although some glass has cut my cheek. But what was that last explosion?"

"Initially, I thought it was a mortar or grenade, but by the appearance of the flooring, it was a bomb planted under the room," replied a shaken and groggy Luke.

The two men became aware of the panic and commotion outside the door.

The explosion had jammed it tightly shut, resisting any attempts to open it.

Cromwell shouted to be heard over the din of the would-be rescue, "We are fine. Take your time and do the job properly!"

Outside the shattered room, John Thurloe, Cromwell's leading minister, screamed at the men around him to dismantle the door and sent others to fetch implements to force it open.

Evan, who had waited in an adjacent room, tried to calm the frantic minister.

Evan took control of the confused troops and courtiers.

"Slow and steady is the best approach. Use the thick sideboard as a battering ram against the wall. Attack the panels with your pikes and halberds! Splinter the wood! Create a hole big enough for our trapped comrades to squeeze through. Forget the door! It is too thick to give way quickly."

Evan was annoyed when Thurloe withdrew from the rescue attempt, and engaged in conversation with a lifeguard.

Suddenly a now ashen-faced minister raised his voice and directed his appeal to Evan, "Captain Williams, you don't have time for slow and steady. There are other bombs ready to explode at any minute. We must get His Highness and Colonel Tremayne out immediately."

A reinvigorated group now armed with axes and machetes quickly carved a sizable hole in the paneling beside the jammed door.

Thurloe poked his head through the gap and emotionally informed Cromwell and Tremayne of the remaining bombs.

Everyone was evacuated to the far end of the garden.

A protective detail of Cromwell's infantry lifeguards surrounded him.

Luke, his two comrades, and Thurloe lingered at the entrance of the bombed building.

Thurloe pushed a young soldier in front of Luke. "This is trooper Tom Archer. He intended to shoot the Protector two weeks past. He came to me minutes ago and reported that a man had placed three bombs within Whitehall. They were all due to explode within minutes of one another. One has obviously just done so."

Luke asked Archer, "What type of explosives is being used?"

"Concoctions of gunpowder, tar, and pitch placed in a basket. Long fuses have been attached to the ingredients. The cords are already lit as the bomber aimed for maximum effect by exploding all the bombs at once."

"Where are the remaining bombs?" demanded Luke.

"I do not know. My task, with that of other marksmen, was to cover the exits and kill the Lord Protector as he runs from the burning building. I was to cover the main door. Others are watching the remaining exits."

Luke turned to Evan. "If the bomber planned this carefully for maximum effect, he would have placed all three bombs close together and in an area where His Highness is known to spend considerable time."

Thurloe interrupted, "Oliver regularly works in a small room next to the one that exploded. Under that room is a unused chapel. An explosive placed there would complete the job that the first bomb began. It would demolish this building completely. If it had gone off close to the first, we would all be dead."

Luke ran down a narrow staircase to the chapel.

To his relief, just inside its door, he found a long fuse that had prematurely extinguished itself.

He turned to run back up the stairs to give the good news to his comrades when a side door opened.

A figure emerged, and before Luke had time to defend himself, the stranger struck him on the head with the base of a large candlestick.

He fell to the floor unconscious.

While Luke was unconscious, the stranger moved into the chapel and relit the fuse.

As he left, he kicked Luke viciously in the face.

Luke bled from the reopened cuts created by the glass shards; and as a result of the kicking, his mouth and nose oozed, continuing trickles of blood.

The kick had surprisingly galvanized the dazed Luke into full consciousness for a second or more during which time he saw his assailant disappear.

He could smell burning cordite and tried to stand, but the effort proved too much.

He fell back, lapsing again into unconsciousness.

The burning fuse neared a gigantic basket of explosives.

Luke, momentarily regaining his senses, dragged himself behind a heavy wooden pew and, as the bomb was about to blow, intuitively curled into a ball.

Nothing happened.

Strad, concerned that his colonel had not reemerged from the damaged building, went down into the chapel.

He found Luke moving in and out of consciousness and the burning fuse within a foot of the basket.

He pulled the fuse away from its destination and half carried, half dragged Luke back up the stairs.

He was placed under a large tree while an apothecary and cunning woman were sent for to dress his wounds.

Thurloe asked him, "Can you tell us anything about your attacker?"

"Only that when he kicked me in the head, it altered my line of vision. He had red hair."

"It fits. Archer said the assassin was a redhead, and my prime suspect is also a redhead. He goes by the ridiculous code name of Yarrow," muttered Thurloe.

Cromwell was still surrounded at close quarters by his infantry lifeguards, who provided a protective shield with their own bodies while the cavalry began a search for the marksmen and bomber.

Evan was alarmed.

He sent an urgent message to the commander of the Protector's personal detail.

"Move His Highness to the garden bench surrounded by dense shrubs. At the moment, he is an easy target for marksmen in the upper stories of the surrounding buildings despite the close body positioning of your men."

Within minutes, Evan was relieved to see Cromwell and his protective shell of lifeguards move away from the crowd and open ground to a sheltered garden nook in the corner of the privy garden.

Evan questioned Archer further.

He had been shackled to give the chief assassin the impression that he had been captured. "Trooper, where is the third bomb?"

"I have no idea."

Evan was distracted by an anguished groan from Luke, who was valiantly trying to stand up.

Luke pointed in the direction of Cromwell.

Luke appeared frozen to the spot and rendered speechless.

Evan followed the direction of his outstretched arm.

A gardener in the distance was pushing a wheelbarrow toward Cromwell's group.

Its cargo of leaves was smoking.

"My god," exclaimed Evan. "The bomb is in the wheelbarrow. The aroma of burning leaves will conceal the smell of burning cord. He has almost reached the Protector."

Without awaiting orders, Strad, Luke's sergeant who had not left his colonel's side since Luke had emerged from the disused chapel, grabbed a musket from one of the sentries, primed it, and fired in the direction of the gardener.

The shot hit the would-be assassin who dropped the barrow to the ground and raced away through the hedge.

All parties were then stopped in their tracks by a sudden and effective explosion that not only shattered the barrow but left a large hole in the manicured Whitehall lawn.

Shrapnel flew everywhere.

The experienced battlefield veteran Cromwell once more dived to the ground—with his lifeguards on top of him.

Eventually, the area was completely cleared, and Cromwell was escorted safely to his private quarters.

2

Next day Luke met Cromwell and John Thurloe in an alcove of the Banqueting House to continue the meeting that had been curtailed by the explosion.

Cromwell was direct. "John will brief you on why you're here, although our experience yesterday epitomizes the problem most succinctly."

Thurloe, chief minister and head of intelligence, responded, "My agents recently uncovered a new and potentially dangerous organization calling themselves the Garden, whose aim is twofold: assassinate His Highness and seize control of sections of the army in order to overthrow the present government. Yesterday's attempt was the latest in a well-planned program."

"Little chance of subverting the army! Although there is discontent within it over rumors that Your Highness will accept the Crown, the bulk of the troops remain loyal," pontificated Luke.

Thurloe agreed, "True of the veterans of the New Model Army, which His Highness commanded for so long. Unfortunately, most of these men are in Scotland and Ireland. Recently, to meet our obligations under a treaty with France, we undertook to provide a new army to fight side by side with the French against the Spaniards in Flanders. We could not deplete our troops in either Celtic nation and have had to recruit two completely new brigades."

"That should be easy. The numbers in the national army have declined over recent years. There must be a ready pool of experienced veterans in need of employment," suggested Luke somewhat naively.

"That colonel is precisely the problem. The experienced soldiers clamoring for enlistment are either men whom His Highness dismissed over the last decade or men who in our recent conflicts fought for the king. The Garden is targeting this new army. My agents have established that one of the officers already appointed to the Flanders contingent is part of the conspiracy, and the leader of the group is a woman who is about to join the household of the general appointed to command this section of the Flanders army. Unfortunately, I have no names."

"The Garden is planning to kill His Highness and in the chaos use this new army to topple the regime before you can recall our loyal veterans from Ireland and Scotland," summarized Luke.

"Even worse! The conspirators expect a small fleet and army of Irish nationalists to assist them."

"That will have little support. Even the men around the king do not want a foreign invasion of England, especially if led by the Irish. How could they raise a fleet and army? Your agents and our military command between them know where every potential Irish troublemaker is located."

"Not quite! There have been disturbing reports from the Indies for months regarding a mysterious fleet and army of Irishmen. Your former deputy, Colonel Cobb, resigned his job as governor of Edinburgh Castle to accept a more junior position as deputy governor and military commandant of Jamaica to investigate. He was convinced that hundreds of Irishmen who disappeared during our campaign to gain a foothold on the larger islands of the Caribbean were being organized into an army by his twin brother, a nationalist fanatic."

"Cobb was always obsessed with the rebellious Irish and his treacherous brother. Is his brother behind this army?"

"Probably! The rumor is given credence by the large number of ships that have disappeared in the last two years in Caribbean waters. If they have not fallen foul to the weather or to pirates as alleged, they would make a sizable fleet to transport the Irish army to England."

"Is there any real evidence?" asked Luke.

"You may in time be able to tell me," answered Thurloe.

"Surely, you are not sending me to the Indies?"

Cromwell smiled. "No."

"Then how am I to probe West Indian affairs from London?"

"The officers that you will shortly join have recently returned from the Indies, and some, according to my spy, are well aware of this rumored Irish force. They are the same officers appointed to train the new army," Thurloe replied.

"What measures have you taken to thwart the Garden and their Irish allies? According to popular rumor, you have an agent in every Royalist and Irish household in the country. It should be very easy to protect His Highness from these horticultural fanatics," Luke half joked.

"Yesterday is proof that I have not closed every loophole. It is more difficult than normal counterespionage," answered Thurloe.

"Why is that?" asked Luke almost mischievously.

"I have agents in most Royalist households and organizations. Their attitudes are closely monitored and their behavior predictable. Leading English Royalists are opposed to any assassination attempt. The Garden, on the other hand, is a maverick organization—a bunch of fervent amateurs led by a woman. Their behavior is erratic."

Cromwell intervened.

"Enough chatter, gentlemen! To ease the problem, the officers who are recruiting and training the new army and their families will be transferred from their London base in Liffey House to an isolated manor at the far eastern end of the Medway estuary, hard against the Chetney Marshes. Austin Friars is a house surrounded by tidal flats and during high tide is cut off from the rest of the world and becomes an island."

"And where exactly do I fit into this?" asked Luke.

"You join the staff of the Flanders army as adjutant and intelligence officer and uncover the identity of both the treacherous officer whose code name is Weld and the female virago who leads and finances this horrific enterprise. She has the appropriate alias of Belladonna."

Cromwell continued, "While Thurloe is present, I want your advice on another matter."

"I have never shirked telling you as it is, at the moment everything seems to be swirling out of control," muttered Luke.

"I agree, and that is why I am trying to settle the nation with a new constitution," interjected Thurloe.

Luke turned to Cromwell, feigning despair.

"With you, Oliver, as king? Surely not! We fought many a battle together to remove the tyranny of monarchy from the land. You cannot betray your comrades and the grand old cause!"

"Luke, your intuitive reaction reflects the problem. My generals, even family such as Desborough and Fleetwood, agree with you—as does my recalcitrant deputy over many years, John Lambert. All my major generals, except one or two, are in this same antagonistic camp. Against John Thurloe's advice, I want to summon all senior officers to London to discuss the issue with me."

"Why do you oppose the idea, Mr. Thurloe? Democratic consultation with his officers has been Oliver's trademark throughout his military career," asked an impertinent Luke.

"If the army's senior officers are all gathered together in one place, it would create a magnificent target for a Royalist or radical assassin. Even if we discount these possible attempts, gathering all the senior opponents of the plan together in London may lead them to take steps against the proposal or even against the person of the Protector. He could facilitate a coup against himself. There are rumors that Lambert is planning such action."

"I thoroughly agree with you. It is a risk not worth taking in the current situation" was Luke's surprising response.

"But I must know the level of loyalty in my senior officers should I accept the Crown," demanded Oliver.

"Then hold off until I report to you on the general attitude of the army command," replied Luke.

"And how do you do that imprisoned on a swamp encircled house in rural Kent, where I am about to send you?" asked Cromwell.

"Because most of the officers there are touring the countryside, recruiting officers and men. I can do the same and use the opportunity to sound out senior officers already within the national army and key garrisons. My new comrades will also pick up a general feeling for the situation, which I can ascertain from them, and report back."

"Agreed! You move to Kent within two days, and your company of dragoons will follow as soon as possible. Leave a small team behind to follow up yesterday's attempt on my life and to take over investigations into earlier assassination attempts from Thurloe's civilian agents."

Thurloe winced. "My only piece of advice for you, Colonel Tremayne, is that the one person of major interest is the person that assaulted you, recruited Archer, and wheeled the bomb-laden barrow toward His Highness: the man the Garden has labeled Yarrow."

Three Weeks Earlier

Yarrow shivered and sweated simultaneously.

On a winter's afternoon, beside the London to Hampton Court road, Yarrow, the code name taken by Miles Thornton—assigned to kill the ruler of England, Scotland, and Ireland—completed the deployment of his assassins.

They lay in wait for their victim.

As Yarrow hid, concealed in a fissure of a large boulder high above the road, he wiped away the perspiration from his eyes. The tension was overwhelming.

He had trouble calming himself.

He had hated Cromwell since, as a young ensign, he had taken part in an unsuccessful mutiny against the general a decade earlier—a rebellion after which Cromwell ordered one in ten of the mutineers executed.

Yarrow's sweating increased as he remembered that fateful day. The tenth man was to be chosen by lot.

They were required to draw a musket ball from the hat of their commanding officer. None of the company could look at their ball until all had been taken. A tenth of the balls were scratched with a cross. He was the second last in line and prayed as he dipped his hand in the hat. Before he could grasp the ball, his companion, his older brother, pushed him aside and grabbed the remaining balls, looked at both, tensed, and quickly returned one to the hat. Thornton reluctantly picked up the last ball.

All men with a marked musket ball were to step forward.

Thornton was initially delighted. There were no markings on his.

His brother stepped forward.

The ball that he had eagerly grabbed and deliberately retained was marked.

Miles Thornton swore he would avenge his brother and protect the revolution from the greed and ambition of the generals, especially Oliver Cromwell. He would save the revolution from this powerful clique.

His brother was summarily executed in line with General Cromwell's order.

Thornton and most of his company were also immediately dismissed from the army without the arrears of pay owing to them.

Five years later, as the army struggled to find recruits, Thornton rejoined under an assumed name. He was sent to Scotland as part of the English army of occupation. Within months, the high-handed attitude of Cromwell's military governor, General George Monk, led Thornton to organize a mutiny.

It was ruthlessly and savagely suppressed.

Thornton fled to Flanders where he met other dissident soldiers imbued with the Leveling and democratic principles of their longtime radical leader, John Lilburn.

Eventually, Thornton made contact with some Royalist exiles, who believed that the first step in the return of Charles Stuart to the English throne was the assassination of Oliver Cromwell. Given the king's reluctance to support such an act, no Royalist leader was willing to provide the funds Thornton needed to effect a successful killing.

Then two obscure courtiers approached him, both claiming to be wealthy peers who would finance his activities through their local agent, an English aristocratic woman.

He returned to England armed with a letter of introduction to the woman who would fund his assassination attempt.

3

Thornton presented his letter as directed to the publican of the Spotted Sow in Newmarket—and remained at the tavern, awaiting a reply.

It came the next day.

He was to meet his potential benefactor in the remains of a manor that Cromwell had razed to the ground—in an old dairy that was the only building on the estate that remained intact.

On entering it, he saw a large table around which sat four men and two women.

Most wore a light fabric mask, which concealed the lower face, while the rest of the head was covered by their hood.

A plump man of short stature rose to greet Thornton.

He, unlike the others, concealed his features with a sack pulled over his head that reached to his shoulders.

A woman signaled for Thornton to take the only vacant seat. "Welcome! Your letter of introduction comes from impeccable sources. We are the Garden, a group of active Royalists who aim to assassinate Oliver Cromwell and control enough of the army to seize power. To conceal our identity, we have aliases. I am Belladonna, and my female companion is Foxglove. The four gentlemen are Thrift, Woodruff, Woad, and Weld."

Thornton responded testily, "I did not put myself at your pleasure to play games with code names and the like. Have you the means to finance my killing of Cromwell?"

"Be patient, my man! You are part of a much bigger enterprise than the murder of the chief regicide. I have spent most of my life abroad and on returning here recently am appalled to find that many leading Royalists are not only accepting the rule of Oliver Cromwell but are falling over one another to serve him. Our leading organization is preaching acceptance of the new regime. The more strident supporters around the Queen Mother are refusing to act without Spanish support, and the king himself cannot, or will not, actively support the overthrow of the current government. I have the means, and you, Yarrow, the name by which we will know you, have the ability to kill Cromwell. This will lead immediately to the overthrow of the regime. Ideally, you will carry out your work within a fortnight. Before you leave here, I will give you the funds needed."

"How do I contact you should the funds be insufficient?" asked the pragmatic Yarrow.

"You don't. You will be contacted from time to time by Woad, who will regularly update your orders and assess your performance. The rest of us in our various ways will concentrate on the second of my objectives: take over the government of the country by controlling part of the army. Weld has already put in train the arrival of a fleet with a small army of Irishmen to assist our cause. Cromwell's veteran troops, the majority of whom occupy Ireland and Scotland, will not be swayed. But by the time they could reach London to rescue his regime, we will be in command. The only section of the army able to be subverted without much trouble are the new troops being recruited to fight in Flanders. Many of the officers are desperate for employment and are not necessarily loyal to Cromwell. Some are fellow Royalists who conceal their past, and many more are veterans who over the years have been dismissed by Cromwell. Weld is a senior officer in this new army and is in the process of subverting the general staff. Woad will be your contact with me."

Yarrow eagerly received a large bag of silver and gold coins from Belladonna and then sent a parting barb toward his benefactor, "My lady, I cannot assassinate the tyrant within fourteen days as you suggest. It will take much observation and planning."

Yarrow brought himself back to the present. This was not the time to reminisce. Weeks of intelligence had revealed that every Friday afternoon Cromwell left Whitehall to spend the weekend in the more relaxed atmosphere of Hampton Court. He traveled by coach with two of his lifeguards, riding well ahead of the vehicle, another one on each side of the coach, and six bringing up the rear.

Yarrow placed five musketeers on each side of the road, all with a different angle of fire. They were concealed behind the only cover available: a number of large boulders. They would pour a concentrated salvo into the coach and immediately escape across the fields to safety. Two other musketeers, located closer to Hampton Court, would initiate the assault.

On a signal from Yarrow, they would create a disturbance as the coach approached. He hoped the leading guards would stop the coach while several of them would ride ahead to investigate, leaving the coach less protected.

Yarrow had hardly deployed his men when the noise of a coach was heard approaching. The assassins tensed. Muskets were primed, and the killers waited for the order to fire.

The coach was on them faster than expected.

Yarrow had no time to fire his pistol, the signal for his men to fire.

It was also too late to activate the musketeers farther up the road to create a diversion.

As the coach came hurtling around the corner, Yarrow sensed a problem. The vehicle was not guarded. There were no lifeguards.

Cromwell, especially in the heightened antagonistic atmosphere of Parliament's offer of the Crown, would not travel without a heavy guard.

The coach rattled past, giving Yarrow just enough time to glimpse its occupants: two elderly women.

After this false alarm, the group settled back to await the arrival of the Lord Protector.

It was getting colder, and light snow began to fall. It would soon be dark.

Darkness did not worry Yarrow. A coach highlighted by its lanterns would make an easier target, and darkness would aid their escape.

Sometime later, the group was alerted by the sound of many horses coming toward them from London.

Yarrow readied his men. Minutes later, a troop of lifeguards galloped past the concealed killers, who were taut and tense—and ready to fire.

But this time, there was no coach.

Was Cromwell disguised as one of his lifeguards?

Yarrow cursed and stood down his men.

He was now worried and perplexed.

Cromwell never made his trip to Hampton Court after dark. But why would a troop of lifeguards be hurtling toward the palace if the focus of their existence was still in London?

Yarrow left his men in place and made his way on foot to the gates of the palace.

His fears were realized. It was well guarded by the palace's usual detachment, reinforced by the Protector's lifeguards.

As he watched from the shadows, a small cart left the palace. Its owner had delivered supplies to the inhabitants of Hampton Court.

Yarrow asked, "Good man, I am sorely disappointed. I had hoped to catch a glimpse of the Lord Protector as he traveled past."

"Good sir, he came by barge, although his guards had to travel by road. They have only just arrived."

Yarrow was disappointed but not downcast.

There would be other occasions.

He returned to his men and paid them half the promised amount on the grounds that they had not completed their task.

The men were openly hostile at this miserly interpretation of their agreement.

A jovial rotund six-footer confronted Yarrow, "Not good enough, sir! There is no such condition in our agreement."

He made a grab for Yarrow's large money purse, gave a groan, and fell to the ground dead.

Yarrow withdrew his dagger from the prone body.

As the men muttered ominously, Yarrow primed his pistol, mounted his horse, and rode off as his men hurled rocks at their departing employer.

Two of these disaffected mercenaries, William Mant and John Starkey, made it to the Golden Swan to spend their newly acquired pittance. They continued to grumble about receiving half the agreed amount.

A small man with an oversized cape overheard their conversation and asked, "Not a good night, brothers?"

William replied, "Mind your own business! Be gone!"

The stranger laughed. "You can't fool me. The constable was here only a few minutes ago warning us that there were highwaymen on the road from London. He saw most of your group enter the Hog's Head while the two of you came here. I am sure the constable would like to know what your group were doing on the London road after dark."

"What is it to you, stranger?"

"Let me say I can do you a good turn."

"And that would be?"

"Whatever you were up to this night, you are not happy with your recompense. I will pay you double if you tell me who was on the road this evening."

John looked at William. Both were in two minds. John responded, "Let us see the color of your money!"

The stranger opened a purse replete with silver coins. William was cautious. "And why do you wish to know these things?"

"I am a government agent hoping to rid the London road of criminal and subversive elements," replied the small man naively.

John was immediately alarmed.

He wanted the money but would have no truck with the government.

He lied in the hope of still obtaining the money.

"We were approached by a stranger who offered us money if we lay in wait on the London road and robbed any rich gentlemen who passed by. Unfortunately, no one appeared, and we arrived here penniless."

"Who employed you?"

"I don't know. All I can tell you is that he recently returned from Flanders and was red haired," revealed an indiscreet William.

The stranger beamed.

He momentarily left the tavern but soon returned with four armed men.

He confronted William and John,

"You have been in contact with a person who has recently entered this country to carry out subversive activity against the government. You will be taken for interrogation to the nearest magistrate."

John glared at William.

Yarrow had only ridden a few minutes toward London when he had second thoughts.

Disgruntled men could cause trouble.

He had been unwise not to pay them the promised amount.

At all costs, he must maintain the secrecy of his mission and obliterate any links to himself.

He feared that some of these men with a silver coin would drink themselves to oblivion in some tavern and in an act of bravado reveal all to the enthralled fellow drinkers.

He turned around and rode post haste in the direction of Richmond where his men indicated they would be drinking.

He caught up with all but two of them in the Hog's Head on the outskirts of the village and paid them the second half of their retainer. They informed Yarrow that the missing men were locals who had gone on to their favorite alehouse the Golden Swan and that they were very vocal about their poor treatment.

Yarrow would take no risks.

Before entering the Golden Swan, he dipped into his saddlebag and drew out a large black wig, which he placed over his short-cropped reddish hair, and replaced his black doublet with one of bright emerald green. He also placed a black patch over one eye. In the dimly lit tavern, the two troublemakers would not recognize him.

He was immediately alarmed to see John and William, the worse for drink, being plied with more alcohol by a small obsequious man.

Yarrow moved to a bench next to the three men.

He was appalled.

But he was prepared.

In case his enemies should capture him, he always carried with him poisonous powders, concealed in plugs of tobacco.

His chance came sooner than expected.

A buxom barmaid leaned over John and William and asked if she could refill their cups.

She took the empty vessels to the barrel of beer.

Yarrow followed her.

He offered to take the refilled cups back to William and John as other customers urgently sought her attention.

He broke apart a tobacco plug, placed some powder in each cup, and returned them to the anxious drinkers.

Just after he deposited the cups, the stranger became cross and moved to the door.

In his absence, William and John gulped down their beer.

The stranger returned with four men—and arrested them.

As they were being led from the tavern, John grasped his stomach and fell to the floor.

The stranger bent over the prone body and in an agitated manner announced that the prisoner was dead.

He turned to William, whose face expressed extreme agony as he too expired on the steps of the Golden Swan.

Yarrow smiled, stepped over the bodies, and returned to London.

4

A week later, Yarrow saw the opportunity for another attempt.

Drinking in the Mermaid, an alehouse not far from Whitehall, he recognized a former comrade from his Scottish days, wearing the uniform of the Lord Protector's lifeguards.

Trooper Tom Archer had participated in Yarrow's abortive uprising years earlier but denied his complicity and, without damning evidence of his guilt, escaped punishment.

Since then, he so impressed General Monk that he was eventually recommended as a trustworthy soldier to join the Protector's bodyguard.

After many drinks, Yarrow cautiously asked, "Has your closeness to Cromwell changed your opinion of the army high command?"

"Yes, until recently, I was very happy to serve the Lord Protector. He finally introduced many of the reforms wanted by us soldiers."

"Not many I'm afraid, but what has now raised doubts in your mind?"

"Our corrupt Parliament, which has done nothing to improve our lot or bring godly rule to the nation, has recently offered Cromwell the Crown. I did not fight constantly for fifteen years against monarchy, suffering many wounds, and losing several friends and family to have it resurrected again by the very men—by the very man—I trusted."

Yarrow refilled Archer's cup over several hours.

Finally, Yarrow dropped into the conversation that one certain way to ensure that Cromwell did not accept the Crown was for him to die. Yarrow added that a mutual friend and leader of past conspiracies against the generals Edward Sexby was about to publish a book showing that killing the traitor Oliver Cromwell was not murder. It was justice.

Archer recoiled from the suggestion, "No, that is not the way of the Lord. If Cromwell rejects the offer and dismisses his civilian advisers, he may yet bring us the heaven on earth that our ministers expect. I would have no cause to kill him. This is not the time to act."

"Tom, whatever Cromwell says or does regarding the Crown, it will be meaningless. The former Royalists who now surround him will slowly and effectively dismantle all the reforms that the Commonwealth and protectorate have enacted—destroy everything you and I have fought for. As a lifeguard stationed at Whitehall, you must see the growing number of aristocratic antiarmy fops who are now his courtiers."

"Maybe, but I will wait on the Lord to guide me. And what would I gain from such an act? I could lose everything, including my life."

Yarrow was temporarily distracted. He now realized that the rebellious democrat of their Scottish days had become a religious extremist. A new strategy was required if he was to enlist Archer as the assassin.

"Tom, you killed many men during your years in the army. You killed some because they were your opponents fighting for the king, but in many cases, you killed them because they were the enemies of God. Cromwell is openly flouting God's will. Your removal of him would not strain or indeed stain your conscience."

"There lies my dilemma! Has Cromwell betrayed the Lord, or is he still the Lord's anointed? The leaders of my church are divided. Until he accepts the Crown, I will not act," replied Tom defiantly.

Yarrow changed his approach once more. "Have you thought about your future?"

Tom became irritated.

"Enough silly questions! A man like me has no need to plan a future. I am a serving soldier in His Highness's cavalry lifeguard. That is what I will do for the foreseeable future unless because of some crisis, I am reassigned to another position in the army."

"And for that foreseeable future, you will be paid a pittance. When your army service is over, you will have nothing. I will give you ten times your yearly wage to kill Cromwell. When we served together in Scotland, you were upset by the way your father was ejected from the family farm because of a poor season, he was unable to pay his rent. My offer will give you and your family a good future."

Yarrow realized that he had finally broken through Archer's resistance by the reference to his father and the loss of the family farm.

Tom now responded with tears in his eyes, "I have no family. Both my parents and only brother are dead, and I have never married. The possibility of regaining the family farm and of marrying and creating a family of my own is tempting."

Yarrow smiled.

Archer had no family. He would not be missed. As soon as Archer killed Cromwell, Yarrow would eliminate him. Any links to Yarrow and the Garden would disappear.

Yarrow continued, "If you agree to my proposition, I will give you half the payment before the event and the rest on the completion of the mission. Here is a gold coin as a token of my good faith."

Tom angrily replied, "A pox on your gold coin. If I appeared anywhere with a gold coin, the constables would be on to me in very short time. A common soldier does not handle gold. If I accept your proposition, pay me in small silver coins."

Yarrow's limited patience was exhausted. He inexplicably exploded, undoing his hours of persuasion, "Don't quibble. You will carry out this mission on my terms."

"And why would I do that?" replied an irritated and very drunk trooper.

"Because it is your only option. Accept and you receive a small fortune, regain your family land, start a family of your own, and live in reasonable circumstances. Refuse and you will be cashiered from the army, perhaps imprisoned, or even possibly executed."

"And why would such dire circumstances occur?"

"Because I will let it be known that you, one of Cromwell's trusted lifeguards, is, in fact, a democratizing leveling extremist from the past and now a religious fanatic who no longer believes that the Lord Protector is God's anointed."

"I will not be blackmailed. The Lord will lead me in this matter. Leave!"

"Tom, you are in a perfect position as a lifeguard to assassinate the Great Traitor. Meet me here again tomorrow night, and we will progress this matter further. Remember, you will be doing both God's work and ensuing your future prosperity."

The next evening, Yarrow hired one of the small rooms at the Mermaid.

He sat there alone, wondering whether Tom Archer would appear. In the light of day, the combination of stick and carrot may not be as appealing to a sober lifeguard.

Yarrow was about to accept failure.

Archer had not appeared.

He rose to leave when there was a knock on the chamber's closed door.

Archer was apologetic, "Sorry, I'm so late, but I had difficulty in breaking away from my regular drinking comrades who wanted me to stay with them. It would not do for us to be seen together."

After a short discussion, Yarrow was delighted with Archer's considered approach.

He had convinced himself that if he eliminated the Protector, he would serve God, the nation, the lower ranks of the army—and his own future.

Yarrow then outlined a plan he had devised to shoot the Protector during his afternoon walk in St. James Park.

Archer listened for some time and to Yarrow's delight suggested that there were problems in his plan.

"It is true that Cromwell takes a walk around the parks of central London late each afternoon. On these walks, a platoon of infantry lifeguards accompany him. I might kill the tyrant, but I would not be able to escape. It would be a suicide mission. Neither your bribe nor the satisfaction of doing God's work is tempting if I am to die."

Yarrow mused inwardly. *If the Protector's men did not kill him, I will.*

"So what is a better approach?" asked Yarrow grudgingly.

"As a cavalry commander, Cromwell rides across to Hyde Park once a week where he can give a horse and himself a thorough workout, galloping along the Serpentine. On these occasions, only six cavalry lifeguards accompany him. Three remain at the beginning of his gallop, and three assemble at the farthest extent of his ride. While he is at full gallop for hundreds of yards across the park, he is not protected."

"How would you effect the deed and then readily escape?"

"I will attach myself to the Hyde Park detail and saunter halfway up the Protector's normal course and conceal myself in the shrubbery. As he gallops past, I shoot him and escape through the nearest gate, which you will ensure is open. It would be ideal if after I kill Cromwell and leave by this gate, you park a cart or wagon across the exit to prevent me being followed by the cavalry. By the time they find another gate, I will be long gone."

Yarrow was delighted with this simple plan and the opportunity it presented to have both Cromwell and Archer eliminated within minutes of each other.

He would ensure that all the gates remained locked.

Some well-paid lackeys would block the relevant exits of the park and shoot Archer as he leaves the scene of his crime.

Yarrow would be well away from the action, drinking in the Mermaid.

Archer spent a lot of time in the stables. His horse was the envy of many of his comrades. It was a beautiful black horse that was strong and swift. Its strength and looks were largely Friesian, but its slighter appearance and greater speed came from its part-Arabian lineage.

Yarrow became anxious when Archer reported that Cromwell had canceled his weekly ride in Hyde Park due to the pressure of business. His enthusiasm for the plan waned further on hearing of Cromwell's growing arthritis and rumors that he may never ride again.

Such fears were not realized.

The following week, Archer sat in behind a detail as it escorted Cromwell into Hyde Park.

As a security measure, when the Protector was in the park, other users were excluded.

Archer became aware of one other small problem. On entering the park and moving out all its visitors, two troopers moved in opposite directions around the perimeter of the park, locking every gate.

Archer noted this activity but breathed a sigh of relief, knowing that Yarrow would reopen the gate nearest to the assassination site.

He then had a moment of doubt. Would Yarrow come properly prepared to open a heavy metal gate that had been securely locked?

As the troopers cantered to their appointed places, Archer moved slowly past the Protector and his rear guard. He had gone twenty yards when the captain of the guard, Asa Glover, shouted at him, "Trooper, stop where you are!"

5

Archer tensed. What did Glover want?

He would have no time to prime his carbine if the situation became difficult.

Glover continued, "Return here, trooper! The Protector wishes to speak to you."

Archer reluctantly obliged.

He would never be as close to the man he planned to kill.

He started to perspire profusely.

He could stab the dictator now and accept the fatal consequences. England would be free from tyranny, and he would receive his heavenly reward. Was God telling him to act?

The Protector spoke gently, "The captain has told me about your fine horse. It looks even better than its reputation. Would you dismount so that I can examine it in detail?"

Cromwell and Archer both dismounted.

Cromwell passed his hands over Archer's horse.

He spoke, "One of my senior officers, Colonel Tremayne, has always ridden black Friesians, but they are much bulkier than this animal. What's its history?"

"It was bred by neighbors of my parents from a Friesian mare and an Arabian stallion."

"Have you ridden it in battle?"

"No, but I have ridden it many a time in Scotland to control riotous crowds."

"May I ride it?" asked Cromwell. "Can it take a hard gallop?"

Archer nodded his assent to both questions.

Cromwell removed the musket slung around the saddle—the very weapon intended to end his life.

He mounted Archer's horse and set off at a canter, increasing slowly to a full gallop. At the end of the track, Cromwell turned the horse and thundered back toward the group of troopers.

He profusely thanked Archer and asked for details about the breeder. If there were any further offspring from the Friesian mare, he would be interested.

The group reassembled for the canter back to Whitehall, except for Glover and Archer.

The captain had picked up the musket that Cromwell had discarded. He waved it under Archer's nose.

"Trooper, explain yourself! Why is a lifeguard carrying a musket in addition to two carbines and personal dirk? You are not a common dragoon. Why are you here? You are not on my roster for today's escort."

"I wanted to shoot some rabbits to improve our monotonous army diet. Many have escaped the warrens of surrounding aristocrats and are infesting the park. I attached myself to your detail to enter the park to avoid trouble."

The captain outwardly accepted Archer's story.

But he was deeply troubled.

On his return to Whitehall, he sought audience with the head of intelligence, John Thurloe, who also controlled internal security.

"What is it, Glover?"

"Sir, it may be nothing, but in this period of heightened security, we cannot ignore unusual occurrences. This afternoon, one of His Highness's lifeguards attached himself to a detail for which he was not listed. He also carried with him a musket in addition to the arms he is entitled to bear."

Thurloe looked alarmed. "Thank you, Captain! Pity help us if one of the Protector's own guards is in the enemy's camp. What's his name?"

"Archer."

"Where does he drink?"

"At the Mermaid."

Thurloe dismissed Glover, suggesting he closely monitor Archer's behavior and as a precaution not roster him for any duties that brought him near the Protector.

Thurloe summoned his top agent, William Acton, and his deputy John Greenwich.

He was apologetic.

"I am sorry to call you in after I transferred your cases to military intelligence. Unfortunately, that unit has yet to arrive from Wales, and there has been a disturbing development."

"It must be serious as you are not known for reversing your decisions," commented Acton undiplomatically. "What's the sudden problem?"

Thurloe outlined Glover's concern regarding Archer.

"He drinks at the Mermaid. I want him watched. List the names of all those who drink with him—or meet him. Archer may be a loyal servant of the Protector or, most worrying, an agent of a group seeking to undermine the government by assassinating him."

Acton and Greenwich watched Archer for the next three nights.

The suspect drank and conversed at length with three of his troop. None of them mixed with the other customers—an attitude that made Cromwell's troops unpopular in many of the drinking houses of inner London.

On the fourth night, the agents' perseverance was finally rewarded. Halfway through the evening, a closely cropped redheaded man entered the room and nodded to Archer.

The stranger went into an adjoining private chamber.

Archer left his companions and followed the new arrival.

Greenwich followed Archer.

Greenwich, with an ear to the keyhole, heard an intriguing conversation.

The stranger was cross.

"It is fortunate that you acted out of conviction and not for a hefty reward. You have earned nothing. I want you to return the down payment I gave you. What went wrong? I waited all night for the joyous news that the Protector was dead to spread across London. I waited in vain. Did you get cold feet?"

"No," answered a deflated Tom.

He described what had happened.

Yarrow swore vehemently.

"Cromwell is protected by the devil. That is twice in a few weeks that well-laid plans have been thwarted by unexpected occurrences. Why did he suddenly take a barge to Hampton Court? Why did he take a liking to your horse and then insist on riding it?"

Archer rejected such an interpretation and advanced one that Yarrow found anathema.

"Maybe it is God who is protecting him?"

His antagonism toward Cromwell was waning.

"Don't be stupid, Archer! Despite this setback, our work must progress. Meet here in a week's time, and I will reveal a new plan!"

Greenwich reported back to Acton, who ordered him to follow the redheaded man as he left the building.

He did but was back inside the tavern within minutes.

A heavy fog had descended, and the suspect had disappeared into the gloom.

Acton reported to Thurloe.

"Was that lad with the fine steed really about to kill His Highness?"

"When I was first informed of this, I thought it only a distant possibility, but Greenwich heard the man confess."

Thurloe was silent for some time and then announced, "Gentlemen, you have done a good job. The army intelligence unit, the Protector's favorite, has now arrived. I will brief their leader Colonel Tremayne in the morning."

The meeting was delayed a day by the attempted assassination of Cromwell through the bombs detonated within Whitehall itself.

Luke would stay at Liffey House for a day or two and then relocate with the rest of the senior officers to Austin Friars in Kent.

Evan and Strad would stay in London and take up the investigation that had been conducted up until now by the civilian agents Acton and Greenwich.

After considerable discussion between these agents and the two soldiers, Tom Archer was released from confinement.

For the time being, his warning regarding the bombing, even though almost too late, was taken as a change of heart by the soldiers although dismissed by the cynical civilian agents as a ploy.

They were amazed at the apparent naivety of military intelligence.

But Evan and Strad were not totally convinced by Archer's change of heart.

He was bait to trap the real plotters.

Tom would accept Strad as a new drinking partner, and if Yarrow appeared, he was to emphasize Strad's ability as a marksman.

For two nights Tom, Strad, and several other soldiers drank together without incident.

Evan found a corner in the Mermaid from which to observe events.

He felt that Yarrow would make contact as soon as possible to find out what went wrong with the bombings.

He was right.

The redheaded conspirator arrived, pulled Tom from the bench, and physically propelled him out of the drinking chamber into a neighboring room.

A few minutes later, Tom reappeared and signaled for Strad to join them.

Evan was delighted.

Yarrow had taken the bait.

Strad would be a marksman in the next attempt on the Protector's life.

Ten minutes later, Yarrow, Tom, and Strad left the small antechamber.

Yarrow indicated by vigorous hand gestures that he was not to be followed.

As he exited, he declared that they would meet again two nights hence.

Evan followed Yarrow.

Strad, unbeknownst to Evan, followed them both at a discreet distance.

Evan, assisted by the pale moonlight, tracked Yarrow as he ambled slowly beside the Thames.

He walked well beyond Westminster Abbey and was soon passing the relatively new large townhouses of the nobles.

Then suddenly, Yarrow disappeared.

Evan ran to the spot where Yarrow was last seen.

He found an unlocked gate beside which was a plaque indicating that this was Liffey House—the very house to which Luke was assigned.

This was too much of a coincidence.

An excited Evan followed a winding path through shrubs and trees of Liffey House until he reached the manicured lawns of this large multistoried building just in time to see Yarrow enter by a side door.

Almost simultaneously, three figures ran from the other side of the house and across the lawn to the path beside which Evan was standing.

Each man carried a sack and in the other hand held a large item: one had a large silver plate, another a massive gold candelabra, and the third a bag that rattled as if full of coins.

The thieves stopped in their tracks.

Evan, with sword drawn, confronted them on the path.

He suddenly realized the futility of his actions.

They would simply turn and run off in all directions.

All three did turn to make their escape, but another soldier slashing his sword wildly through the air blocked their retreat.

Strad had finally overhauled Evan and summing up the situation had moved in behind the thieves.

Taken completely by surprise and caught red-handed, they meekly obeyed Evan's order to move quietly to the gate. On reaching the street, Evan was delighted to hear the watch moving slowly toward them.

The thieves were also delighted.

Common gossip was that the military tortured their prisoners.

To be handed over to the watch and incarcerated in a civilian prison was the lesser of two evils.

This more positive outlook for their immediate future was quickly quashed.

Evan discussed the situation with the watch.

Two of them assisted the soldiers to escort the prisoners to Whitehall, where they were placed under military guard in a small cellar.

The thieves were terrified.

A night in complete darkness, in a windowless rat-infested room, would weaken their resistance to interrogation.

Evan had no interest in their robberies.

He wanted information about the mansion they had just robbed: Liffey House.

6

Early next morning, the thieves identified themselves to Strad as Harry Haybittle, Wally Coyfe, and John Garrett.

They were ordered to spread their ill-gotten gains across the floor of the makeshift cellar prison, withdrawing from their pockets and various bags attached to their bodies jewelry far more valuable than the large items they had openly carried from the house.

These worldly wise criminals were well aware of the various jurisdictions across London and the relative harshness or leniency of each authority.

They were not happy to be in the hands of the military.

They tried the humble contrite approach, meekly asking Strad why they were confined in Whitehall with soldiers as their jailers. Military prisoners were usually sent to the Tower and petty criminals such as themselves spread across numerous London jails.

Strad was blunt. "What difference does it make, lads? You stole goods worth a fortune by breaking in to a house after dark. In every jurisdiction in the land, that is a hanging offense."

Evan arrived in full military uniform, emphasizing his rank and status in a further attempt to overwhelm any resistance the trio might have to cooperating with the army.

He signaled for the thieves to sit on the floor against the far wall and for the guards to leave the room.

Harry panicked. "Please, sir, send us to a normal prison. We are simple thieves who struck it lucky. We mean no harm to the government or to its officials such as yourself."

"Just be quiet! My sergeant and I will inspect your loot once again."

"Take the loot, sir, and let us go!" pleaded Wally.

"These goods will be returned to their owner General Liffey, but you will get you wish. You will be transferred out of our control and sent before the justices of the Liberty of Westminster where they will have no option other than sentence you to be hanged," Evan announced slowly and with a theatrical flourish.

He suddenly spied one of the small sacks from which the valuable items had been removed but which did not appear to be empty.

He upended it.

He shook it vigorously, and out fell a bundle of letters carefully tied by a green ribbon.

"Why did you conceal these documents?" asked Evan.

Wally explained, "Sir, none of us can read or write. We did not know if they had any value, but just in case they did, I put them in my bag with the jewels."

Evan and Strad left the cellar and ordered breakfast for the prisoners. The soldiers adjourned to a neighboring room and divided the letters between them.

After two hours of reading, the task was complete.

The letters were to General Liffey during his period of service in the West Indies from his Royalist sister, Lady Myra Ashcroft. Their contents were singularly concerned with family matters and contained nothing useful to military intelligence.

Nevertheless, they raised a major concern.

The worrying issue was not the content but the source.

They were all sent from the Royal Court in exile as it moved from Paris to Cologne and more recently to places in Flanders.

Later that day, Evan consulted John Thurloe regarding Liffey House and its resident general.

He was surprisingly informative.

"Tremayne is to take up temporary residence there. He may have already moved in. Liffey House is the London estate of the Irish peer, the Earl of Liffey. It is occupied by an able officer of our national army, the earl's second son, Major General Christopher Liffey. Liffey recently returned from service in the West Indies and a week ago was appointed to command a section of the army that is currently being recruited to fight the Spaniards in Flanders."

"Is Liffey loyal?" asked Evan.

"Probably, although there are a number of factors that could undermine such a positive assessment. First, he has been out of England for over six years. He was intensely loyal to General Cromwell at that time of his original appointment to Barbados, but how he has reacted to Oliver creating the protectorate and now thinking of becoming king, I do not know. Second, his father, the earl, and his eldest brother and sister have remained staunch Royalists. They all chose to go into exile rather than remain in republican England. Third, his service in Barbados brought him into contact with Spaniards and many high-ranking Royalist prisoners of war. They may have influenced his views."

"So the presence of Yarrow in Liffey House is no great surprise?"

"Nothing in London is a surprise. You are more likely to be betrayed by pretended friends than by open enemies. Did the thieves tell you anything useful?"

Evan explained the discovery of the letters probably sent from the Royal Court.

"Don't alarm yourself regarding their origin. Myra Liffey, the general's eldest sister, married Nicholas, Lord Ashcroft, Charles Stuart's head of security. She moves with the Royal Court. If you come across any coded letters, give them to me, and I will have my experts decipher them."

Evan smiled, relieved that the origins of the letters had no sinister connotations and noted that "Colonel Tremayne knows Lord Ashcroft. They were briefly on the same side during Luke's French adventure four years ago."

"Your commanding officer knows the most interesting people," remarked Thurloe sarcastically.

Thurloe, who had been casually thumbing through the letters that Evan had given him, remarked as he left the room, "All these letters are more than a year old. Liffey must have recent mail from his sister that could be more useful to us. Ask Tremayne to obtain it!"

Evan bristled.

He did not respond but thought to himself, *I have a better plan that will not jeopardize Luke's position.*

He discussed the situation with John Martin and Strad.

He was still cross.

"The less Thurloe knows about what we do, the better. I do not trust him. He dislikes Luke to start with."

"The feeling is mutual," commented Strad.

After a brief discussion, the soldiers decided on a plan that would remain a secret between them—and Luke.

Evan immediately went to Liffey House to put Luke in the picture.

Meanwhile, Strad assembled the company of dragoons and selected two groups of twelve men.

An hour later, one of these groups led by John Martin escorted the three prisoners from their confinement within Whitehall across Westminster to meet their fate at the hands of the local magistrates.

For some unaccountable reason, John took his men and their prisoners through a large section of woodland, overgrown with shrubs and small trees. Then in a magnanimous gesture to his ill-fated prisoners, he had his men dismount and allow the three thieves, temporarily freed of their shackles, to take one last walk together, accompanied by a single trooper.

Suddenly, a dozen hooded horsemen rampaged through the wood, grabbed the prisoners, and galloped away while John and his men seemed at a loss as how to respond.

All John could do was to lead his troop back to Whitehall and report to Evan.

Both men took a glass of celebratory mulled wine.

Five minutes later, a troop of horse led by Strad returned to the Whitehall barracks, leading two hooded men.

These men were placed in the cellar recently vacated by the three thieves.

Evan was curious.

He admonished Strad, "Why are there only two prisoners? What happened to the third?"

Strad, relaxed and pragmatic, acknowledged the error.

"My mistake, Captain. My men raced through the woodland intent on snatching up the three men. They thought they had accomplished their mission. It was only after we had reassembled on the edge of the woodland that I realized there was only two."

"No real harm done. Let's interview the lucky duo!" said Evan.

Evan and Strad entered the cellar and removed the hoods of the prisoners.

The two men gasped with surprise.

Harry exclaimed, "We are back in the same cellar as earlier today, and you are the same officers who questioned us this morning. What is going on?"

Evan replied, "Let me tell you a story! Three thieves escaped from the army's custody and disappeared into the mists of London. The army sergeant who recorded their names, and their alleged crimes, seems to have lost the paperwork detailing the incident. As far as the army is concerned, these men are free—in fact, they were never here."

"If we were never here, or if we were and have escaped, why are we still here, as what appears to my simple mind, as prisoners? And where is Johnny Garrett?" asked a confused Wally Coyte.

"I thought you might be able to tell me," said Strad. "When my men galloped through the woodland, they claimed they only saw two men walking beside the mounted trooper."

"True, when the three of us heard the noise of horsemen at a gallop descending on us, Wally and I thought the worst. They would mow us down and kill us. We kept walking, hoping that the end would be quick. Johnny dived to the ground and rolled under a bramble. Your men missed him."

"Why are you here? you ask. For reasons of national security, I need a person who knows the layout of Liffey House to accompany me there tonight. As a reward for such a service, you will both walk out of here free men."

Wally responded almost too quickly, "Harry knows the mansion backward. Johnny and I only followed his lead."

Harry confessed that he knew the house, having spent much time there a few weeks earlier as a glazier's assistant.

Evan led the two men from the cellar.

"Wally, follow this soldier to one of the rear entrances of the palace and disappear. Harry, come with me!"

Back in his chamber, Evan called for refreshments; and while Harry enthusiastically drank his beer, the former began his interrogation, "How many people live in Liffey House?"

"Until the return of the general a month or so ago, the house was deserted, except for an Irish couple who have acted as caretakers for years. They employed some of us locals over the years to maintain various parts of the establishment. Several windows had been broken during that severe storm last autumn, and I helped with the repairs."

"Have things changed since General Liffey took up residence?"

"Not very much. The general expects to leave for service in Flanders at any time. He has given rooms to five or six of the officers who served with him in the Caribbean and will again in Flanders. He employs a dozen or so soldiers as servants to manage the house. But he has only opened up part of the mansion. That is why it was so easy to steal what we wanted. Those currently living in the household never use the rooms where much of the silver and jewelry is held."

"Do you know anything about the senior officers staying with the general?"

"Nothing at all."

"Has anything unusual occurred in the last week or so?"

"Yes, the night before we burgled the building, I scouted through the house and grounds. I was surprised to find several additional rooms had been opened up at the opposite end of the house. A man whom I have never seen in the daylight lives there. We waited till he left the house on the night of the robbery before we risked entering the building."

"Although you have never seen this man in the daylight, can you describe him in any way?"

"I caught a glimpse of him as he entered the Broken Bell, an alehouse across the road from Liffey House. He was small with short-cropped reddish hair."

Evan was delighted—and changed his emphasis.

"Was the general at home on the night of your robbery?"

"Yes, and for most nights, we had the house under surveillance. He spends his evenings until very late in his library."

"That could be our problem. I need access to any letters that Liffey has received in recent weeks."

"Then the library will be the place where they are filed. Wally said one of the drawers in the general's desk was filled with papers. We will need to be very careful. He retires late and then only into the next chamber, which he has made his bedroom. A servant patrols the house after the general retires and ensures that all doors and windows are locked."

"If that is the case, how do we get out?" asked a perplexed Evan.

"The locks are on the inside. Once in, we can get out, but if out, it is impossible to get in. You need to enter the premises earlier in the evening and wait until the house—and, in particular, the general—retires," suggested Harry.

7

As soon as darkness fell, Harry led Evan expertly into Liffey House and to a deserted part of the rambling building.

Evan was not content to stay still for three or four hours, waiting for Liffey to vacate his library.

He left Harry and explored the deserted rooms.

The general and his staff, including the elderly caretakers, occupied the northwest quarter of the second floor.

The mysterious visitor seemed to use two ground-floor chambers in the southeast corner.

Four-fifths of the rooms had been closed for over a decade ever since the earl escaped to the continent following the king's defeat at Naseby. The dust and cobwebs were intermingled with masses of rat droppings and constantly disturbed by the destructive actions of the rodents themselves.

Since Liffey's arrival, the doors of these unused rooms had been left open to allow six or seven recently obtained cats to deal with the vermin.

Evan was glad that he had discovered the feline community.

They made as much noise as a human and could, if stumbled upon, alert the household to an intruder.

He was in two minds about a large ginger tom that followed him everywhere, weaving itself around his legs.

This cat could give him away or, conversely, provide him with a scapegoat if noises alerted the household.

For the moment, there was no need to bludgeon it to death—a thought that had entered the cat-hating officer's mind.

The ground floor was eerily quiet as Evan made his way in almost total darkness toward the area occupied by Yarrow.

Eventually, he saw at the end of long passageway faint beams of flickering light.

As he approached the source, he could hear someone moving about in the dimly lit room.

He moved closer to the half-opened door.

Then he heard an outer door slam and footsteps heading toward him.

He retreated back into the shadows.

A man opened the door fully and greeted the new arrival.

The newcomer brushed aside the cordial greeting and responded with a damning criticism, "My arrival was supposed to coincide with an uprising provoked by the assassination of Oliver Cromwell. You have now failed on three occasions, and none of the officers upstairs have been converted to our cause."

The visitor entered the room and in shutting the door plunged Evan into darkness once again.

Evan moved quietly to the door, treading cautiously as the ginger tom rubbed against his legs.

He placed his ear against the large empty keyhole.

The new arrival continued his attack, "Yarrow, not only have you failed on three occasions, but your people rose prematurely in Wales and were decimated. The Garden is losing confidence in you. Religious fanatics and democratic revolutionaries are clearly not up to the task. How far have you involved us Royalists in your plans? We fund you."

Yarrow replied, "I contact the Royalists I need, a small group of Londoners who import arms and ammunition. I await the Royalist agent on Liffey's staff to make himself known to me."

"Why haven't you made first contact?" asked the visitor.

"I was not told who he is, and to maintain the highest levels of secrecy, he was to approach me."

"At least you understood that part of your instructions. I am that agent John Blair or, in the Garden's vocabulary, Woad."

"Why wait so long to reveal yourself?" asked Yarrow provocatively.

"I too have to await orders before I act. A senior officer on Liffey's staff, Weld, is our leader. It may be the new man who arrived yesterday, a Colonel Tremayne. Only Belladonna knows his identity. My role is to seek out powerful former Royalists who have temporarily achieved key positions in the Cromwellian regime. When I receive any useful information from them, I will let you know. As they have regular contact with the Protector, they will be in a perfect position to facilitate your next attempt."

"I have already organized another attempt on the life of Cromwell," lied Yarrow, anxious to maintain his freedom of action.

"No, my dear Yarrow, I have orders from Belladonna to take over the responsibility for, and planning of, any assassination. You will do nothing until you receive my orders."

"Is Cromwell's death no longer the number one priority for the Garden?" asked an impertinent and coldly furious Yarrow.

"For the moment, our immediate aim is to convince General Liffey, or one of his general staff, that it is time to change sides and lead an army coup to replace Cromwell and recall the king."

Yarrow was lost for words. He had not expected to be pushed aside.

He verbally attacked his visitor, "You will be lucky. My intelligence is that, despite his sister's marriage to a leading Royalist, Liffey remains loyal to Cromwell and is delighted with his appointment in the Cromwellian adventure with the French against the Spanish Netherlands."

"That is why my role is now critical. I am a junior officer attached to Liffey's staff and moved into this house some weeks ago. I was informed like you that there was already a Royalist on the staff, but he has failed to make contact. Belladonna is not happy, both with the failure of this senior officer to contact me and with your three failures to remove the tyrant. She has decided that she will only finance future attempts by you to kill Cromwell if you act directly under my and, ultimately, her supervision."

"Is all the work I have already put into the next plan to be wasted?" asked a deflated and angry Yarrow.

"No, if this plan is well advanced, it would be a pity to cancel it. What did you have in mind?"

"I have converted one of the Lord Protector's lifeguards to our cause and am about to employ an ace marksman, a friend of the former, to assassinate the Protector from a distance. This man can really shoot. It was his accuracy that rendered a previous attempt by us a complete failure."

Blair visibly winced.

He was silent for some time.

Yarrow was irritated. "What's your problem, Woad?"

"Clearly, it is you, you fool!"

Yarrow's growing anger rose to the surface, but before he could explode into a torrent of abuse, Blair continued, "I am shocked by your revelation. You are a fool, not because you failed but because you relied on Cromwellian soldiers. You cannot trust any current soldier at Whitehall or most of his retired veterans. Thurloe has proved his uncanny ability to infiltrate all organizations that oppose the Protector. Your two soldiers are probably Thurloe agents. Your operation needs a complete reassessment and overhaul."

"What do you mean?"

"There will be no immediate assassination attempt! End all contact with these soldiers! Completely disappear! Leave here immediately I depart. Are you clear? Surprisingly, this may be good news for you."

"What do you mean good news?" seethed Yarrow.

"Your past failures were not due to your incompetence but to Thurloe's foreknowledge of your plans."

"Those soldiers give me an excellent entry into the palace of Whitehall," persisted the unconvinced Yarrow.

"Did you not hear me? You failed because Thurloe knew what you planned. More serious is the probability that you are now well-known to the government. A change of identity is essential. For a start, dye your hair—a red head is too easily remembered—and await further orders."

"This is unfair," protested Yarrow.

"Calm down and disappear! Even though I control future assassination attempts, you, in a new identity, will carry out the actual killing. I will contact you when I am ready."

Evan heard footsteps within the room moving toward the door.

In his haste to move away, Evan backed into a suit of armor that went crashing to the floor. In seconds, the door was thrust open; and the two conspirators with swords drawn, one also holding a lighted taper, burst into the chamber.

John Blair called into the otherwise darkened room, "Come, show yourself! Yarrow, move to the far door to prevent his escape!"

"No need to panic, Captain. Here is your intruder!" announced Yarrow, happy to discomfort the now-edgy Blair.

Yarrow picked up the large ginger tomcat that he caught urinating on the newly collapsed armor.

"Get that filthy animal out of my sight. Make sure there is nothing left in the house that can be traced to you and leave before dawn. I will return upstairs to my quarters by an indirect route through the garden."

Blair departed, but Evan had obtained a good picture of him before he left the lighted room.

He would recognize him when they met again.

Yarrow carried the cat down the hall toward the exit.

Evan took advantage of Yarrow's movement to escape and rejoin the patient Harry who was dozing peacefully on a gigantic bed.

Fortunately, his snoring had not been heard by any of the denizens.

Meanwhile, Yarrow maintained the rage.

Blair's performance had not been completely convincing.

He seemed confused about some aspects of Yarrow's designated role and provided no proof of his identity as Woad other than declaring it.

Yarrow had a worrying thought. What if Woad was himself a Thurloe agent?

It was a brilliant plan by Cromwell's master manipulator. Prevent an assassination attempt by simply canceling it.

As a symbol of his defiance, Yarrow picked up the ginger tom he had deposited in the garden and reentered the house, suggesting to the feline that it might find Blair—and urinate over him.

The general eventually retired for the night, although several of his guests continued to play cards by the warmth of a smelly but effective coal fire.

Harry led Evan into the library where the latter soon located the general's desk, which was a new French model with a myriad of secret drawers.

Harry was apologetic.

He had no idea how to access the desk other than smashing its locked drawers.

Evan smiled. "Don't worry, Harry. A friend of mine has one of these, and he entertained me recently by showing how the various hidden drawers and compartments were opened. Let's hope I remember enough of his demonstration to find the most recent letters."

He did.

He placed them in a leather bag, which he had slung around his neck, and pulled down the short hood that now covered most of his face.

Almost simultaneously, the door of the library swung open.

Three armed soldiers with swords in one hand and tapers in the other entered the room, followed by several officers led by Colonel Tremayne.

Evan did not hesitate.

He ran at full speed toward the double doors that led from the library onto a balcony.

Luckily, the doors gave way, and Evan hurtled over the balcony into the darkness below.

The soldiers raised the alarm, and lights began to appear throughout the house.

Soon dozens of men crisscrossed the garden.

A soft evergreen shrub broke Evan's fall, and he was able to run down a cobbled path toward the road.

He reached the side gate, and just as he entered the thoroughfare, he tripped over a body lying across the path.

He turned the body over.

He was appalled.

He recognized the victim.

It was Blair.

Blood was trickling out of numerous stab wounds.

As Evan bent over him, Blair stirred slightly and muttered almost incoherently a single word—or so Evan surmised.

It sounded like *marriage*, but it could have been *carriage*.

There was a sudden expulsion of air.

Blair was dead.

Next morning, Evan and Strad carefully examined the letters and papers that had been stolen from Liffey's library.

These were much more political than the earlier communications.

They were largely from his eldest sister pleading with him as governor of a West Indian island to change sides—to denounce the protectorate and declare for the king.

He had obviously not done so.

Unfortunately, there were no copies of his replies.

Another group of papers proved more interesting. They were the last month's notes for later entry into a diary.

It was a personal account of the issues Liffey faced.

It was dominated by his genuine desire to command the protectorate's army in Flanders in its joint operation with the French against the Spaniards.

It was clear that Liffey's service in the Americas had stiffened his opposition to and dislike of Spain.

What was of even greater interest to the intelligence officers were several references to unnamed officers on his staff whom he suspected of dealing with the king or, even more dangerous in his eyes, with the Spaniards.

After several hours of reading, Evan decided that despite his misgivings, he must report the latest development concerning John Blair and Yarrow to Thurloe.

Evan was amazed at Thurloe's reaction.

He put his head between his hands and then hammered his desk several times with a closed fist.

"Wait here, Sir Evan. I must inform His Highness immediately."

Thurloe left the room.

Evan was confused by the overreaction to the news he had brought.

8

Within minutes, a servant entered the room and asked Evan to follow him to the Protector's reception chamber.

Both Cromwell and Thurloe were present.

The Protector did not waste time.

"Mr. Thurloe has updated me regarding your adventures in Liffey House and the death of Blair."

"Your Highness appears unduly interested in the fate of another would-be assassin. I overheard him plotting and planning with that redheaded scoundrel, Yarrow, to kill you."

Thurloe interrupted, "What you heard, Captain, was my agent John Blair trying to discover all that Yarrow knew and at the same time render him ineffective. The conversation you reported from Blair was almost word by word my instructions to him."

Cromwell took up the case. "John has hundreds of agents across the land in most gatherings of our enemies. I do not want you or Tremayne wasting time uncovering our own men. Please inform Luke that Blair was one of us but that he should keep that information to himself."

"On the bigger issue, do Liffey's letters suggest that he should be cashiered or imprisoned?" asked Thurloe.

"No, the general in this case is loyal. Or to be precise, we have no evidence that he is not."

"Yarrow was expecting to make contact with a Royalist agent on Liffey's staff. Liffey himself suspects that one of his officers is a Royalist or Spanish agent. Luke should also be informed of these developments without delay," demanded Cromwell.

"Before I depart, do either of you know why Blair spent his dying breath enunciating a word like *carriage* or *marriage*? What could be its significance?" asked Evan.

"Only the more obvious. Perhaps Blair discovered that an attempt would be made on His Highness during a marriage or as he rode somewhere in his carriage. I will double the guard on any trips taken in a carriage and give you a list of any future marriages His Highness has agreed to attend," Thurloe replied.

Cromwell ended the discussion by reminding Evan that with Blair dead, Yarrow may choose to ignore his new instructions and do his own thing. "An organized conspiracy is much easier to uncover than the erratic behavior of a lone wolf. Watch Yarrow day and night!"

Evan sent Strad to update Luke, who, in turn, visited Liffey.

He was welcomed into the library where he handed the general his authority from Oliver Cromwell to act in the name of the Protector and, if necessary, override all other jurisdictions, military or civil.

The general perused the document and commented, "And why is a senior officer on the Protector's personal staff engaged on intelligence business, seconded to my Flanders army as a simple adjutant?"

Luke diplomatically explained that the government suspected that one of Liffey's officers was a clandestine Royalist, planning both the assassination of the Protector and a simultaneous uprising created by gaining control of the very army that Liffey was establishing.

Liffey responded gravely, "Alas, Colonel, your fears are justified. While in the Caribbean, I suspended two officers who were in touch with Royalist or Spanish agents. I daily received requests from family and unnamed sources to denounce the Protector and declare for the king."

"Now that you have a commission to form a significant portion of the army for Flanders and are appointing your own staff, these requests will intensify."

"Yes, it is already occurring. Since my appointment was announced, I have had dozens of letters recommending people for appointment."

"That is why I am here. Royalists will fall over themselves to receive such an appointment. Hopefully, they will overreach themselves and reveal their true colors."

"Should I appoint doubtful candidates and lead them into a trap?"

"No, our enemies are not fools. Recommendations of obviously Royalist sympathizers can be rejected. The real enemy agents will have a much better cover, and we may not be able to discover them unless they make a mistake."

"Let's hope you can catch them before they act against Cromwell and his government," concluded Liffey.

Luke changed his line of questioning. "Tell me about the people who already comprise your staff and share part of this house with you. Let's start with the stranger at the other end of the house."

"Never met him. Apparently, my caretaker responded to a letter from my elder sister to house one of her acquaintances in the far wing while he carried out some business in London. I may have been a little naive because recently we have had several robberies, and a body of a junior officer, Captain Blair, was found just outside our gate, presumably killed while trying to stop one of robbers from the night before last."

"I know of the robbery. I was one of the officers that confronted the two thieves."

"Did they kill Blair?"

"No! Blair was a government agent who had gone some way to untangle the intrigues beginning to build up around you."

Luke remembered too late that such information was to be kept secret.

Liffey momentarily looked surprised but then asked, "How do you know that the robbers are innocent?"

"General, those intruders were also government agents trying to flush out a would-be assassin who goes by the alias Yarrow, the man who lives in your house."

"Good god! Liffey House, home of an assassin! I hope my sister did not know the intentions of her friend. That information confuses the situation. Did the murderer intend to kill Blair, the serving soldier who may have created personal enemies, or did he eliminate a government spy whose cover had been blown?"

Liffey struggled to conceal a strange look that momentarily dominated his face.

Luke was perplexed by this but responded to his comments, "You are right. It does complicate the investigation into his murder. What do you know about Blair?"

"Very little. He was not one of my West Indian staff."

"So where does he fit in?"

"My men and I returned to England in the hundred-gun ship of the line *Defiance*. It had been part of the English fleet sent to apprehend the Spanish treasure fleet but had been ordered to detach itself from the fleet and cruise the Caribbean in search of Spanish galleons engaged in interisland trade. After several months in this role, it was ordered back to England at the very time that I received similar orders. On the homeward voyage, while still in Caribbean waters, the *Defiance* came across a Spanish merchantman laden with goods and ammunition. It disabled the Spanish vessel and boarded her, finding five English prisoners in the hold. The three sailors were immediately incorporated into the crew of the *Defiance* while I offered to take responsibility for the two officers: Blair and Peebles."

"Did these officers explain how they came to be prisoners aboard the Spanish merchantman?"

"I spoke to neither at the time. The captain of the *Defiance* conducted the interrogation after which he kept both men in isolation until we docked, but he did give me a short report. Blair was part of a raiding party against one of the Spanish forts on the

American mainland and had been captured on what was clearly a failed mission. Peebles claimed he was traveling between Barbados and Jamaica when his ship was blown off course and sank. He was rescued by the Spanish merchantman that the *Defiance* attacked."

"Since their residence here, have either acted strangely? Were they close friends?"

"Exactly the opposite. There was constant tension between the two men, and they avoided each other's company. Blair was overgregarious, annoyed some of my officers, and was overinquisitive. I now know why. Peebles kept to himself but did not hesitate to imply that Blair was not whom he claimed to be."

Luke realized he was wasting his time asking about Blair. At the first opportunity, he would seek the full story from Thurloe.

"Is Peebles here? I would like to talk to him."

Ten minutes later, Major Peebles sat opposite Luke who had taken over Liffey's office for this important interview.

Luke went straight to the point.

"Major, I am Colonel Luke Tremayne, head of the Protector's personal intelligence unit. I have been alerted to the murder of Captain Blair, and as you may have known him longer than anyone else here, I need to ask you a few questions."

Robert Peebles was a tall blond-haired, well-built man who stared for some time at his inquisitor. His first words revealed he was Irish, as was Blair. Luke had mastered their accent nearly a decade earlier.

"Colonel, are you the Luke Tremayne that served in Ireland as a cavalry commander and at one stage had a Simon Cobb as your deputy?"

"I am. You know Cobb?"

"Yes. He is my current commanding officer."

"Why would Simon go to the far ends of the earth? He was never one to seek rewards and titles."

"Sir, you may have observed in your days with him that he was obsessed with his twin brother who betrayed his family. According to Simon, that brother now threatens the current government by leading an Irish nationalist conspiracy against England being launched from the Caribbean."

Luke could not hold back a tear as he recalled that it was Simon's twin brother who had murdered one of the few women he had truly loved.

He changed the subject. "How did you come to be aboard that Spanish merchantman?"

"Cobb has told me much about you. I feel free to talk to you. Do not reveal any of what I am about to say to any other officer in this household including Liffey. I want your word as a gentleman that my information will remain within your unit. In addition, I would like you to get a message to Jamaica to inform Colonel Cobb of my current situation and the need for further instructions."

Luke did not like those he interviewed imposing conditions, but his suspicion of the Liffey household and Peebles's relationship with Simon Cobb made him sympathetic.

He agreed to both requests.

"So what are you doing for Cobb, and why is it so confidential?"

"Cobb sought the position in Jamaica because he had heard rumors in Scotland that the Irish rebels expected an armed fleet and army to emerge out of the Indies and push the English out of Ireland."

"I have heard similar rumors. Did Cobb have or obtain any solid evidence?"

"Once in the Caribbean, he certainly received information that increased his obsession."

"What do you mean?"

"Cobb interviewed many of the Jamaica garrison that had been part of General Venables's army, which had conquered the island, and many naval officers who commanded several of the warships left behind by Admiral Penn to patrol the surrounding seas. What emerged was a disturbing picture. Over the past two years, two thousand men and eleven warships had disappeared. The authorities chose officially to believe the men had deserted, or had been killed, although their deaths were not recorded and that the ships had sunk without trace on one of the many uncharted reefs or during unpredicted hurricanes."

"Simon did not accept this analysis?" asked Luke.

"No, he believes the missing men are nearly all Irish and are hiding on one of the many islets in the Caribbean or on the American mainland and that the ships are at anchor somewhere, ready to collect these men and sail for Europe."

"Can he prove any of this?"

"That colonel was my task. I was sent to all the English islands in the Caribbean to ascertain the whereabouts of their Irish prisoners. I discovered that many Irish officers exiled to Barbados had disappeared, and similar patterns occurred elsewhere. Cobb was right. Most Irish officers had disappeared while most of the English Royalists could be accounted for."

"But that did not necessarily mean they have made their way to a secret rendezvous to be part of an Irish army?"

"No, but if a large mysterious fleet were to be discovered, Cobb's suspicions will appear more credible."

"Was such a fleet discovered?"

"I believe so, but I cannot be sure. When the ship I had taken to return to Jamaica encountered the fierce storm that blew it off course and, ultimately, onto reefs in some unknown part of the Indies, I am sure that just before my ship went down, I saw through the tumultuous waves at least eight ships riding at anchor inside the reef that destroyed my ship. It was only a momentary glimpse before I was hurled into the water and swept away clinging to a large water barrel until discovered a day later by that passing Spanish merchantman."

"You doubt what you saw?"

"I had been hoping to discover such a fleet for weeks, and maybe in that moment before what could have been imminent death, I saw what I wanted to see. Who knows?"

"Well, if you worked with Cobb long enough, his obsessions might become contagious. Tell me about Blair."

9

"Not much, but from the beginning, I did not trust him."

"Just a feeling, or did you have evidence?"

Peebles clearly hesitated before answering, creating suspicion in Luke's mind.

Could he believe what Peebles was about to say?

An answer finally emerged from a suddenly wary Peebles, "Both. Blair and I were kept apart on the Spanish ship. I did not know he was aboard until just before the *Defiance* attacked us. I heard the Spanish officers sound the action bell, and almost simultaneously, Blair was thrown into my dingy brig."

"How did Blair explain this sudden arrival?"

"He had been imprisoned in a similar cabin elsewhere in the ship, but on sighting the English warship, the Spaniards needed all the men they could spare. To have prisoners spread throughout the ship, requiring separate guards, was not the most efficient use of their limited resources."

"You didn't believe him?"

"Initially, it appeared reasonable. The captain of the *Defiance* questioned some of the captured sailors, many who were Portuguese conscripts. They claimed that until the attack Blair had a separate cabin and ate with the Spanish officers. Blair denied it, claiming that he had had a serious altercation with the Portuguese, who now made unfounded allegations against him."

"Difficult to prove one way or another," Luke mumbled.

"There is more. Since his arrival here, Blair has been very outgoing regarding the mission on the American mainland that led to his capture. Since our capture of Jamaica, its governor has been the only English official empowered to mount military missions on the continent. I have never heard of the one in which Blair claims to have participated."

"Anything else you can tell me about Blair?"

"Yes, before we met on the *Defiance*, I had seen him on various islands in the Caribbean although at that time I did not know who he was. Given what I know now, I would certainly have followed up his behavior. He was always with senior officers of the various English administrations or with powerful local planters and merchants."

"He moved in high circles?"

"Yes!"

"And since you both have been in England?"

"He has ingratiated himself with the senior officers although at times irritating them—and humiliated the more junior."

Luke brought his questioning to an end.

He must see Thurloe and obtain the full story of Blair's mission in order to assess the value of Peebles's information.

First, he needed to tie up two loose ends.

Luke went to Liffey.

"Sir, release into my custody the robber you hold! He is also a government agent. My unit needs to debrief him."

Liffey had Harry brought to him.

Luke thanked the general and escorted Harry from the room.

Immediately they reached the garden, Luke told Harry he was free to go. Luke watched as the petty criminal disappeared into the bustling throng of passersby.

Luke continued on to Whitehall to discuss Blair's murder with Evan before confronting Thurloe.

Blair's murder was baffling.

Was he murdered for reasons other than being uncovered as a Thurloe spy?

"If Blair was seen as the Royalist agent who had taken control of the assassination attempts, was his murderer another government agent who did not know the real situation?" asked Luke.

Evan was pragmatic. "Or equally plausible, his murder may have nothing to do with high politics. Did the local thieves kill him? They may have gone back for more loot unbeknownst to us and were confronted by Blair."

"I don't think so. Remember, he was killed during the short period Harry and you were both in the house searching through Liffey's papers. Those lads were conniving thieves, not killers."

"It may have been an accident. Harry's friends could have been waiting outside for Harry to reappear and somehow fell into dispute with Blair. After all, his body was found at the end of our planned escape route," recalled Evan.

"If so, Blair's murder need not concern us being unrelated to plots to undermine the government or assassinate the Protector."

"Another possibility is that Blair was murdered by Peebles," added Evan.

"That need not be a major concern either. If Peebles is an intelligence officer working for our governor of Jamaica, his removal of a Royalist agent as Blair appeared to him fitted his brief."

"But what if their roles are the reverse of that outlined by Peebles? What if Blair was the government's agent, which we know he was, and Peebles the Royalist spy? Peebles murdered Blair to conceal his real loyalties, which the latter was about to reveal."

Evan continued, "Peebles may have murdered Blair, but I heard Blair announce from his own lips to the man we know has made three attempts on the Protector's life, Yarrow, that he was taking control of such attempts. Blair was presenting himself as a Royalist and central to the assassination conspiracy. Who knew otherwise? Peebles?"

"All that is what Thurloe wanted Yarrow to think," said Luke.

"Or that is what Blair wanted Thurloe to think," continued Luke as if he had just experienced an epiphany.

Neither man put into words the catastrophic possibility.

Was Blair a double agent whose real loyalty was to the king?

Luke chose to focus on the immediate.

"Blair is dead, but we may have an experienced assassin very close to Liffey in Peebles. He may not be the real Peebles but an impostor. If the latter, he is taking a great risk that someone will see through the pretense."

"Not much of a risk!" scoffed Evan. "It will take months for us to obtain proof from Jamaica that this is or is not the real Peebles."

"Not so. I can have proof within the hour. Most of Penn's fleet that took part in the conquest of Jamaica lies at anchor at various English ports. Most of the sailors have been demobilized, and many of the ships have been decommissioned. However, the admiral's flagship lies in the Thames, a few minutes' walk from where we are."

"How will that help identify Peebles?"

"Because until they left Jamaica, a detachment of the admiral's sailors provided part of the bodyguard for the governor of Jamaica—a role that they played jointly with my friend Colonel Cobb and his assistant, Major Peebles."

"Great. I will find any sailors who were in that guard and can identify Peebles and bring them here," volunteered Evan.

Luke was silent for some time but eventually spoke, "Evan there is yet another possibility. Was Blair murdered by mistake? His killer mistook him for Peebles. Our enemies were aware that Peebles might reveal Blair as a Royalist or Spanish spy and sent orders for his execution, but their agent confused the two recent additions to Liffey's household."

"Hardly likely. The men were quite distinct in appearance—Blair a small wiry figure with black hair, and Peebles a tall blond."

"Darkness may have obliterated these differences in the eyes of a paid killer who was not familiar with either man. This interpretation would best suit our purpose," concluded Luke.

"What! To have a killer on the loose who, when he discovers his mistake, will try again?"

"Precisely. He will try again, and we will be ready for him."

"We have ignored another explanation that would suit us even better—the one you passed over earlier with Blair as a double agent. He remained a Royalist and Spanish spy while convincing Thurloe he was one of us. A Royalist who thought he might inadvertently give the game away killed him or more likely because he had failed in his mission. All the assassination attempts on Cromwell have coincided with the time Blair has been in the country," suggested Evan.

"Maybe Blair and Yarrow were in this together?" mused Luke.

"From the conversation I overheard, Blair was only then imposing his authority on Yarrow. This was to be a partnership for the future, not one from the past," Evan explained.

Evan left for the docks, and Luke visited Thurloe.

"What can I do for you?" Thurloe asked as he ushered Luke into his small antechamber.

"Details of Blair's mission and any of his findings that may help me solve his murder."

"Don't confuse your priorities, Colonel! Solving the murder of Blair is of little importance. Preventing the assassination of His Highness and the subverting of his new army are the issues."

"But, sir, the solving of Blair's murder may be essential if we are to forestall the enemies of His Highness. What exactly was his mission for you in the Indies?"

"I sent Blair to the Caribbean several years ago when I received information that imprisoning high-ranking Royalist officers and hundreds of Irish nationalist prisoners on the various islands in the area may not have been a good idea. These enemies of Cromwell were forced together by us into situations that provided them with ample opportunities to plot against the government, with little chance of being caught. More recently, following our partial defeat in establishing more colonies in the area, Blair reported that thousands of men and dozens of ships had just disappeared. The authorities put the loss of men down to disease and of the ships to inclement weather.

Blair heard increasing rumors of a Royalist-Irish army being gathered together and trained on one of the many islands and of a fleet being readied to transport them to Europe. His attempts to uncover the precise details of these activities were complicated when your old friend Cobb began a similar investigation through the person of Major Peebles."

"So Peebles and Blair were on the same side doing the same job?

Did Blair's activities bear fruit?"

"Blair was brilliantly successful, but while he and Peebles were doing the same work, they would not appear to an outside observer to be on the same side."

"What do you mean?"

"Under my instructions, Blair presented himself as a Royalist and successfully infiltrated the cabal of Royalist officers that were planning the insurrection."

"So Blair may have recognized one of them on Liffey's staff?"

"It is possible, but that officer would not have murdered Blair unless he knew that the latter was one of my men. He would have sought Blair out, and the two of them would have planned together the subversion of the army they were creating. That was my plan."

"How was it that Blair infiltrated the Garden and became the agent Woad?" asked Luke.

"He received a letter of introduction to a wealthy English woman who it was assumed was financing the Caribbean operation."

"Identity?"

"No names were provided. He was to present his letter to the keeper of a public house in Newmarket and await instructions. This he did, and he attended the inaugural meeting of the Garden."

"His death at this time must be a major blow to your operations. Did you give him any special instructions when he arrived at Liffey House?"

"Yes, he was to be overfriendly but at the same to provoke the officers who had been in the Indies, especially Peebles of whom we knew least, to the point that in a moment of temper they might reveal something of interest."

"He was ordered to provoke, irritate, and annoy?"

"Yes."

"He apparently succeeded. On another matter, did the government plan a colony on the mainland of America, and did it authorize the collection of Royalist and Irish officers from outlying islands to settle it?"

"Yes, it was my response to the posed threat. The government would round up the Royalist officers and Irish troops still left on the islands. Remove them from their pleasant detention and send them to a disease-ridden part of the American mainland where they could not easily escape to join any planned rebel army."

"Mr. Thurloe, the more you tell me, the more I am sure you were fooled. You gave Blair authority and opportunity to gather together potential troublemakers. He moved them to a secret location to form a rebellious force instead of isolating them on a mosquito-ridden part of the American mainland. You told him to instruct Yarrow in the very terms that his Royalist masters would have used. Blair was a double agent, and his true loyalty was to Charles Stuart."

"Do you have conclusive evidence of this?" asked a troubled Thurloe.

"No, but it would explain a lot."

10

Next morning, Peebles waited in a small alcove in Liffey House, awaiting a meeting with Luke.

Evan with two other men took up a seat on a bench against the opposite wall.

The two other men covertly observed Peebles.

After a few minutes an orderly admitted, Evan and his two companions to Luke's chamber.

The orderly also apologized to Peebles, indicating that the colonel would see him in a few minutes.

Luke was excited. "Straight to the point. Is the man in the next room Major Peebles, an officer on the staff of the governor of Jamaica?"

The two sailors in unison answered, "That is the missing major."

"What do you mean *missing major?*" asked Evan.

"Whenever his commanding officer Colonel Cobb wanted him, he was absent. Very quickly, he was known behind his back as the missing major."

"Was that because of his responsibilities? He was often sent on secret missions by his superiors," Luke asked.

The two sailors sniggered. "Sorry, sir," replied the taller of the two tars. "The only mission Peebles cared about was to cuckold every officer in the Caribbean."

"So Peebles liked women?" queried Evan.

"Only married women, ideally with an income of their own."

"Surely, this created disharmony among the officer community?" asked Luke.

"We returned to England before much of this became common knowledge. Peebles has probably returned here to escape one or more of those irate husbands."

The two sailors uttered bawdy asides as they left by a back door.

Luke and Evan decided not to confront Peebles with any of the information the sailors had provided and content themselves with clarifying his work for Cobb in Jamaica.

The subsequent interrogation produced of little interest.

After Peebles departed, Luke informed Evan that he had shaken Thurloe's confidence by suggesting that Blair was a double agent loyal to the would-be king.

Evan was less amused than his colonel. "That could make our task much more difficult—the top government intelligence organization penetrated by the enemy."

Evan returned to Whitehall to continue the surveillance of Yarrow.

Luke sent orders to John Martin to organize the move of the intelligence company of dragoons to Austin Friars.

That afternoon, Luke met again with Liffey.

He explained that while uncovering the Royalist agents who plotted the assassination of Cromwell and the subversion of the Flanders army was his priority, he had to solve Blair's murder.

Liffey promised full cooperation and gave Luke a list of his senior officers and their responsibilities: Peter Marlowe and Richard Grey each commanded an infantry regiment and David Halliburton the cavalry. Anthony Audley was adjutant and artillery advisor, responsible for liaison with the army command and the provision of supplies. Timothy Redmond and Robert Peebles had no specific roles assigned to them.

Luke arranged to meet each of them separately before the move to Austin Friars.

Sir Peter Marlowe was the first officer interrogated.

"Did you know of Blair before he was rescued by the *Defiance*?" asked Luke.

He was initially pleasantly surprised by Sir Peter's positive response.

Luke waited for Marlowe to elaborate, but nothing was forthcoming.

Luke quickly sensed that to extract information from Marlowe would not be easy.

Luke continued with what could prove a fruitless interview.

"Where did you meet Blair prior to his rescue?"

"I've never met him!"

"But you said you knew him?"

"No, I did not. I said I knew *of* him, but we never met."

"Then explain the circumstances in which you knew of him," asked an exasperated Luke.

"As lieutenant governor and military commandant of the colony of Barbados, one of my duties was to visit the outlying islands of the southern Caribbean to inspect and resupply the small garrisons we had established on them. On one of these islands, our garrison commander reported that they had been visited by an English warship carrying an officer claiming to be a Captain Blair with authority to remove all Irish or Royalist officers that the garrison held in captivity.

"I visited several other islands and found that Blair had preceded me there. On one island, a garrison commander who had complied with Blair's request expressed serious doubts about Blair's identity. He claimed to have fought with a Captain Blair in Ireland, and this was not the same man."

"There were many Blairs fighting in Ireland. It is not an uncommon name," Luke replied.

"After Liffey invited Blair to stay here in his townhouse, did you question him on this matter?"

"Yes, over a game of cards, I asked him directly whether he was the Captain Blair who sailed the Caribbean collecting Irish and Royalist officers. He readily admitted this role and claimed and that he was collecting them to colonize part of the American mainland on behalf of the current government. Apparently, for security reasons, they wanted to remove potential troublemakers from the smaller island communities."

"Is that believable given your knowledge of the Indies?" Luke asked.

"Check with Thurloe! Liffey was never informed of any such enterprise. Young Peebles, who claimed he was the governor of Jamaica's right-hand man, also claimed his superiors had no knowledge of such a plan."

"Actually, they are both wrong. Thurloe confirms that this was a government plan, but I have no evidence as to where these Irish troublemakers finished up. Did Blair get on with you and the other officers?"

"Peebles did not trust him, and the two avoided each other. Blair tried to turn us against Peebles by hinting that he was a Spanish spy and had been planted on the Spanish merchantman that then sailed deliberately into the path of the *Defiance*. On the other hand, Peebles said that Blair was the Royalist and that the papers he was expecting from Jamaica would prove his loyalty to the government."

"Did Blair upset anyone in particular? Was he particularly close to any of them?"

"He was close to Timothy Redmond, but I believe that was due to the fact that they were the most junior officers at Liffey House—a captain and a lieutenant."

"Rank, a sensitive issue?"

"Yes, Liffey, as the second son of a wealthy earl, places great emphasis on position and status. There is now a strong possibility that he will succeed to the earldom. His father is at death's door, and his elder brother is childless and seriously ill. His desire to serve the Protector in Flanders is driven by an inferiority complex that he and the rest of us obtained our current rank through relaxed service in the tropics rather than through the battlefields of Britain and Europe."

"Anything else about Blair and your fellow officers?"

"Yes, Blair provoked Halliburton. Halliburton is an excellent card player, and his constant success at Blair's expense led to hints from the latter that David must be cheating. When challenged by David, Blair denied he had expressed any such views. David was going to challenge Blair to a duel to redeem his honor."

"Let me summarize your comments. Our victim is the Blair who collected Royalist officers in dubious circumstances, Peebles questioned his past and present loyalties, and Halliburton was irritated by his accusations of cheating at cards."

An orderly terminated their discussion, informing the officers that young Redmond had been attacked and was at death's door and that Audley, who in his youth had been a battlefield surgeon, was tending the victim, pending the arrival of a physician.

Luke found Audley at the scene of the crime.

Both men immediately recognized each other from their school days. The Audleys were a Kentish family that had moved into Cornwall, taking over a number of estates near the ancestral home of the Tremaynes. The children of the local gentry went to school on the estate of the most powerful local aristocrat, Lord Hanes.

Tony Audley and Luke Tremayne had been the best of friends.

Luke asked rhetorically, "Are you really the Anthony Alexander Audley that went to school on the estate of Lord Hanes in the early thirties?"

"Yes, and you are that boisterous blond boy who used his blue eyes to have all the girls falling in love with you. You and Lord Hanes's daughter Elizabeth were very close. If I remember correctly, her father was mightily relieved when you were packed off to fight for the Dutch Republic. I heard only last year that you and she, a recent widow, were to marry, and you were to take over her father's extensive estates, making you one of the wealthiest men in England."

"I did renew my acquaintance with the Lady Elizabeth, but the nature of my work is such that I could not settle permanently in one place with a wife."

"That sounds like an excuse, Luke."

"Maybe. Let's talk about old times over dinner. For the moment, how is Redmond? Is he still alive?"

"Just."

"Do you know what happened?"

"No! I simply found the body."

"How did that come about?"

"Redmond was to see the general. An hour after the appointed time, he had not appeared. I had just completed my meeting with Liffey, so he asked me to look in on the missing man. Outside Redmond's quarters, his newly appointed valet told me that Redmond had not appeared for breakfast and that his bedchamber was locked. After continuous knocking failed to arouse him, I sent for keys that might open the door. Eventually, the aged caretaker arrived and after considerable trial and error found one that opened the door."

"What exactly did you find when you entered this room?"

"What you see now. The room was bathed in sunlight, and those large windows overlooking the garden were wide open. At first glance, I assumed that Redmond had locked the door from the inside and then disappeared through the window. That is until I tripped over a large ornamental cushion that had fallen from the bed. Beside it and half hidden was a body. It was Redmond. I examined him. He had been stabbed in the chest probably as he lay sleeping on his back, and the would-be killer then rolled him off the bed and half covered the body with the cushion. There was also a massive blow to his head. His skull appears badly dented, and you can see a large pool of blood has spread across the floor."

"Has he been conscious at any time you were with him?"

"No, I initially thought he was dead, but I then discovered he was still breathing. I have summoned a physician and informed Richmond's relatives who have a mansion just around the corner."

"I have no time for physicians. Give me an apothecary or army surgeon any day."

"This physician meets your requirements. He has an unusual background. He was an army surgeon in his youth, as was I."

The physician and Redmond's uncle arrived at the same time.

After a careful examination of the wounded man, the physician cleaned the wounds and covered the most open of them.

He concluded that any further intervention on his behalf would be useless.

Only time would tell whether Redmond would regain consciousness—let alone recover. And if he did, he may not be normal.

He suggested to Redmond's uncle that he prepare himself for the worst.

The uncle went to the door and summoned a number of his own servants who carefully placed Redmond on a stretcher.

Redmond would die or recover or linger on in a vegetable state in his uncle's home.

Luke reported the matter to Liffey and asked, "Did Marlowe ever tell you of a mysterious ship collecting Irish and Royalist prisoners from outlying islands?"

"Yes, he thought it was either a scheme by the governor of the newly conquered island of Jamaica to supplement its meager population or to remove troublemakers onto the disease-ridden American mainland where they would conveniently die."

"Did he tell you the officer collecting the prisoners was Captain Blair?"

Liffey went quiet.

He then bent the quill in his hand in half and muttered, "Damn it, he did not. And why would that have been?"

Why indeed! thought Luke.

11

Next day Luke was back at Whitehall, where Evan had more information on Blair.

"He was also asked by Thurloe to monitor the performance of both General Venables and Admiral Penn in their dramatically acrimonious and unsuccessful assault on Santo Domingo, the capital of Spanish Hispaniola. Then he is listed as missing in an assault on a small garrison on the outskirts of that city. Venables's adjutant noted that a surprisingly large number of officers went missing on this rather innocuous affray—and all of them were Irish.

"He implied that Blair and his largely Irish regiment had deserted. From this point, Blair officially disappears but under Thurloe's secret orders continues to recruit Royalist and Irish prisoners from the lesser islands of the Caribbean for the governor of Jamaica while infiltrating various groups of conspiratorial Royalists."

"We now know all we can about Blair except for the most critical point of all. As a double agent, with whom did his basic loyalty lie?" asked Luke.

On return to Liffey House, Luke was amazed at its transformation. The doors and windows were open, the coverings had been taken off the furniture, and there seemed to be dozens of servants engaged in transporting goods and cleaning the house.

Luke made his way through this activity toward Liffey's office.

As he approached the general's door, he heard raised voices.

The general's antagonist shouted, "You are a fool, Christopher! Your attempt to raise morale by this gesture will backfire. She is a troublemaker who will have us at each other's throats as we were in Barbados."

A man stormed out of the room, slamming the door with unconcealed ferocity.

He was so angry he did not to notice Luke.

It was Liffey's second deputy, Colonel Richard Grey.

Luke waited a while and then knocked gently on the door.

A voice shouted from within, "Go away, Dick. I have had enough of your complaints."

Luke pushed the door aside and announced himself.

Liffey apologized, "I thought it was Dick Grey returning. He and I have just had a major argument. As you have noticed, I am renovating Liffey House and removing most of its furnishings, at least temporarily, to our new base at Austin Friars in Kent. I have brought in dozens of servants from my family's country estate, Liffey Grange, to assist the move and serve us in our new headquarters. I have invited my officers to bring their families to Kent until we embark. It will keep individuals happy and, in general, raise morale."

"Grey disagrees?"

"Yes, something happened in Barbados, and he developed an obsessive hatred of Penelope, Peter's wife, and, to a lesser extent, of Ursula, Audley's daughter."

"Is Grey married?" asked Luke innocently.

"Yes, but unhappily. Many Royalist peers, to protect their property, married their daughters off to up-and-coming Cromwellian officers. The Earl of Rede married his daughter and heiress Evadne to Richard Grey, an obscure Norfolk gentleman. She never came to Barbados."

Then he added gravely, "Dick has serious problems with women."

Luke would follow up on that comment. It could open up the more intimate life of the returning colonial officers and their families.

For the moment, he concentrated on his immediate priority. "Tell me about Timothy Redmond."

"Tim, when a young child, was taken by his father to St. Kitts. The father became a wealthy planter, exporting most of the island's sugar to England, although the Redmonds had money before the St. Kitts enterprise. The wider family are London merchants and strong financial supporters of Parliament, and now of the Protector. Young Tim found little to attract him on Kitts and came to Barbados seeking employment. I offered him a commission, and he was delighted, even more so when he heard we were all returning to England. He was so keen to remain one of us that he requested to stay here rather than reside with his uncle in the next street."

"So any attack on Redmond, if political, would be the work of an antigovernment group or individual?"

"Possibly, but I doubt if the motives are political. It has probably more to do with Blair. They became great friends during the voyage and were largely inseparable here, leading some of the men to suggest an unhealthy relationship. I don't know about Redmond, but Blair was overtly a ladies' man, although his profligate behavior in this regard may have been a cover for unnatural tendencies."

Liffey was called away, and Luke sought out Grey, whose alleged *difficulties with women* intrigued him.

Grey appeared anxious to talk to Luke and invited him to his chamber where servants produced a range of cold meats and tankards of freshly brewed ale.

Luke found it difficult to begin an interrogation while chewing at a large turkey leg.

He began gently, "Colonel Grey, tell me about yourself!"

"Call me Dick. A man in your position hardly ever interrogates unless he already knows most of the answers. Your reputation goes before you."

"I know you fought bravely in Northern Ireland under General Monk, and when he was transferred to Scotland to become its military governor, you and your commander Lord Liffey were probably disappointed to be sent to Barbados instead of following Monk across the Irish Sea. I have also heard that you are married to the heiress of a penurious earl, and although your own pedigree is not so impressive, your family wealth is immense."

"Yes, my lowly pedigree is often flung back at me. My father was a yeoman but an exceedingly wealthy one. He became the richest landowner in our part of Norfolk with property also in Suffolk and Essex. On his death, the local community condescended to consider me a gentleman. When the wily but impoverished nobleman, the Earl of Rede, married off his daughter to me, my local standing rose. But it hardly compares with my colleagues here—an earl's son Lord Liffey, a viscount Lord Audley, a knight Sir Peter Marlowe, and a landed gentleman of impeccable pedigree David Halliburton, esquire."

"Despite what you obviously see as a distinction in rank, do you get on with these men?"

"Very well! One great advantage of the new national army formed in 1645 was its emphasis on military merit rather than status. All the senior officers here are imbued with the same egalitarian attitude as loyal servants of the Protector whose own origins are lowlier that all of them—except me. My comrades are not a problem. It's their families who consider me inferior."

"That is rather childish. Your wife outranks them all. Is that why you object to Liffey inviting the families here? I overheard part of your argument with the general earlier this morning."

Dick nodded assent as he refilled Luke's empty tankard.

"I also heard you mention one woman as a troublemaker. Who is she?"

"In the eyes of the Lord Jesus, Lady Penelope Marlowe is destined for hell given her persistent breach of the commandment 'Thou shall not commit adultery.'"

Luke suddenly realized Grey was a Puritan.

How extreme was he?

Luke probed, "Are you a Fifth Monarchy man? I have just come from fighting some of your misguided brethren in Wales who rose against Cromwell despite half their leaders opposing such action."

"Yes, I am! It is the role of the army to prepare the way for Christ's coming by removing the reprobate and supporting God's chosen leaders such as the Lord Protector. No, I do not subscribe to the view of those Welsh rebels that the Protector himself should be removed to make way for the direct rule of the saints."

Luke changed the direction of his questioning. "Tell me about Blair"

"Until he was picked up by the *Defiance*, I had never met him or heard of him, which, given his behavior here, was probably to my advantage."

"You were not impressed?"

"The man was an impostor. He reminded me of the very worst of our cavalier opponents. I know that not all our fellow officers are God-fearing servants of the Lord, but Blair was a worthless reprobate. I had already suggested to Liffey that he be omitted from our command structure for Flanders. We knew nothing of his past, and Peebles hinted that he was probably a deserter and a Royalist. There are plenty of good officers available. We did not need him."

"If Blair was murdered by one of your comrades, who would you consider the most likely perpetrator?"

"Liffey, Audley, Halliburton, and Marlowe are honorable men who would have challenged him to a duel and dispatched him according to knightly protocol. Audley or Halliburton were about to do exactly that."

"They took their cards seriously!"

"Another of the devil's pastimes! Halliburton appeared so incensed with Blair that after a few acrimonious games, their paths hardly crossed. For most our time here, David has been scouring the countryside, trying to recruit a regiment of horse that will not weaken the government's establishment in England. Peebles is a possibility. The man keeps to himself. He seems politically reliable, but I really know nothing about him, except that he detested Blair."

"Could Redmond have been Blair's murderer?"

Dick Grey laughed. "That quean. He doted on Blair. On the other hand, I am sure Blair did not return Redmond's attention. As a rejected lover, the boy could have killed Blair. On board the *Defiance*, it was thought that both Redmond and Blair were faggots. However, since arriving at Liffey House, Blair showed a decided preference for women."

"You could be right. Redmond felt rejected and killed Blair as part of a lover's tiff? If Redmond was as you suggest, why did the general appoint him to his staff?"

Dick laughed again. "Well, may you ask? Redmond was a callow youth with no military experience. When he first arrived at Government House in Barbados, I could not help thinking of the young drummer boys appointed to Royalist regiments for no other purpose than to satisfy the lust of the officers temporarily deprived of female companions. I was shocked as none of my colleagues are that way inclined. I asked Christopher why he had appointed such a person to his staff. He claimed he did not know of the boy's proclivities in advance. He was simply doing a good turn for the boy's father—apparently an old friend. The father thought the army might make a man of the boy."

"Who attacked him?" Luke asked.

"None of us. If my fellow officers objected to his behavior—which, apart from his fawning over Blair, was not obscenely overt—they would have given him a good beating or asked Christopher to expel him. With Blair's rejection of his advances, he may have sought a lover elsewhere and was murdered by this new friend."

"Richard, I cannot rule out your fellow officers for either Blair's murder or the attempt on Redmond," responded Luke.

"Why not? None of my comrades would feel compelled to kill two inconsequential reprobates such as Blair and Redmond."

"Blair may have confided some damaging information about one of you to Redmond, and the victim of this information had to remove both men to keep his secret."

"What sort of secret could any of us be hiding?"

"A possibility is beginning to emerge. All of you spent much of your time in the Caribbean inspecting the outlying islands. You did something on St. Kitts, Nevis, Antigua, Barbuda, or elsewhere that could destroy your reputation. Blair traveled from island to island, collecting Irish and Royalist officers and men for the governor of Jamaica to help settle the newly acquired colony. Blair could have discovered something incriminating about one of you."

12

"Luke, if you knew anything about those small Caribbean islands, you would know there is no room for any disreputable or disloyal activity to go undetected. You could not keep anything secret from the closely knit community of planters and their wives."

"Now you are being naive, Richard. No matter what the location, there is always occasion for rape, adultery, murder, extortion, fraud, or treachery—just to start with."

"No, you are on the wrong track, Colonel. Apart from Peter, we are all very wealthy men with no need to increase our assets by immoral means. We are all honorable men who would not act criminally. If there were any grounds for blackmail, it could only be deep in the past and concern someone close to us rather than any of the senior officers themselves."

"You get on well with your fellow officers?"

"I have worked with Marlowe for over a decade. We were both officers on Monk's staff in Northern Ireland, and both of us hoped to follow him to Scotland. Instead, we were sent to the Indies. We have been a little estranged recently, given my attitude toward his wife. The others I have known for the five years we were in the Caribbean."

Luke completed his questioning and made his way back to his own apartment.

He realized that Grey's religious convictions, unlike that of many of his sectarian brethren had given him a very rosy if not naive view of the world—women excepted.

Later that evening, Anthony Audley and Luke dined alone.

Luke asked, "What have you done since you finished school? If I recall correctly, you were the scholar destined for Cambridge."

"Yes, I went to Cambridge and studied mathematics among other subjects, but my real interest moved to invention. I built a model mill that can be powered by steam. It will revolutionize manufacture. Industry will no longer be locked into areas where wind and running water are available to turn the wheels."

"How then did an aristocratic inventor finish up a Parliamentary soldier in the Caribbean on the staff of the governor of Barbados?"

"When the Civil War began, unlike my neighbors but like you, I joined the armies of Parliament. Initially, I used my knowledge of the human body gained at Cambridge to act as a battlefield surgeon, but I soon became more interested in artillery. I made several improvements to our cannons and ammunition. I rose through the ranks as an artillery officer and was sent to the Caribbean to inspect the new fortifications and to ensure that we had sufficient reliable cannon to defend our recently obtained possessions.

"I was also going through a humiliating divorce in which my former wife's indiscretions were public knowledge. It was less traumatic to be out of the country.

"After all, I had the only possession I wished to retain from that horrible marriage with me: my daughter.

"Last year, Father died, and I became the ninth Viscount Audley. I came home earlier than the other officers to take up my new responsibilities but promised Christopher that if he received a battlefield assignment, I would advise him on artillery matters but would not play an active role. I resign my commission as soon as Liffey leaves for Flanders to take up seriously my role as local lord and national politician."

"In whose interest?"

"The Protector's! My father and the wider Audley family supported Parliament when most families in Cornwall actively or covertly supported the king. Even the Tremaynes, apart from you, did not openly support Cromwell or the army. Now with the creation of an Upper House, nominated by the Protector, the family's loyalty is to be rewarded with my membership of this new body."

"Are any of your fellow officers Royalist sympathizers?" asked Luke trying to catch Audley off guard.

"Before I answer, I have one question for you. Why are you really here? Although I have been in the Caribbean for years, I am aware of your reputation as Cromwell's right-hand man—special agent, hit man, and trusted confidant. Why would such a person accept a position as adjutant in an army of raw recruits?"

"My appointment here is in line with my lifetime role of protecting Oliver Cromwell and aborting any plots against governments supported by the army. Someone associated with Liffey is organizing both an assassination attempt and a coup against the regime. Your group of officers is the center of attention. So which of your comrades should be my prime suspect?"

"Luke, the far-flung islands of the Caribbean created situations where betrayal and disloyalty could easily occur. Most of the officers stationed on Barbados spent considerable time inspecting the outer islands well away from the scrutiny of their colleagues. While inspecting the artillery on Anguilla, I was approached by a man claiming to be an agent of the king and offering me vast sums to betray Barbados to the Spaniards by revealing the strength and placements of our artillery. All of us have been tempted, but it would have been very difficult to conceal our acceptance of such offers. From the very beginning I suspected only one of us might succumb: Marlowe."

"Evidence?"

"Nothing that would stand up at a court martial. Marlowe's description of several of his trips to distant islands did not fit my knowledge of times and places. There was much time not accounted for. What was he doing in those periods?"

"Did you call him out on these matters?"

"Yes! He acknowledged the discrepancies but hinted that the time was spent with a woman, and he preferred that I forgot what I knew."

"Did you mention your suspicions to others?"

"To Christopher who indicated he would watch Marlowe more carefully."

"Tell me about Blair and Redmond."

"Both unpleasant types. Redmond was a callow youth who attracted lascivious males. I protested when Christopher appointed him to the staff. I was proved right when we picked up Blair on our journey to England. Redmond became devoted to this mystery man whose sexual appetite was beyond comprehension. Male or female, it did not seem to worry him. I am glad I did not know him in Barbados. He would not have been able to keep his hands off my daughter, and I would have had to kill him."

"Was it their sexual activities that got Blair killed and Redmond seriously injured?"

"Could be! If so, the murderer was probably one of their casual acquaintances and not one of the officers at Liffey House."

"What do you make of the other shipwrecked soldier Peebles?"

"On the surface, a dedicated soldier of the Protector, except that I have a lingering doubt about his story. He claims he is a senior officer in the employ of the governor of Jamaica. I visited Jamaica to advise them on artillery emplacements just before my return to England. I spent a lot of time with the governor and his deputy, an Irishman named Cobb, and I never heard the name Peebles mentioned. I was present at a number of conversations where the latest intelligence reports were discussed. None came from Peebles who claims here that he was the senior intelligence officer of the Jamaican administration."

"Peebles did work for Colonel Cobb, but he was absent so often that the rank-and-file called him the missing major. These absences might account for your paths never crossing. I am checking his detailed claims. Colonel Cobb is an old friend of mine, but return post to the Indies can take half a year. You expressed your doubts concerning Marlowe. What about Grey?"

"I have nothing but praise for Dick Grey. He has risen through the ranks by his own ability, although he was elevated socially through a marriage well above his station. His current wealthy situation is due to his and his wife's efforts and not simply inherited. I have never doubted his loyalty to our cause."

"There are many loyal soldiers, including some of my best friends, whose loyalty is currently being tested by the attempt to make Cromwell king. My current task is to uncover potential assassins. This is now a hundredfold more difficult as the most loyal of men can be turned into the most venomous of enemies over this one issue. Could Grey fit into this category? He is a religious man, and I have just come from suppressing a sad uprising of his religious brethren in Wales."

"I don't envy you. We all could defect if current circumstances go badly awry. I hope the army high command and people close to Cromwell, such as yourself, can convince him not to turn his back on those of us who have followed him all these years.

"Have you been approached by any senior officers to take a major part in this growing campaign to thwart the civilian push to make Cromwell king? Has Marlowe or any of the other officers received high-ranking visitors recently?"

"Dozens. As soon as Christopher's appointment was announced, senior officers throughout England began visiting him, seeking positions in the new army. Most are sick of garrison or administrative duties and want to get back into battle. Two of the former major generals offered their services. One visit that upset Christopher was from General Lambert's adjutant."

"Did Liffey elaborate on his reaction?"

"He certainly did. He claimed it was bad enough to select the right men for the task that lay ahead without his work being undermined by Cromwell's former deputy and the army's most popular general."

Luke let out a long-controlled whistle. "Good god, John Lambert does not accept the hereditary protectorate, and Cromwell will soon be forced to dismiss him."

"Liffey served on at least two occasions under Lambert. I could only guess that the adjutant's visit was a request from Lambert to join the campaign against Cromwell accepting the Crown."

"Or, even more seriously, to join a campaign to remove the Protector if he makes the wrong decision," muttered Luke.

"Heaven forbid! You have a very dark view of your fellow man. It must be the job!"

Luke ignored Audley's observation and commented, "There is one aspect of your interview that I find troubling. You have nothing but praise regarding Dick Grey, yet your daughter and Grey have had serious differences."

"A purely personal matter. My daughter made certain complaints regarding Grey. He and I spoke on the matter, which was resolved with good will on both sides, although I admit my daughter is still unhappy."

"What was at issue between them?"

"It was a matter of honor and intensely personal—not something that needs to come within your purview."

Luke sensed that Audley felt strongly on the issue and decided not to pursue it—at least at this time.

He changed the direction of his questioning. "We have discussed all your fellow officers except David Halliburton. Any comments?"

Luke sensed a momentary hesitation and then noticed that Audley had involuntarily clenched his fists and veins bulged on his forehead.

"I saw very little of him on Barbados. The cavalry had a reduced role in the Indies, often sent to outlying islands to bring rebellious plantation workers under control. With our attack on Dominica and Jamaica, they were seconded to General Venables's invasion force and then remained in Jamaica well after my departure to England. Since his return, he has been crisscrossing the countryside, trying to raise cavalry for the Flanders campaign without reducing the existing cavalry establishment."

"He spends considerable time with former soldiers?"

"Yes. I see the problem. He could be raising regiments of cavalry that comprise of men who resigned or were expelled from the army because they disagreed with Cromwell."

Luke nodded. "We have seen easier days."

13

David Halliburton was of slight build. Luke wondered how such a small man could control the heavy cavalry beasts that were his day-to-day companions. Unlike most Cromwellian officers, he wore his black hair long and dressed flamboyantly.

There was no concession to the dominant Puritan fashion that spurned broad lace collars and cuffs.

Luke knew Halliburton. He had commanded this young cavalry officer in Ireland some years earlier.

Luke recalled his surprise when Halliburton relinquished his Irish position for a post in the West Indies—hardly the path for rapid advancement.

David greeted Luke as an old friend, "Colonel, we met many times when you were my nominal commander in Ireland, although much of my work there was with General Monk in the north, and you were often away on secret missions."

"I remember you well, David. I was surprised that you did not stay in Ireland, where my many absences would have led to your rapid promotion, or follow Monk to Scotland, where your cavalry skills would have been much appreciated in bringing those Highlanders under control. Self-exile to the Caribbean was not a good career choice."

"My decision was very personal. Suffice it to say, I am now back in England and full of enthusiasm for the forthcoming conflict in Flanders. I had the odd encounter with Spaniards in the Americas and cannot wait to resume conflict with them."

Halliburton paused before taking the initiative, "Your presence here is hardly discreet. Everyone pretends you are here to find who killed Blair and assaulted Richmond. Equally, everybody seems to know that your real purpose is to uncover the Royalist spy and potential assassin that the government and our own commanding officer suspect is within our own general staff."

"No comment! For the moment, let's concentrate on the murder and assault. Who did it?"

"Redmond is easy. Any of my fellow officers could have done it. He was a quean."

"Any of your fellow officers in a relationship with Redmond? Was he murdered to keep the affair a secret?"

"No, none of my comrades are interested in men. Most of them have enough problems with women. Redmond associated with the lowlife of Barbados and, since his arrival here, with the London riffraff. He may have discovered something against one of us. If he did, I would not be surprised if he used his knowledge to blackmail one of my comrades, and they may have retaliated."

"Whom might it be?"

"Anyone! Redmond's appointment to the staff and his return to England with us was a great surprise. One explanation is that he was blackmailing Liffey. Peebles showed an immediate disdain toward Redmond and gave the impression that such lowlife should be exterminated."

"What about Blair?"

"A womanizing card cheat who was murdered before Audley or myself could challenge him to a duel. No one could substantiate any of his stories, although Marlowe did recall that a man called Blair was sailing the outer isles, rounding up Royalist and Irish officers to take them to Jamaica as part of our colonizing activity. I was seconded to Jamaica in the months after the original conquest and never heard of any such forced migrants arriving, although the concept was widely mooted. Peebles did not pull any punches. He told us that Blair was a Spanish spy, and when the Spanish merchantman picked him up, Blair was not a prisoner on board that ship but an honored guest. It was only when the *Defiance* hove into sight that he was cast into the brig alongside Peebles."

"While you were on Jamaica did you meet Peebles?"

"No, but Cobb mentioned him on several occasions. He was away on a secret mission for the Protector. I did hear rumors that his mission was of a more personal kind: the seduction of married women. The Peebles at Liffey House showed no such inclinations, although Blair made up for all of us in that area."

"You mentioned earlier that your comrades had difficulties involving women. I have heard that Colonel Grey had some trouble with Lady Penelope Marlowe and Lady Ursula Audley."

"Some English gentlewomen seem to lose their modesty and decorum when forced to live in distant colonies. Penny Marlowe is a lively, seductive woman who has many male friends. The extent of that friendship remains a mystery, but many a Barbados planter, truthfully or otherwise, claimed a very intimate relationship with her ladyship. Dick Grey detests her, which has led to strained relations with Sir Peter."

"What about Lady Ursula?"

David suddenly became nervous and muttered almost incoherently, "On the surface, she appears an ice-cold innocent, but she did become embroiled in some way with Dick Grey, which surprisingly brought him and her father closer together."

"And what about yourself, David? Did you have a relationship with either of these women?"

Again David hesitated and appeared agitated. "It was another relationship that forced me to give up my ambitions and flee to the Indies. I was not going to complicate my life by getting involved with the womenfolk of my closest comrades. I do not look forward to Liffey's request that their families move into Austin Friars, our new barracks in Kent."

"You are the second officer to consider it a bad idea. Why?"

"There were tensions in Barbados even though all my comrades and all their families were rarely present at the same time. Liffey will assemble all of them together for the first time under one roof. Even Lady Evadne is expected to attend—a privilege we did not have in Barbados. Liffey is up to something. That in itself is worrying."

"What possible motive could Liffey have other than providing his closest staff with a brief period of domestic bliss before combat?" probed Luke.

"In the very early days of the Parliamentary army under the Earl of Essex, Liffey was one of your lot. He was a special agent and spy for Essex. He is now obsessed with the belief that one of us is a Royalist plant, and he is determined to root him out before we embark. Putting us altogether with our families is a last-ditch attempt to unsettle and then unearth this spy. He has even asked Lady Penelope to bring friends to act as companions to the bachelors among us if we refuse to involve our female friends and relatives."

"Grey and yourself seem to have a strange attitude toward women, but let me raise another matter. You have spent the last month or so recruiting the cavalry regiment to fight alongside the French in Flanders. That brings back memories for me. My first military experience was in a Dutch cavalry troop when I was just a lad, fighting the Spaniards in Flanders. The flat terrain gives the cavalry a distinct advantage over infantry on one hand, but the prevalence of walled towns gives you little chance of an open battle. Audley's artillery will have a field day. Enough of nostalgia! What type of men have you recruited?"

"I know your concern. With His Highness refusing to allocate regiments of the loyal national army to our expedition, I have had to create a new regiment from experienced cavalrymen. Such men by definition include large numbers of both former Royalists or cashiered members of the Parliamentary army."

"None of them lovers of the current government! Have you no safer option?" mused Luke.

"Colonel, the only other option is to conscript raw youths who may be good horsemen but who have no experience of conflict. Would you ride into battle with such men?"

"Given that even senior previously loyal officers in the national army are contemplating a coup against Cromwell if he persists with his plan to become king, how can you ensure that your new regiment will not become part of such a coup?"

"The rank-and-file troopers have never had strong political views these last five years. My recruiting sergeants tell me that most the men they have enlisted are doing so because they enjoyed the soldier's life and miss the regular pay and conditions that facilitate the fulfillment of their lusts. Monk taught me a simple lesson. Ensure the loyalty of your senior officers and support them in the imposition of tight discipline on the men. I have personally checked on the political views and detailed experience of most of the officers. I am still finalizing this part of my program."

"Monk's approach has certainly worked in Scotland. Let's hope your similar approach here is as successful. My guess is that Cromwell's opponents would find subverting pockets of the national army still stationed in England very difficult. A newly recruited unit does provide their best opportunity. Give me the names of the officers you have or are about to appoint, and I will find out as much as I can about them."

"Good. I will bring you a list tomorrow. The government must be very concerned, even alarmed, about the army we are raising if you have been sent here."

"Yes, this new army is a loose cannon. His Highness should have drawn it from elements of the existing army. I am sure Monk could have spared some veterans from Scotland, and Venables's men from the failed Caribbean expedition, instead of being demobilized, could have been retained for immediate service in Flanders."

"Exactly what are you doing?" asked Halliburton.

"It sounds deceptively straightforward: solve the murder of Blair and the attack on Redmond, ascertain the loyalty of my fellow officers, and unearth any conspiracies against the government, especially plots to assassinate the Protector. Do you doubt the loyalty of your fellow officers?"

"Up until this campaign for Cromwell to accept the Crown began, I would vouch for their loyalty to the protectorate. Nearly all of us fought in the Irish campaign. I knew Marlowe and Grey during that conflict. In the Caribbean, you were in an environment where meeting with Royalists was a frequent occasion. This is what gave Liffey the obsession that one or more of his officers was a Royalist or Spanish spy. Then again a couple of the officers including me had seen service in Ireland. As you know, it was quite common for troops of a defeated Royalist or Irish Confederate army to enlist in the companies of the victor. Maybe some soldiers want to change back to their original loyalties?"

"Who is most likely to succumb to Royalist pressure?"

"Of the three I suspected, one is dead: Blair. Another, Redmond, will soon to join him according to reports, and the only one left is Sir Peter Marlowe. But it is only a guess."

"What about Liffey himself? He is the son of a Royalist peer, and his sister is married to the king's security chief."

"Anyone can change their position, but Liffey has sacrificed a lot to support the Parliament and more recently the Protector. If you suspect Liffey because of his aristocratic Royalist upbringing, you will have to suspect half or more of Cromwell's current council. Former Royalists will soon be in the majority."

"You don't seem to be troubled by this."

"No, unlike most officers, I have no objection to Cromwell accepting the throne. I fought against the tyranny of one man, Charles I, and the corruption of subsequent Parliamentary cabals. I am loyal to Cromwell and what he stands for. The abolition of monarchy was not one of my priorities, and its return in the form of King Oliver would be preferable to its return with another Stuart. If Cromwell does accept the Crown, it will make it much harder for the Stuarts to return. Most of the more powerful Royalists will have given their loyalty to King Oliver."

"Given your surprising views on this matter, David, who of your comrades is most opposed to Cromwell accepting the Crown?"

"That is easy: Dick Grey."

"Any others?"

"No, Liffey and Audley are aristocrats, who, though intensely loyal to Cromwell, would not greatly be concerned if they served him as Lord Protector or king, and Marlowe could be a Royalist devoted to the Stuart cause."

"And yourself?"

"I am a professional soldier who will fight for any government that accepts the views you and I have embraced for the last decade and a half."

14

Yarrow, initially unaware of Blair's death, reluctantly followed his orders. He burned papers and letters in a small grate, bundled his few possessions into a sack, and next morning headed across town to find new lodgings—and a new identity.

He paid a young boy who roamed the vicinity of Liffey House to keep him informed of any major changes by leaving messages for him at the Red Hart.

At the Red Hart, he told the alehouse keeper, "I have friends who may come looking for me. Here is a shilling, which I will add to every time a friend leaves a message for me here."

The Red Hart was not the accommodation that Yarrow sought, but it would provide a base for receiving and sending messages, which in no way revealed where he was living. His new home was the more salubrious inn: the Three Bells.

This arrangement meant that only those he wanted to find him could do so. He would visit the Red Hart regularly to collect or send messages, always ensuring that no suspicious strangers were lingering in the vicinity.

Yarrow would have been distraught if he had known that immediately he left Liffey House, he was followed to the Red Hart and subsequently to the Three Bells.

On his first visit back to the Red Hart two days later, he received a message that Blair had been murdered.

His death created a dilemma.

Yarrow was freed of immediate supervision and from the recent instructions that he resented, but it left him without immediate orders and more importantly without sufficient funds.

Despite his misgivings, he would contact the Garden.

He left for Newmarket and took up accommodation at the Spotted Cow where he left a message with the landlord that he needed to meet with someone from the Garden.

Three days later, he was jostled by a furtive little man in the drinking chamber and told to avoid the usual meeting place at all costs and to present himself at a dilapidated stable near the finish post of the racetrack an hour after dusk the following day. He must wear a mask or hood to conceal his identity from the other conspirators.

Next day, as Yarrow entered the building, a woman with her face concealed by light silver hood with holes for the eyes and mouth spoke, "We are now all here. You are always the last to arrive Yarrow. Let me remind you all that our lives and the success of our mission depend on absolute secrecy, which includes concealing our true identity as far as possible from one another. Your faces must be hidden and your identity concealed behind our aliases. For those with a bad memory I am Belladonna."

"Is this really necessary?" asked a plump man hidden in the shadows,

"Absolutely, my dear Thrift. The man who entered this building last has made three attempts to kill Oliver Cromwell. Each of them failed not because of his incompetence but because Cromwell's right-hand man John Thurloe had an agent in our group who forewarned the authorities. If any one of you here is an agent of the Lord Protector, when you leave this meeting you may have a general idea of our enterprise, but you will have no names or description to give substance to your report."

Yarrow's eyes had finally adjusted to the poor light, and he became aware of five people in the room other than himself, two of them women.

The taller of the females asked in an imperious manner, "I am surprised that the enterprise is to continue. Support for it has declined rapidly."

"It is for that very reason, Foxglove, that we must continue with renewed vigor," replied Belladonna.

Foxglove retorted, "I do not see your logic. The king himself is against the project. The leading Royalist organization in England, the Sealed Knot, is against it, the most senior aristocratic Royalists in England are opposed, and as a result Spain has withdrawn her promised help. Your secret alliance with the anti-Cromwellian Puritans represented here by Yarrow is a catastrophe. They rose prematurely in Wales and were crushed. That episode showed clearly that many of our Royalist friends are quite happy to support the Lord Protector and are indeed flocking to join his administration."

"That is precisely why we must act—and act quickly. If Cromwell stays in power another year, most of the landowners of England will have come across to his administration and will readily serve King Oliver."

Yarrow felt moved to comment, "Lady Foxglove is confused. My people did not rise prematurely. They rose according to a schedule drawn up by Royalists on the continent in consultation with leading disaffected Parliamentarians. They were crushed because the promised concurrent Royalist uprising, and Spanish aid did not eventuate. Spanish troops were about to land in Wales but were turned back on orders of a senior Royalist who as far as I know may even be in this room."

Belladonna replied, "Yes, Yarrow, your people were betrayed but not by anyone in this room. The villain was a devious Papist peer who has great influence with Spain and in the court of Charles II. This enterprise to kill Cromwell and bring down the government is in our hands and our hands alone. It has the support of a few aristocrats currently on the continent, but they will not reveal their position for fear of reprisals from the cowardly courtiers who simply await the English people and army to recall Charles II."

A man who had not previously spoken announced he was Woodruff and asked, "If we are to continue to act, what now are our roles?"

"The Garden has two related objectives: assassinate Oliver Cromwell and overthrow the republic. Yarrow will execute the first with some assistance from one or two of you. The second part of our plan—which involves a section of the army rising against Cromwell to be assisted by a fleet and armed troops from abroad— will be handled by Weld and myself," replied Belladonna.

"Ridiculous," uttered Foxglove. "You are daydreaming. Every time we place our hope in the army or some part of it turning against Cromwell, we are disappointed. It remains intensely loyal to him, and any dissidents are immediately removed. Where are you going to find an army that is not dedicated to Cromwell or its own rule?"

"It is in the process of being created. We are acting to fill it with men and officers who are not devoted to Cromwell. The new army, raised to fight alongside the French in the Netherlands, is being recruited afresh from officers with mainly colonial service and men who are sacked Cromwellian troops or former Royalist soldiers, waiting for revenge," replied a man who identified himself as Weld and who had a distinctive military bearing.

"What about the navy?" asked Foxglove. "We know that Spain will not help. Nor will Venice. The Dutch, always ready to attack, are at the moment too scared of a combined Anglo-French fleet to become involved."

"Never worry, my dear. A small fleet and army are already sailing to Europe."

"Where from?" asked Woodruff.

Weld smiled. "Thurloe and his military associate, Colonel Luke Tremayne, who has been attached to the new army precisely to uncover our conspiracy, would love to know that detail. Thrift handles our contact with the fleet. The rest of you need not know any details."

"Surely, this complicates our situation," announced a concerned Woodruff. "I know Tremayne. He is ruthless and often acts without regard to morality or the law. Thurloe must be aware of our plot to have sent a person of that status to the very army you hope to subvert."

Weld replied, "That is why we are making last-minute changes to the original plan. You would have noticed that Woad who attended our last meeting is absent. He was killed in yet to be explained circumstances. He was to assist in subverting sections of Cromwell's senior staff especially those in charge of the newly raised army for Flanders and to oversee Yarrow's next attempt on the tyrant's life. I will take over his role among the general staff. Until his death, he and I shared the same accommodation, and Lady Belladonna, given the fortuitous circumstances that will soon place her in the same critical location, will oversee both aspects of our conspiracy. All orders will be between Belladonna and the individual agent involved. The least you know about one another and your roles, the safer we are from being infiltrated by Thurloe and Tremayne. Two of you have already been assigned to render Tremayne's activities less dangerous and, above all, transparent to us."

Belladonna took aside each of the group and individually outlined in detail what she expected of them—instructions that were heard by no one else.

After she had completed her briefing, Weld spoke, "Any questions?"

Yarrow, never entirely convinced by Woad's final meeting with him, asked, "Lady Belladonna, what were your exact instructions to Woad to be conveyed to me?"

"Why do you ask?"

"Because Woad may have been the government agent who was betraying us to Thurloe."

"Ridiculous! I personally recruited Woad in the Indies years ago. He has been serving our cause for years," declaimed a perturbed Weld.

"My last orders to Woad were to make himself known to you, supervise your activity, and require your assassination plans to be referred to him for approval," answered Belladonna.

"Then if Woad was genuinely one of us, his murder may be a Tremayne inspired extralegal assault on our numbers. I may be next," uttered an alarmed Woodruff.

Yarrow privately agreed with Woodruff.

Yarrow thought as he left the meeting the simple answer to the Tremayne problem was to kill him, but would any of these Royalist fops give him such an order?

The new orders he had been given were clear—and limiting.

His initial reaction was to ignore them.

He did not wish to await Belladonna's approval before embarking on any assassination attempts.

His Leveler prejudices did not sit well with obeying a group of amateur Royalist conspirators who had yet to prove they could achieve anything.

He also fumed at his treatment at the two meetings of the Garden. He was reprimanded for arriving last, but he arrived at exactly the time he had been told. He was no fool. This Royalist cabal had the real meeting before he arrived. In their eyes, he was simply a paid assassin—a hired hand.

He no longer saw himself as the Royalist puppet, Yarrow.

Code names and the wearing of masks did not appeal to a veteran soldier who had a clear mission to kill Cromwell. He would plan and execute this without waiting for specific orders from a woman.

He would be more effective in killing Tremayne and Cromwell as a lone wolf—as Miles Thornton.

All these thoughts he had to put aside for the moment, given Belladonna's specific new task, for which she already paid him a considerable amount of money.

He intuitively checked his hidden purse, well concealed within his clothing, for the numerous gold coins he had received.

He was to present himself at the causeway leading to the manor of Austin Friars on the eastern arm of the Medway estuary near

Chetney Marshes, at high tide on the afternoon of Wednesday, two weeks hence.

A servant of Belladonna would approach him and give him further instructions.

He was to wear a sprig of Yarrow and wear a wig or hat that would conceal his red hair, which was becoming a liability.

15

Before he left for Kent, Luke met Thurloe to exchange information.

Luke reported that Yarrow was at the Three Bells but using the Red Hart as a contact address. He left London temporarily and went to Newmarket where he stayed at the Spotted Cow.

"Unfortunately, according to my sergeant who performed this feat of tracking, the quarry evaded his surveillance, disappearing from the Spotted Cow for several hours. Yarrow is now back at the Three Bells."

"I can fill the gaps in your sergeant's story. My agents have been watching the Spotted Cow for months. It is the conduit through which the Garden communicates with its members. The real identity of these people still eludes us. Blair, before he died, reported that he had been instructed to monitor the assassin Yarrow, which gave me an opportunity to direct him to push this control a little further than Belladonna intended. He also claimed that he had been instructed to await contact from Weld, who he believed is a senior officer currently at Liffey House.

"If Yarrow attended a meeting of the Garden during the period he disappeared from the Spotted Cow, then it is most likely that

Weld was also present. I will find out where all the officers at Liffey House were at the time of that meeting."

"Liffey House is not the ideal location to monitor these types of situations. The move to Austin Friars will make your task much easier," commented Thurloe.

"How so?"

"Austin Friars is an isolated estate in the eastern extremity of the Medway. It is on a small area of elevated land against the Chetney Marshes. The manor is built on an island except for very low tide when it is accessible on a long narrow causeway from the mainland. Entry to the island will be easy to control."

"My dragoons are ready to move. They will patrol the perimeter of the estate, as well as man the causeway to prevent unauthorized exit or entry."

"An excellent idea, but you will need boats to effectively seal the island from sea borne intrusion."

Thurloe continued, "You have to keep some men in London to monitor Yarrow."

"Evan and Strad will handle that."

"Good! I hope you don't object to my next move."

Luke was well aware that a suggestion from Thurloe was either an indirect order or a fait accompli.

Thurloe called for drinks, and the two men adjourned to a long cushioned bench against one of the walls. After pouring a red Spanish wine into a large glass goblet, Luke quietly asked, "And what is your next move?"

"I have added one of my best agents, Captain Jared Castle, to Liffey's staff as the army's intelligence officer—in effect, your assistant. When your unit was created, I suggested Castle as your deputy, but His Highness, aware that your first mission was in Wales, insisted on a Welsh deputy. But with Sir Evan in London, you could well do with Castle's assistance at Austin Friars. Before you protest, Castle has another asset. His wife, who is another of my best agents, will accompany him. She will be invaluable as your eyes and ears within the large coterie of wives, daughters, and female friends that will gather at Austin Friars. You will find Jane Castle not only a most attractive woman but an effective operator."

Thurloe gave a knowing smile, which disconcerted the usually unflappable Luke.

"With two of your agents seconded to me, what is left for me to do?" asked Luke with tongue in cheek.

He did not expect an answer, but surprisingly, Thurloe responded, "I have asked Liffey to vary your duties as adjutant. You will become the officer responsible for the women at Austin Friars. This will put you in a better position to observe them, hear their petty complaints, and gather valuable evidence."

"Anything else I need to know before I leave for Kent?"

"Yes, before he died, Blair gave me three pieces of information that could be vital to your investigation. I have not kept you fully in the picture up until now, but his murder has changed the situation. You will need all the information he and I have gathered."

"From Blair's information, despite your inbuilt prejudice in favor of the army, one of the officers on Liffey's staff is definitely a traitor. Our plan for Cromwell to accept the Crown may have shaken the loyalty of his previously most ardent followers."

"That is very true, Mr. Thurloe. And that is why you must prevent it happening! Oliver without the army is nothing."

"And Oliver without the law will struggle to survive. If he accepts the Crown, he will have the support of all the traditional buttresses of monarchy. Blair, before he was murdered, gave me other pieces of information. If Weld cannot persuade officers to his cause, he will murder those who refuse to cooperate and replace them with others who will. I expect many more murders at Austin Friars."

"Thanks!" said Luke sarcastically. Any more pieces of enlightenment?"

"The plot is controlled and financed by a woman, the Lady Belladonna, who arrives at Austin Friars in the immediate future from where she will supervise both aspects of her plot."

"She must be a partner, daughter, or female friend of one of the senior officers whom Liffey has invited to Austin Friars for the months before embarkation to Flanders. So I am to solve the murders of Blair and Redmond and discover the identity of Weld and Belladonna before they can implement their plans."

"And the last piece of relevant news is the most worrying of all. I have come up with a possible interpretation of Blair's last word, which sounded like *marriage* or *carriage*. It was, in fact, Harwich, which the locals pronounce *harridge*."

"Why is that of concern?"

"Harwich is one of the Haven ports. The estuaries of the Stour and Orwell provide the best harbor between Whitby and the Thames-Medway estuaries. Since 1652 the government has been fortifying the area and building a dockyard at Harwich. Our agents on the continent have reported that the Dutch see Harwich as the ideal port to land an invasion army. On the other hand, it is an ideal port from which to launch our forces for Flanders. Up until now, this fallback position, should our activities on the Medway and the Kentish coast prove inadequate, was only known to His Highness, myself, General Desborough, and Blair."

"Why did Blair expend his last breath to murmur Harwich?"

"Perhaps he has discovered that this Royalist-Irish fleet and army gathered together in the Indies will attempt to land at Harwich rather than in the Medway—an invasion timed to occur simultaneously with Weld taking over the army for Flanders and turning it against us."

"Mr. Thurloe, who do you, with the evidence gathered from your many agents, think murdered Blair?"

"Dozens of reasons have been put to me. The Garden may have discovered he was my agent, Weld may have become jealous of the trust Belladonna was placing in Woad, one of his fellow officers disconcerted by his card-playing and womanizing activity, the local thieves in search of more loot, Redmond or any homosexual friend of either or an unknown enemy from Blair's deep past. Don't waste time on Blair if it not related to your two urgent aims: stop the plots to kill Cromwell and prevent the subversion of his Flanders army."

"I won't waste time on Blair, but you may also be unwise to base your strategy on what Blair has told you. If he was a double agent with his ultimate loyalty with the king, his information may be partially or completely false."

"If he was a Royalist agent, why would he try to warn us with his dying breath about the threat to Harwich?"

"To tempt us to move our resources from the London and Medway area to Harwich. An excellent strategic ploy."

Luke thanked Thurloe for his candid discussion but refrained from asking one more question regarding Blair. Was he murdered on the orders of Thurloe who, despite his overt denials, may have finally accepted that he was a double agent serving the exiled king?

Thurloe's real position, as on everything, remained a mystery.

Austin Friars, Kent, a Week Later

Liffey moved out of London with enthusiasm.

Austin Friars was a large house. Before the Reformation, it had been a large friary of the Augustinian order.

The general was determined to fill it with the families of his officers.

Luke was delighted with this as it was vital to uncover the real identity of the Lady Belladonna, the driving force and probable brains behind the dual conspiracies to murder Cromwell, and take control of his new army.

Liffey, Marlowe, Grey, and Halliburton made up the core of senior officers who would lead the army into Flanders. Audley, who was taking a major role in the planning and preparation, would need to be replaced well before departure by another artillery commander.

The cautious Liffey refused to allocate Peebles a role, although he was invited to Austin Friars with the others.

Luke had only been in residence for two days when Liffey summoned him.

"Luke, you have a slight change of role."

Thurloe had forewarned him of the changes.

"Whitehall has appointed Captain Jared Castle to the army. He is a young officer who can speak Dutch, German, Spanish, and French—the ideal qualifications for an intelligence officer in our situation. Sir Peter Marlowe is very enthusiastic about the appointment."

The last sentence worried Luke.

Had the master spy and infiltrator of enemy organizations, Thurloe, been outfoxed at his own game once again?

Was Castle, like Blair before him, a double agent, whose basic loyalty was to Charles Stuart?

And was Marlowe's endorsement of the appointment an indication that he was Weld? Was Castle the first of Weld's anti-Cromwellian officers that he intended to place in key positions?

Luke returned to his second-story apartment and watched the waters of the Medway recede.

His time for reverie was cut short.

Coaches, wagons, horses, and dozens of servants crossed the causeway even before the last trickles of the estuary had drained away.

The invasion of Austin Friars by the families and friends of the officers had begun.

Liffey's experiment was under way.

There were so many people heading for Austin Friars that a considerable number would have to wait until the next low tide not due until the following morning.

Although it suited his purpose, Luke viewed this invitation to numerous wives, lovers, and sisters as dangerous.

Men preparing for war are not necessarily appreciative of a family presence, especially to the additional pressures and tensions to which they might be exposed.

Luke was sure that Liffey had an ulterior motive, but what was it?

To avoid the chaos that ensued as the guests settled in, Luke did not eat in the old refectory that was now the formal dining hall for the greatly expanded household.

A servant brought supper to his room.

Luke had just finished the roasted half chicken and downed a large glass of mulled red wine when there was a loud knocking on his door.

Ever cautious, Luke placed his hand to his sword.

He invited his unexpected guest to enter.

They did.

The first to enter was young officer resplendent in the red uniform that was becoming the fashion for officers close to Whitehall.

A tall woman, whose striking beauty immediately derailed Luke's thoughts, followed the soldier into the room.

The young man acknowledged Luke and announced, "Captain Jared Castle reporting for duty and transferring to you your new orders from Mr. Thurloe and His Highness."

Luke was quietly pleased.

He initially assumed that Castle would act on his own initiative and report everything back to Thurloe despite the latter's statement to the contrary.

Instead, Castle was to be Luke's agent in Austin Friars.

Castle handed Luke a sealed letter and at the same time introduced the woman by his side.

"Colonel, this is my wife, Jane, whom Mr. Thurloe believes will be of great assistance in discovering the secrets of the many women who seem to be taking over this house."

Luke bowed to Jane Castle and then suggested, as it was late, he would talk to both of them in the morning after he had read his orders.

The instructions were clear and repeated the information that Thurloe had given him in London.

Young Castle will officially be the intelligence officer attached to Liffey's staff. You will continue in your role of coadjutant. It is anticipated that the conspirators will not be as careful when they think they are dealing with an inexperienced young man. You are to use your known appeal to women to ingratiate yourself into the confidence of as many women that you can. Your task is simple. Discover the identity of Belladonna and the traitorous officer Weld. In the process, you may find out who murdered Blair.

Your deputy Sir Evan Williams and your sergeant Stradling will remain here at Whitehall to investigate Yarrow and his role in the attempts to assassinate the Protector. In the end, hopefully, both the assassination attempts of Yarrow and the conspiracies of Belladonna and Weld will be explained by what you discover at Austin Friars. You will make whatever use you can of Mistress Castle who has worked for the government on previous occasions and who, according to His Highness, is your ideal woman.

The last complication Luke needed was an ideal woman.

16

Early next morning, Luke met the Castles in his apartment. They had been well briefed and knew as much, if not more, about the situation than he. Luke decided that Jared should overtly have no contact with him.

Jared was, as of now, the unit's intelligence officer. Luke's role as the government's top agent at Austin Friars would be downplayed.

Jared would report informally to Luke through his wife.

Luke would have been devastated had he known that his role at Austin Friars was well-known to the conspirators—conspirators who would in no way be fooled by the appearance of young Jared.

When Jared left the meeting, having been summoned by Liffey, Luke continued his discussion with Jane.

It was obvious that she was an experienced and effective agent.

His lustful intentions were immediately repelled.

"Initially, His Highness thought that you and I should fake a relationship so that our constant meetings would have a reasonable explanation that fitted neatly into your womanizing reputation."

"And who was the moralizing pedant who killed off such an enjoyable plan?" asked Luke.

"Thurloe! He thought that if you embarked on an affair with me, it would undermine his plan that you make yourself attractive to as many women of the household that you could, in order to gain the maximum information."

"Thurloe does not understand women. My experience suggests that my pursuit of you would have engendered more interest in me by others," commented an arrogant Luke.

Jane gave an enigmatic smile. "Thurloe also modified His Highness's view on another matter. The Lord Protector wanted us to report to Liffey on the progress of our investigation. Thurloe is not convinced of Liffey's loyalty, and he is not to be kept informed."

"For once, I agree with Thurloe. This whole charade of friends and family, especially the emphasis on women, must have a purpose that for the moment, I cannot fathom. Why has Liffey done this?"

"Thurloe said almost exactly that the other day. He is suspicious because Liffey, despite promises to the contrary, has not forwarded in advance the names of the people who will reside here. Consequently, Thurloe has only been able to provide us with information concerning the women who were in the West Indies, namely, Penelope Marlowe and Ursula Audley. When we know who is here, I am to send the names to Mr. Thurloe, although you and I will discover the facts more quickly through idle chatter with these women and their servants."

"When does Liffey force us all together?" asked Luke.

"At supper tomorrow night. Jared told me that by then all the guests will have arrived and all the senior officers will be on base."

"Despite Thurloe, I will try to charm you," whispered Luke with a twinkle in his eye.

"And I might succumb to your charms," said Jane as she left the room giggling.

For the next few hours, Luke wandered around the manor and its outbuildings, ambled around the perimeter of the island, and crisscrossed the estate, almost falling victim to the rapidly returning tide.

As he reentered the reception hall, a soldier informed him that the general wished to see him.

Liffey went straight to the point.

"Luke, I have invited the wives, daughters, and women friends of my officers to live here until their men folk embark for Flanders. You know that one of my reasons is, in line with your presence here, to create a situation where any clandestine Royalist may be more readily revealed. To give you a reason to be constantly in the company of these women, I have told each of them personally that you are responsible for their safety and comfort while they are here."

"How many women are here?"

"Eleven."

"Who are these unfortunate victims?" asked Luke, only half jokingly.

"Three are associated with me: my sister Isadore, my potential wife Lady Lydia Veldor, and her mother Sophia, Baroness Veldor."

Luke was genuinely surprised.

"My lord, I was not aware that you had a sister Isadore. I know of your elder sister who is married to Charles Stuart's chief of security—a gallant if misguided officer."

"Isadore is the only other member of my family who gave her loyalty to Parliament and now the Protector," commented Liffey.

"Nor did I have any inkling that you were contemplating marriage."

"Since both my father and elder brother had entered into a period of serious ill health, I will probably inherit the earldom within the year. Consequently, in terms of maintaining the succession, I have a duty to marry. In the light of my enhanced prospects, several aristocrats have approached me regarding the suitability of their daughters. Baron Veldor is one such father. That is why I invited Isadore. She will give me her honest view on the suitability of Lady Lydia. Also, given Isadore's strong political position, she will probably intuitively uncover any Royalist sympathies among any of the other women. She may be of some use to you."

Before Luke could politely reject the help from yet another potential sleuth, Liffey continued, "Young Dora expressed a desire to meet you alone before the other women are gathered together. She awaits you in the antechamber."

Liffey, followed by Luke, moved into the adjoining room where he was momentarily taken aback by the woman that rose to greet him.

Luke had expected a strong supporter of the Protector would have emphasized her allegiance by conforming to Puritan habits of dress and coiffure.

Isadore dressed as if she was at the French court, considered the height of fashion, where she would have captivated every male from the king down.

Luke was apprehensive. Why had Liffey thrown his attractive young sister into the situation so early in the investigation? What was he up to? Was this an attempt to divert him from his priorities?

Isadore was much younger that her brother, probably in her midtwenties.

Luke signaled for her to take the larger of the chairs in the room while he drew up a smaller one and placed it opposite her.

He did not waste words.

"Lady Isadore, I cannot possibly understand why you want to see me. Our paths have never crossed, and given my activities, I cannot see how I can be of any assistance. Did your brother put you up to this?"

"No, he did not."

"What did he tell you about me?"

"That you are a personal friend of the Protector and that you have been sent to help Christopher uncover a traitor among his officers."

"If that is the case, why would you want to see me? I'm sure you can not name the traitor."

"But I might be able to lead you to him."

"Lady Isadore, I appreciate the thought, but I cannot allow you to waste your time here as an amateur detective trying to unravel a complex series of events. To be blunt, you could complicate the issue for both your brother and myself."

"Colonel, I have no intention of becoming a sleuth seeking the undercover Royalists at Austin Friars, but I have a small trunk of letters written by Christopher from the Indies, where he meticulously details his thoughts about the loyalty of his men. During his time in Barbados, I also wrote to and received letters from some of his officers. Your professional eye may pick up hints of disloyalty that an innocent maiden has missed."

"You have them with you?"

"Yes, the trunk arrived with the rest of my possessions."

"Does Christopher know about the letters and your offer for me to read them?"

"Not yet, but if you discover anything of use, I will tell him."

"Why are you doing this? Is there a price I have to pay?" asked Luke with a flirtatious wink.

"My brother is in danger of making the biggest mistake of his life. Ever since it became generally known that my father and eldest brother where both seriously ill and that Christopher may soon become the Earl of Liffey with extensive lands and wealth, he has been inundated with proposals of marriage from a range of peers, mainly Royalists, who have put forward their daughters. The Royalists will use this gathering and my brother's emotional vulnerability to fill Austin Friars with their supporters. I do not trust my obnoxious future sister-in-law and, even more so, her extremely wealthy and dominating mother."

Luke responded, "Baroness Veldor is a very wealthy woman, but she is also a stalwart of the protectorate."

"Says whom? When Christopher told me that he was inviting Lydia and her mother here, I insisted on coming to keep an eye on them. I am sure that in your search for a Royalist agent, you will discover information regarding the Veldors that will help me protect my brother. In return for my letters, I want that information."

"Isadore, do the Veldors follow the horses?"

"Lady Veldor races illegally at Newmarket."

"Is she also a keen gardener?"

Isadore laughed.

"I doubt if she even notices the garden. My one visit to Veldor Lodge suggests that her horses and currently the promoting of her daughter are her only interests."

"What about Baron Veldor?"

"He has been in exile on the continent for years. He surrendered in 1645 and was not punished when he guaranteed not to take up arms for the king. He broke this promise in 1648, and even before the defeat of the Royalist forces, he ran back to the continent."

"If he is such a committed Royalists, how is it that his property has not been confiscated by the government and Lady Veldor reduced to poverty?"

"Lady Sophia's father fought for Parliament, and a large proportion of the current Veldor wealth and land came through Sophia on her father's death. This is why the property has not been seized."

"Thank you, my lady. I will send a man to your rooms to collect the letters. Your comments have been very helpful, and I shall honor our agreement to give you any personal information relevant to your brother's proposed marriage."

Luke returned to his room, pleased with his conversation. Isadore's information regarding the horse-racing activities of Sophia and her extensive wealth made her the prime suspect as Belladonna, although her lack of interest in gardening was a disappointment.

Next morning, Liffey gathered his senior officers: Marlowe, Grey, Halliburton, Audley, Castle, and Tremayne. The noticeable absentee was Peebles, toward whom Liffey had exhibited an inexplicable dislike.

The general outlined the plans for the immediate week and informed the gathered group that Luke would be responsible for their families and friends and that the new man Jared Castle would oversee the intelligence activities of the unit and assist in uncovering any disloyalty among the newly recruited troops.

He then asked Jared to address the group.

"Gentlemen, given the requirement to increase security at every level, I must know where every officer will be for the remainder of the week. I will approach you individually after this meeting concludes and before this evening's grand banquet."

Luke smiled to himself, having instructed the young officer to approach each of his comrades with such a question but in the process try to discover where they had been in the week just past. Anybody who had been near Newmarket or Harwich would be of especial interest.

Liffey's banquet was a lavish affair that reflected his status and was a harbinger of the massive wealth he could expend when his father and eldest brother died.

The whole affair was organized down to the last detail, and table placings were a reflection of Liffey's thinking—or, in Luke's case, of Isadore's interference?

He found himself seated next to Sophia, Baroness Veldor.

Sophia began the conversation with a provocative opening gambit.

"Colonel Tremayne, your reputation goes before you. His Highness must be very worried to send someone of your status to Austin Friars, or are you here simply because my future son-in-law is obsessed with traitors in his command?"

"Neither, Lady Sophia! After my adventures in Wales at the end of last year, this assignment is essentially a holiday. I have, in fact, relinquished the intelligence role for the new army to young Jared Castle. You will already have been informed that my new role is to liaise with the families of the officers, answer their inquiries, and solve their problems."

"That fools none of us. You are here to seduce the younger women and charm the more mature into inadvertently giving you information that Christopher, or more probably Thurloe, seeks."

"If that is the case, my lady, I shall look forward to our first encounter. Your reputation also goes before you. I am heading for the Cambridge area in the near future, and I know you have a large stable of racing horses that make use of a loophole in the law to continue to race at Newmarket. One of my weaknesses is a need to wager. Are any of your horses racing this coming week, and what advice would you give me regarding my betting?"

"Colonel, as a cavalryman, you know horses better then I."

"Our military horses are built for strength and stamina, not for speed.

Your steeds are fast and interbred with the new Arabian stallions!"

"Yes, but you are misinformed regarding Newmarket. My horses only race on the private properties of a few select friends. Next Thursday, I have my favorite stallion, Ebony, racing on my own estate Veldor Lodge. If you are interested, I will write you a letter of introduction to my steward, Barnaby Brett, and my neighbor. The latter will put his best horse, Caesar, against mine. Put your money on Caesar if the track is wet. If not, Ebony will win by a mile."

17

Luke was bemused. If Sophia was Belladonna, she was playing an intriguing game with him. He would accept her offer, which would introduce him into the tight group of East Anglian racehorse owners.

He decided to shake her equilibrium.

"Baroness, if I am here to assess the loyalty to His Highness of those around Christopher, you would be my number one suspect as the traitor."

"And why would that be?" replied Sophia with no sign of alarm or even discomfiture.

"Why is your Royalist husband willing to put his daughter forward as a probable wife of a dedicated Parliamentary and Cromwellian soldier such as Liffey? To the outsider, it looks suspicious, especially given the timing. The commander of a new Cromwellian army would be the obvious target for dedicated Royalists to win over to their cause. What better way than through a new wife?"

"You have been a spy catcher too long! You read conspiracies into normal aristocratic marriage negotiations. My family has always been Parliamentarian, so to marry Lydia to Christopher would make my relatives very happy. Baron Veldor and the Earl of Liffey are great friends—and admittedly ultra-Royalists. They are both currently courtiers to young Charles Stuart, but their extreme views are largely anathema to most of those at court. Despite Christopher's misguided loyalties in their eyes, a marriage alliance between the two families overrides any political gain or loss."

At this point, Sophia's attention was diverted by a question from across the table.

Luke turned to the woman on his other side, whom he had studiously avoided during his discussion with Sophia, but that woman had listened to every word spoken between them.

She teasingly rubbed her leg against Luke's while demurely gazing at her silver platter and the arms of her family.

It was Isadore Liffey.

"I hope you heard something of interest, my lady?" remarked Luke playfully.

"Enough to conclude that you have been outfoxed. The ploy to get to Newmarket was too obvious, and Sophia called your bluff. Go to Veldor Lodge and lose a fortune by backing the wrong horse!" teased Isadore.

Luke ignored the flirtatious young woman.

He surveyed the long table.

It had been arranged according to social status rather than military rank.

Close to Liffey at the head of the table were the aristocrats: his sister, the Veldors, Audleys, and, by dint of his wife, the Greys. In the middle were the gentlemen—the Marlowes and the Halliburtons—and at the far end the commoners: the Castles and Robert Peebles.

The obvious physical isolation of Peebles visibly reflected Liffey's distrust of the man. If Peebles was Luke's old friend's agent, he could be put to some use. It was stupid of Liffey to create unnecessary enemies.

He would speak to both of them as soon as possible and try to remove the unnecessary tension.

After that mediation, he would take advantage of Sophia's offer and head into Essex and Suffolk.

Liffey might not be too happy with him leaving the women and families of his comrades, whose welfare he was specifically appointed to supervise, but he would argue that he was following up information provided by Sophia that was pertinent to his real mission.

It was after nine the following morning that Luke caught up with Peebles.

"Robert, I'm glad I found you. I am at a loss as to why the general has failed to use you since your arrival. I can only assume that someone has poisoned his mind against you. Or it may be simply that you are not one of his old guard from Barbados."

"Thank you for your concern, but my isolation appears to be at an end. Last night, I received a note from the general ordering me to report to Colonel Grey at ten o'clock this morning to take over the training of the latest batch of would-be musketeers."

"Great news! I noted in Thurloe's dossier that you had a reputation of being a very effective battlefield commander of musketeers during the suppression of the Irish. Venables should have used your skills in the Indies. His infantry tactics, discipline, and effectiveness were at an all-time low. I'll walk with you to the training area."

Recruits had been training at Austin Friars for several weeks before the arrival of the senior officers.

While the senior officers were accommodated in the manor itself, the noncommissioned officers—sergeants and corporals— lived in a variety of outbuildings.

The ordinary soldiers had erected numerous six-man tents that covered the northern half of the island.

The musketeers were being trained in both the handling of their muskets and in battlefield tactics by an array of loud-mouthed sergeants.

The training area was on the slightest of slopes leading to what was an excuse for a ridge on this otherwise flat island.

After weeks of drill, today in the presence of senior officers, the men would practice with live ammunition.

As Luke and Peebles approached the several detachments of musketeers, who were each divided into three ranks of six men. They reacted to the orders their corporals, "Take up your match, open your pan, blow off your loose powder, open your charge, shorten your scouring stick, ram home, draw forth your match, blow your match, give fire."

"That brings back memories! It is a pity that we are still using matchlocks. Our European opponents have adopted various types of flintlocks. They are safer and lighter," said Peebles.

"And more expensive. I know. My dragoons are equipped with snaphances that rely on a spark caused by driving flint onto a steel base."

"Luke, I must talk to you after I finish for the day. At dinner last night, I was astounded to recognize a person whom I met previously in a context that would suggest that their presence here could be a problem for you."

"Who was it?"

Before Peebles could answer, Dick Grey greeted them from afar.

After a brief discussion, Grey introduced Peebles to the recruits.

Peebles explained to the recruits that for the first time they would actually load and fire their muskets instead of going through the relentless drill manual time and time again.

He then signaled for the noncommissioned officers to resume the drill.

He stood beside the first group of eighteen men and was joined by Luke.

The first rank of six men fired, but two had trouble in that their match went out. They then withdrew to the rear, and the second row fired. This time, five were successful, but the sixth man dropped his musket. With the second rank moving to the rear, the third group fired with one musketeer firing well after the other five.

As a cavalryman masquerading as a dragoon, Luke could not resist to comment, "You do have your work cut out. They are indeed raw recruits."

Peebles took the comment with good humor and replied seriously, "I will have to speak to the general. Firing and withdrawing to the rear is outmoded. Why have we not adopted the Swedish tactics of thirty years ago? The first rank kneels and fires, the second row crouches and fires, and the third row stands and fires. By then, the first row is ready to fire again from their kneeling position."

The musketeers in training were ordered to start again and to complete a sequence of three shots each.

A cacophony of musket fire and the overwhelming smell of burning cord and gunpowder filled the air.

Peebles turned to Luke.

Suddenly, the former's face was transformed into a macerated mess, and Luke felt a sharp pain in his shoulder.

Peebles fell to the ground.

They had both been shot.

Luke, with blood pouring from his upper arm, ordered the recruits to cease firing and for everybody to remain where they were.

Dick Grey sent for a military surgeon.

Luke tried to comfort the prone Peebles, who to his experienced eye would not survive. He had received at least two shots to the head.

By the time the surgeon arrived, he was dead.

Dick and Luke, with a patched-up arm, assessed the situation.

"Who was the target: Luke, Peebles, or yourself?"

"It was Peebles. No one including myself knew I would be here. On the other hand, both you and Peebles received a note purporting to come from the general, ensuring that Peebles would be here for the beginning of training with live ammunition at ten o'clock sharp," observed Luke.

"Where did the shot come from? You were both standing well back behind the trainee musketeers. Their officers would have noticed if two or more of them had turned around and fired in the opposite direction to their comrades," concluded Grey.

"The shots came from well behind the ranks of musketeers, probably from behind one of those tents," said Luke.

"The general will be furious to know there are armed killers running loose on this so-called secure base!"

"Dick, the trainees are still in their positions. Have your men ascertain who should have been on the training field but for some reason had remained in his tent."

"The killers may not have been any of the enlisted troops. Someone could have come across at the last low tide and hidden here, awaiting their chance to kill Peebles," replied Grey.

"Yes, a man lured to his death by a note that I am sure was not sent by Liffey."

As Luke, holding his disabled arm with his other hand, and Dick Grey walked slowly back to the manor, Luke was surprised to see two men riding toward him that he immediately recognized as his deputy Sir Evan Williams and loyal sergeant Strad.

Neither bothered to dismount.

Evan asked, "Has anything usual happened in the last twelve hours?"

Luke introduced his men to Dick who replied, "Yes, a senior officer was murdered, and your own colonel was wounded in the shoulder."

"What are the two of you doing here? You had strict orders to remain in London and monitor the activities of our friend Yarrow," asked Luke.

"That is why we are here. Yarrow visited the Red Hart daily to leave or send messages. He clearly received urgent instructions yesterday. He immediately left the Red Hart, did not bother to return to the Three Bells, hired a horse, and after knocking on a couple of doors in the Tower Hamlets was joined to two other men. All three carried, neatly wrapped in cloth, what I suspect were muskets. To cut a long story short, we followed them and they led us here. Unfortunately, they were sufficiently ahead of us to make the crossing late last night before the causeway was covered by the tide. We had to wait until now."

"Well, Yarrow and his assassins may have made it onto Austin Friars, but they will not leave it. Our dragoons guard the perimeter of the area and ensure no one leaves or enters without our approval. Evan, assume command of our men from John Martin! Strad, come with me! I will brief you and get a message to Thurloe."

Dick and Luke reported the incident to Liffey who confirmed Luke's fears that the note had not been written or dictated by him.

Luke was pessimistic.

"This is more serious than it appears. Peebles was executed because someone here did not want Peebles to tell us what he knew concerning their activities in the Indies. As soon as he or she recognized Peebles, they sent a message to Yarrow in London, and notes, falsely purporting to come from you, were delivered to Peebles and Grey, setting the trap. The use of Yarrow suggests that the death of Peebles concerns the Garden and is therefore central to my mission."

"Did Peebles give you a clue as to who concerned him?" asked Liffey.

"No, not even the gender."

Liffey appeared to be relieved.

He was silent for some time, finally declaring, "I will immediately order a full muster of every person at Austin Friars. If the killers are still here, there will be nowhere for them to hide."

"Their leader will also find it difficult to conceal his red hair," remarked Luke.

Later that day, Liffey reported to a meeting of his senior officers, "My muster was disappointing. There was no excess of troops in training. In fact, nine men have disappeared, probably deserted. While we found no additional men, there were seven wenches hidden away in tents or in the servants' quarters of the house. And all the redheaded men were presented to Luke's sergeant for identification. None were Yarrow."

"They must have escaped before you sealed the perimeter," remarked Dick.

"Not necessarily. The one area in which my muster was faulty was the household staff of my guests. Some of the women did not know how many servants they had brought with them but then vouched for every retainer they thought belonged to them. The person who organized the killing could simply lie about his or her servants. The only good news from Castle, who conducted that aspect of the muster, was that he found no red-haired male servant."

After the meeting ended, Luke informed Liffey that despite that day's events, he would leave for East Anglia the next morning to follow up information that he had received from Sophia—information that could be relevant to what had just occurred.

Liffey was displeased, but Luke pointed out that his deputy Sir Evan Williams was able to carry out in his absence whatever was considered necessary.

Luke's departure was delayed.

As the tide had receded, one of Luke's patrols discovered two bodies half submerged in the mud.

Strad identified them as Yarrow's two accomplices.

Luke was disturbed. There were three marksmen who shot at Peebles and himself. Perhaps the third marksman had deliberately aimed at him.

Was he on the Garden's hit list?

The two killers had both been shot through the back of the head.

A gold coin was found on each man.

Sometime later, three discarded muskets were also found, half hidden in the mud.

Everything was accounted for—except Yarrow.

18

Luke missed low tide. Jared took the opportunity of this delay to report on the movements of the senior officers.

"Bad news I'm afraid. You'd have hoped that by locating one or two officers near Newmarket at the time of the last-known meeting of the Garden, unearthing the real identity of Weld would have been easy. All five officers—Liffey, Marlowe, Grey, Audley, and Halliburton—were absent from Liffey House and recruiting either in the London area or East Anglia. If we accept what they told me as true, each of them could have made the Garden's meeting in Newmarket and returned to where they said they were."

"Thanks, Jared. It was worth a try."

"There was one piece of information that did surprise me. Audley told me that he saw Peebles in Cambridge."

"That is surprising. Peebles was not allocated any responsibilities by Liffey. He would have no reason to be in Cambridge."

"Unless he is running a separate agenda for the deputy governor of Jamaica," commented Jared sharply.

"It's a pity he did not confide in me," Luke remarked soulfully.

"Did he tell you anything that might be useful?"

"Oh yes!" lied Luke, suddenly alert to Jared's unexpected interest.

The more people who thought he knew more than he did, the higher the chances of a misstep by the conspirators.

Luke was surprised that Castle did not ask the obvious follow-up question: what did he tell you?

Instead he made a more mundane observation, "Sir, is it not strange that the two officers murdered were the two men rescued by the *Defiance*—the two senior officers associated with Liffey that were not part of his Barbados establishment?"

"It suggests that Peebles and Blair, despite their overt differences, were both murdered because they had information that was dangerous to the murderer," Luke replied.

"What they clearly had in common is that they were both government agents—Blair working for Thurloe and Peebles for the deputy governor of Jamaica," declaimed Jared with unnecessary vigor.

"If there is a common political motivation, it may simply be the eradication of government agents. You had better be careful, Jared! You could be next," joked Luke.

Jared gave a weak smile.

Luke continued, "None of the senior officers you interviewed admitted to you that they were in the Harwich area?"

"Yes! Audley was in Harwich, advising on the new fortifications."

After Castle left, Luke sought out his old school friend Anthony Audley.

"Anthony, you told young Jared that you had seen Peebles in Cambridge last week. Did he say why he was there?"

"Yes, he was quite open about it but asked me not to divulge it to his fellow officers."

"Why the secrecy?"

"He was on his way to Newmarket to wager a considerable amount of money on the horses. I lectured him on the dangers of losing a fortune, but he cut short my moral diatribe by claiming that it was not his money. He was betting on behalf of another."

"Whom he did not name?"

"Of course not."

"On another matter, you have recently been in Harwich. The government is worried about the situation there. What's the concern?"

"The civilian wing of the government, basing its decisions of the advice of Thurloe and his many agents, has long argued that any imminent invasion of England by Spanish or Dutch forces in support of the exiled Charles Stuart would need a safe haven for the invasion fleet and a ready access to London. They were convinced that the Medway was such a haven."

"And what do the upper levels of the military think?"

"The army agrees with Thurloe."

"Who then does not?"

"The navy! Admiral Blake convinced Cromwell five years ago that the navy needed a dockyard and naval base that would service the North Sea fleet and be of particular use in any war with the Dutch."

"Even Thurloe now agrees on this last point. He told me his agents had discovered that should the Dutch invade, their first choice for a landing was Harwich," said Luke.

"Yes, he has come late to the party but I suspect purely as a fallback position. Should the Medway fall into enemy hands, it would be imperative that our fleet has a North Sea base. Portsmouth is too far away, and London, if the Medway fell, would be blockaded."

"Where would an enemy force land?" asked Luke.

"The Spaniards and the Irish would aim for the Medway. It is so much closer to London. But this is a risk for any invader. The London garrison could make it to Medway in hours, and an English fleet could bottle up the enemy in the Medway estuary quite easily. And the tides, converting much of that estuary into mudflats, would create a serious navigation obstacle. If it's the Dutch Thurloe may be right. The estuary of the Stour and the Orwell would suit the lighter Dutch fleet very well."

"Anthony, your thoughts on Peebles murder?"

"Nothing to do with a Cromwell assassination or the subversion of the army we are creating. He was too far removed from the action. He was an outsider. If the answer to your basic problem lies in developments in Barbados, Peebles was never one of us. He probably lost the money that he wagered on behalf of another at Newmarket, and the aggrieved punter took his revenge."

Luke decided that with Peebles's death and the information provided by Castle, there was no need to visit East Anglia. Instead, he would take steps to flush out Belladonna by a collection of well-chosen lies.

He asked Liffey to assemble all the women guests in the great hall.

When they were all present, he spoke, "My ladies, when Lord Liffey assigned me the responsibility for your welfare and safety during your stay at Austin Friars, I was delighted with such a sinecure. How wrong I was! With the murder of Major Peebles and other information Captain Castle has obtained, I believe one or more of you are in mortal danger."

"Poppycock colonel! Some here may have great pretensions about themselves and their current or future status, but none of us are so important that a crazed killer would murder us," interrupted an imperious but not unattractive tall woman whom Luke realized was Lady Evadne Rede.

"Lady Evadne, a proper and pertinent interruption, but danger to your person does not come from your past or current activities. It comes from what you may have seen or heard even in the brief period since you have been at Austin Friars. Major Peebles and Captain Blair were both murdered because of what they saw or what they may have known, which would have endangered the life or reputation of the murderer."

Evadne responded, "We have only been here a day or so, and I for one have not yet conversed with any of the ladies present. What could we have possibly seen in such a short time that might endanger our lives?"

"You might have noticed something usual when you were waiting for the tide to recede or as you came across the causeway. For example, strangers talking with your servants? Have all the servants you intended to bring actually arrived? Have you lost any?"

Some of women laughed, leading Luke to respond tersely, "This is no laughing matter. The Peebles killer is still on the estate and possibly hiding as a servant to one of you. Therein lies your danger. If you happen to be the unlucky person, with an extra servant, he might murder you in your bed to prevent you alerting me."

Luke was pleased. His plan was working. The mood of the meeting was changing. Nonchalance and boredom had given away to apprehension and, in some cases, palpable fear.

He concluded the meeting on a more positive note.

"I will visit each of you to see if you can remember anything that might help me. My men will guard your persons."

"I, for one, will not have a guard spying on my every movement," announced a woman with flowing brown hair, whose very low-cut bodice left nothing to a lustful male's imagination.

Luke wondered how this gathering of mainly Puritan women would react to such a French style of dress and coiffure.

The objector was Lady Penelope Marlowe.

Before they dispersed, Luke arranged to meet Evadne and Penelope the next day.

Luke ended the meeting and left, but the women did not disperse.

Later that evening, Jane Castle reported to Luke on what happened after he left the room.

"That was a ruthless and nasty performance, Colonel. You almost had me in fear, and you certainly frightened many of them."

"But did it have the required effect. Did any of them reveal information that might be helpful?"

"I'm not sure, but it did reveal something about the group. Immediately you left, Lady Sophia, perhaps by virtue of her age, which must be approaching fifty, took charge. She explained that you had clearly exaggerated the danger, but as long as the murderer was on the estate, it was prudent to follow your directions, and she would be accepting a personal guard."

"Did Penelope respond to this pointed comment?"

"No, but the rest of the group did. They all glared at her, probably affronted by her attire. She is the odd one out. Maybe the weak link that could reveal much more?"

"Of her body, hardly, of information, maybe. Did anybody else speak to the group?"

"Yes, and this is where I embarrass you. Lady Evadne gave a very favorable outline of your career and that they should not be fooled by the presence of my husband. You were His Highness's top man, and you would not have been sent here unless there was a problem of national importance. From information she had gleaned from her unresponsive husband, you were here because the government suspected a Royalist plot to oust Cromwell by the use of the army being trained at Austin Friars. She even, perhaps subconsciously, persuaded the other women to open up to your questioning."

"What did she say?"

"That as Cromwell's top agent, you were discreet. Any private matters that you might unearth would remain a secret, especially from their fathers and husbands. Again, she looked directly at Penelope Marlowe."

"Lady Evadne Rede may not be unbiased. Her husband detests the Marlowe woman. What about the other eight younger women who must all be aged between twenty and thirty?"

"None of them said anything and in general seem confused and bewildered by the situation, but how they responded to one another may give us some useful perspectives."

"What do you mean?"

"Lord Audley's future will be fraught with difficulties. His daughter Ursula ignored her equally young prospective stepmother, Felicity, who in turn appears to be dominated by her sister Grace. David Halliburton's friend Rose Grant seems completely overcome, being placed among such high-status women, and her cousin Veronica openly resents being placed among her social superiors. My advice to you Luke is to approach the Grant women as a fellow social inferior. You, like both of them and me, are an untitled commoner."

"Jane, as a commoner, do you see social snobbery and status as a major divisive factor in this group?"

"Definitely."

"That I will play on," announced Luke.

He brought the discussion to an end.

Jane seemed reluctant to leave.

Luke took advantage of the situation. "Join me for drink?"

Jane smiled teasingly and took Luke's hand.

"Jared is absent tonight. I am sure, despite orders to the contrary, that he has gone to London to report to Thurloe. In the circumstances that you outlined to the women earlier today, it would not be safe for me to sleep alone."

"And we both have had such a busy day—let's forget the drinks."

19

Evadne Rede received Luke in a very spacious apartment. Liffey had certainly favored this fellow child of an earl.

Status appeared important to both of them.

Evadne invited Luke to sit at a small table, the surface of which was entirely hidden by platters of sundry eats.

"Luke Tremayne, you won't remember, but for a few months a quarter of a century ago, we were schoolmates."

"At Lord Hanes's school on his Cornish estate?" asked a surprised Luke.

"Yes, but not for long. My father was a friend of Lord Hanes, and for a few months when I was about ten, I stayed with Lord Hanes while my parents traveled on the continent. I became a friend of Elizabeth Hanes and have remained so since."

Luke gave an embarrassed sigh.

Evadne continued, "Well, may you sigh. I know that in her late teens Elizabeth was besotted with you, only to have her heart broken when you enlisted in the Dutch army. And now more recently, you have done it again. You met the newly widowed Elizabeth and renewed your close friendship. Poor Elizabeth hoped for more and wrote to me, anticipating marriage. How could you refuse my dearest friend and incidentally one of the richest women in England?"

"As the wife of a longtime-serving officer, you know that marriage in such circumstances is not ideal. While I continue my current work, I cannot marry."

"Forgive my impertinence! Yes, I fully understand your position. I *am* in the very position from which you wish to spare Elizabeth."

"Why didn't you go to the Indies with Richard? Was it your status as an earl's daughter that prevented you from lowering yourself to life as an army wife, especially in the horrid humidity of the Caribbean?"

"I should take offense at such a statement. My marriage was a marriage of convenience, arranged by our parents, but that does not mean I wanted to be separated from my husband."

"Then why were you?"

"Perhaps you should ask why Richard left me for so long, but I will answer your rather loaded question. Richard's father built up a vast fortune by stint of brilliant estate management. The dozens of properties that he farmed directly or through tenant farmers whose leases were advantageous to the landlord required constant monitoring and supervision. My father-in-law was well aware that Richard had no head for business, and he slowly taught me the art of property and business management. On his death, I expected Richard to resign his commission and return to East Anglia to take up his thriving inheritance. The large number of properties developed by the Greys and the reinvigorated traditional estates of the Redes amounted to a veritable fortune."

"But he did exactly the opposite?"

"Yes, he accepted an offer from the new governor of Barbados, his friend Christopher Liffey, to join his staff. I owed it to my late father-in-law and to our future to remain in England to manage our network of estates."

"Did you communicate regularly with each other during his five years' absence?"

"Yes, he wrote to me on the first of each month."

"I had not seen Colonel Grey as a romantic. Did any of these letters contain suspicions of a Royalist hidden among his comrades?"

"All of them! Richard is obsessed with evil, which in recent years is manifest in nefarious Royalist officers pretending to be loyal to Parliament and the Protector. He sees them as agents of a Satanic design to destroy God's kingdom and England's special place in it."

"Yes, he is a Fifth Monarchist—unusual and dangerous for a senior officer."

Evadne smiled. "Very perceptive, Luke! In all my letters to Richard, I tried moderating this growing religious zeal."

"At least, he still sees Cromwell as God's general, given the task of preparing England for the coming of the Lord. His more fanatical brethren have recast His Highness as the devil determined to thwart the work of God's chosen."

"You are very conversant with the ideas of these fanatics."

"A few months ago, I helped suppress a rebellion, which included Fifth Monarchy fanatics determined to destroy the government."

"Since his return to England, I fear Richard's religious obsessions have intensified. He has not yet visited his family estates, and when not at Liffey House or recruiting for the new army, he attends the more radical parishes of his religious brethren in London."

"That is a worry! Some of those parishes have fanatical preachers who no longer see Cromwell as God's anointed. Let me return to the letters that Richard sent you during his time in the Indies. Did he name any officer he suspected of treason?"

"Yes, over the five years, everybody on the staff, except Audley, was at one time seen as the prime suspect. To be fair to Richard, he followed up his suspicions and was ready to concede that in most cases they were groundless. Since his return, he told me all his fellow officers are exceptionally loyal to the Protector, with the possible exception of Peter Marlowe."

"Did he ever acquaint you with some problem he had with Audley's daughter, Ursula?"

"Yes, but I did not get the full story. Ursula, as little more than a child, did something quite silly, if not outrageous. Richard discovered it and reported the facts to her father. Ursula never forgave Richard, but her father is forever grateful. Ask them both directly!"

"You don't think Richard got himself entangled emotionally, if not physically, with the young girl?"

Evadne laughed.

"Without being cruel to my husband, Richard has no idea of a physical relationship. Our marriage has never been consummated. To protect his feelings, I have allowed rumors to circulate that I am infertile, which I am not."

Luke thought it wise not to follow up Evadne's last comment. How did she know?

Evadne sensed Luke's thought process and blushed.

Luke quickly changed the subject.

"My lady, I know you have not associated much with the other women that Liffey has gathered here, but do you have any comments that might assist my investigation?"

"I know two of the women here quite well. The Baroness Veldor and more recently her daughter move in the same social circles as I do within Suffolk and surrounding counties. The fortune of the Veldors relies on Sophia's ability and determination. Her husband is more than useless. She and I are in similar circumstances. In the absence of our husbands, we managed and improved the family estates."

"Is Sophia the driving force behind the marriage of Lydia and Christopher?"

"It is not that simple. Sophia certainly sees the future is with Cromwell, and to marry her family into an earldom whose imminent holder is a senior officer in the Protector's army meets her desire to maintain both high social status and political correctness."

"But you have your doubts?"

"Sophia and Lydia hate each other. The baroness was surprised and angry that her daughter returned to England. The marriage arrangement was inspired and negotiated by two aging Royalist peers: Sophia's husband and Christopher's father."

"So you would not suspect her of being the Royalist agent Belladonna?"

"At another time maybe, but for the moment, the best future for her and her family lies in supporting the Protector."

"And Lydia?"

"Unknown regarding her allegiances but a strange if not disturbed woman. As a young girl, she was sent away to an enclosed convent in France, although the family are not Papists. With her father in exile on the continent, he, and not Sophia, was the dominating influence on her upbringing. He is an ultra-Royalist. He may have indoctrinated his daughter with similar sympathies. Her mother grudgingly accepted her return home, only when the Liffey betrothal was mooted, and I imagine under immense pressure from her husband."

"So Lydia could be an unhappy returning exile and a reluctant bride-to-be to an eminent Cromwellian general?"

"Most likely, but Lydia cannot be the wealthy Royalist Belladonna dispensing funds for the overthrow of the regime. She is totally inexperienced and lacks any funds of her own," concluded Evadne.

"Maybe, but she could be the conduit through which Veldor and Liffey and their wealthier Royalist friends feed money into the conspiracy. She seems to be her father's daughter first and foremost," muttered Luke.

"Regarding the other women, I know of Ursula Audley and Penelope Marlowe only through the biased letters of my husband. From what I have seen, his views of Lady Marlowe as a high-class trollop may be justified. Her habit yesterday was outrageous and a very poor example to the younger women. She does not have any money to fund a coup, but as you suggested regarding Lydia, Penelope could well be a channel for funds from other Royalist sources—from her many lovers. She is trouble."

"And Ursula?"

"A spoiled aristocratic brat. I have no evidence, but I don't trust her. There is just something about her that doesn't seem right. I would have your people watch her closely. Maybe these Royalist agents with herbal names are father and daughter: Ursula and Anthony?"

"Even your obsessed husband frees Anthony of any suspicion."

"I was only half serious, but if you establish a firm link other than the obvious connections between the women here and Christopher and his senior officers, it might make your task easier."

"You say you know nothing about the other women. You have been a great help with explaining some of issues of the great aristocratic houses such as your own and the Veldors, but the Audleys are of your class. You know nothing about Anthony's betrothed Felicity Harrison and her sister Grace?"

"Luke, the Harrisons are a West Country family. Our mutual friend Elizabeth Hanes would probably know a lot about them. Why not visit her?"

"Evadne, I hope you are not subverting my mission to a bit of matchmaking."

"Not at all! You do not have to absent yourself from here for long. She is currently staying in her London townhouse. You could be there and back in the same day."

Luke smiled and moved on. "I don't expect you to know anything about the obscure gentry family the Grants—Halliburton's proposed in-laws—and there is a remaining aristocrat, Isadore Liffey."

"An admirable young woman who is very protective of her brother. As she is part of the Anglo-Irish aristocracy, I know little about the family. She is feisty and determined and I am sure will be a match for the Veldors in their attempt to completely snare her brother. Even more so than the Veldors, I understand all her family, except Christopher and herself are active Royalists."

Luke was reluctant to end the interview.

Evadne had proved to be an intelligent, understanding, and warm woman whose closeness to his friend Elizabeth Hanes rekindled beautiful memories.

20

Luke took Evadne's advice and visited the enticing Elizabeth. She was surprised and delighted to see her friend—and the enduring love of her life.

After a moment of hesitation, Luke took Elizabeth in his arms and gave her a long passionate yet gentle kiss.

"Enough!" Elizabeth teasingly proclaimed as she slowly freed herself from Luke's embrace.

"I am sure, given your long-held convictions, you are neither here to seduce me or offer me marriage, although I am favorable to both. It must therefore be work."

"You know me too well, Elizabeth. I have just had the great pleasure of meeting and conversing at length with your friend Evadne Rede, who suggested I visit you for help with my inquiries."

"I am not sure that I can be of any help. Evadne is a matchmaker and is well aware of our on-and-off relationship. She probably manipulated this visit for that sole purpose."

"I am well aware of Evadne's attitude toward us. She would have been delighted if I had come here with a marriage proposal."

"Then how can I help you, Colonel Tremayne?"

Luke explained the general situation at Austin Friars, "As usual, I am investigating murders and trying to unravel a conspiracy against the government. At least one of five men and one of nine women are involved in the plot. Two of the women and one of the men according to Evadne are well-known to you. We both went to school with Anthony, now Viscount Audley. I have already questioned him and also talked about our schooldays, but what can you tell me about his life since he went up to Cambridge?"

"Not much! I lost contact when he went to Cambridge, and I moved to Somerset on my marriage. My Cornish relations continued their social contact with the Audleys and were devastated by the actions of his first wife."

"What happened?"

"Six years ago, after fifteen years of a very volatile marriage, his wife became the mistress of the mad Marquis of Flint, openly flaunting her charms not only to the dithering old peer but to his three predatory and lascivious sons. Anthony sought haven in the Caribbean."

"He obtained a divorce by a special act of Parliament, recently inherited his father's title, and now seeks to remarry."

"To beget a male heir to carry on the title! You males are all the same! Who is he to marry?"

"Lady Felicity Harrison."

"You can't be serious?"

"What's wrong with Lady Felicity?"

"Her aunt, her mother's sister, was Audley's first—and disgraced wife."

"That is intriguing. Why would Anthony wish to marry into the family that disgraced him? Is Felicity a particular beauty? He does not need the money, so her inheritance would be irrelevant. Perhaps her family needs Anthony's status and wealth?"

"There may be some truth in that comment. Felicity's much older sister, Grace, was married at a very young age to the then-dashing Earl of Merrick. Her father provided a massive dowry, which nearly bankrupted the family. It was hoped that the family connection with the Merricks would quickly recover the invested funds. Merrick was an obsessive gambler and lost not only his own inheritance but the Harrison contribution as well."

"What happened to Merrick and his marriage? Lady Grace has accompanied Felicity to Austin Friars identifying herself as Lady Grace Harrison, not Grace, Countess Merrick."

"As an impoverished Royalist, Merrick escaped to the continent. Either his luck changed at the gambling tables, or he inherited a vast fortune from some distant relative. The last I heard of him was that he was living in more lavish and comfortable conditions than Charles Stuart and serving him as a devoted courtier."

"And the marriage? Has his change of fortune affected his relationship with Lady Grace?"

"Who knows? Merrick is certainly in a position to finance a coup against the government. He is still married to Grace who never held strong political or religious views, but she could easily be your Belladonna acting on behalf of her husband."

"And that might explain why she attached herself to her sister and has come to Austin Friars. Merrick is a gambler. Did his gambling take any particular form?"

"Although he played every sort of dice and card game and wagered on cockfights and bear baiting, his overwhelming weakness was horse racing. He spent more time at Newmarket than on his family estates."

Luke could hardly contain himself.

He took Elizabeth in his arms and kissed her, exclaiming, "You may have solved one-half of my problem. Did the Countess Grace accompany her husband to Newmarket?"

"I have no idea. You must ask her."

"Would Felicity be a party to her sister's plot?"

"I doubt it. Anthony is a leading Cromwellian peer, and I have it on good authority from my friends on the Council of State that he is about to become a member of the new Second Chamber with the responsibility of ensuring that the Protector's friends on that body act together to enhance the Protector's interests. Under Cromwell, Audley has power and status. Under the Stuarts, he would lose everything. The Harrisons have already lost a fortune in marrying off one daughter. They would not wish to lose their chance of redemption with their second."

Luke accepted Elizabeth's invitation to stay for supper and the night.

She made it clear that without a proposal of marriage, they would sleep apart.

Next morning, Luke returned to Austin Friars, determined to interview the Harrison sisters.

Before doing so, he quizzed Jane about them.

"Simple! They do not like each other, and Grace does not like Audley, her sister's betrothed."

"Is she here to wreck the proposed marriage?"

"Probably."

"I could do without these subplots. Isadore Liffey is here to scuttle her brother's marriage to the Veldors, and now Grace is here to kill off her sister's nuptials to Audley."

"Don't relax, Luke. These could be deliberate ploys to conceal threats to national security under the cover of dynastic squabbles."

"You are right. Lady Grace Harrison is here using her unmarried name. She is in reality Grace, Countess Merrick, and her husband is a wealthy Royalist currently serving Charles Stuart in Cologne. She could well be our Belladonna."

Luke met Felicity in the enclosed herb garden of the old friary.

She was no beauty. Short, almost plump, with straw-colored flowing locks and round faced—but with intelligent eyes and a perpetual smile.

After a few questions, Luke realized that Felicity was a happy person who adored her much older future husband. She shared his interest in inventions. For a woman, she had received an extensive education through a number of highly qualified tutors.

Audley was clearly looking for a soul mate in his old age rather than a replacement empty-headed and promiscuous beauty of his first marriage.

Luke asked, "How did you meet Viscount Audley?"

"He was married to my aunt. When he returned from fighting, he threw himself into experiments. He had several rooms devoted to his discoveries. As a young girl, he showed me these inventions, and I became very interested in what he was doing, even though because I was a girl, my relatives scoffed at me."

"And how did your betrothal come about?"

"After my aunt betrayed him and he left with young Ursula for the West Indies, my father looked after his then-modest manor, and with Anthony's permission, I was able to use his laboratories. When his father died and he inherited vast estates, he visited these old rooms full of his experiments. He said he was moving all his equipment to Audley Castle, and he would like me to come with him. At first, I thought he meant as a fellow scientist, but he quickly made clear that Parliament had annulled his marriage to my aunt, and as a new peer, it was essential for him to have a wife and produce a male heir. He proposed to me. I later discovered he had already spoken to Father."

"Was your family happy with this proposal?"

"Everybody was delighted, except Grace."

"Why? I would have thought she would have been delighted that you had found such a suitable match."

"Jealousy. Her own marriage is a disaster. She married a Royalist earl who was also a Papist and cannot divorce him. I—the younger, bookish, and plain daughter—will be the wife of a powerful peer and loving man while she, the beautiful seductress, will remain in reality a barren old maid."

"Harsh words, Lady Felicity. So why is she here? To scuttle your marriage?"

"Maybe, but Grace, despite her attitude to the engagement, is not devious. Her presence here nevertheless mystifies me. When Liffey invited me, I had the option of bringing with me as a companion mother, sister, or friend. Mother was coming, but at the last minute, Father insisted that I bring Grace."

"Did you ask him why?"

"Yes. He said that Mother was not well, and the North Kent coast with its the mudflats and cold North Sea winds would endanger her health even further."

"Do you believe him?"

"No. I questioned my mother who said Father had received a proposition that he could not refuse if I took Grace with me. I was curious and asked several of the servants about recent developments concerning my father. It seems that Grace received a parcel from the continent. It was a large wooden box, which Father's valet told me was full of gold coins."

"Where did the box of gold coins come from?"

"From Baldwin Merrick, Grace's husband."

"So they still communicate?"

"Yes, ever since the Earl of Merrick regained his fortune, he has supported Grace and, according to Father, is making amends for the financial losses he caused us years ago."

"So why are the Merricks still apart?"

"The earl cannot return to England as long as Cromwell rules, and Grace refuses to live on the continent."

"Felicity, you have been very helpful. I am sure my old friend Anthony, and you will be very happy."

Felicity left the garden seat, and true to her scientific interest, she began to examine the various herbs.

As Luke left the garden, she pointed to a plant growing in the shade. "Colonel, this is belladonna. And what is disconcerting some of it has recently been picked."

21

Grace consented to an interview on her terms—a cozy afternoon chat in her apartment.

She immediately took the initiative, "Colonel, questioning the women is a complete waste of time."

"And why is that?" asked Luke, cautiously weighing up his opponent.

"Liffey is obsessed that one of his officers is a Royalist spy and that one of the women here is his accomplice, and Cromwell had sent you, his top agent, to uncover their plot."

"And how is investigating this a waste of time?"

"You have been doing this for too long. You create a conspiracy where none exists. Even if Liffey's belief is correct and one of his officers is a Royalist your presence here, with other government agents and troops, have all suspects carefully monitored, if not closely supervised. As soon as they step out of line, you will act. Why would a woman financing a coup come to the very place where the government expects her to be? If I were financing an insurrection, I would have others act for me. I would be as far away from the action as possible and not expose myself to possible discovery."

"So all I need to do is put a personal guard on the five senior officers and watch their every move?"

"Why not? Questioning the women, their servants, and other soldiers will get you nowhere. Some women here, while loyal to Cromwell, have brothers and fathers who are Royalists. Others have relatives who fought for the Parliament but refuse to back the protectorate, and in recent months, I am sure there are many who back the protectorate but not if Cromwell becomes king."

"What are you trying to say?"

"Examining our backgrounds and past political and religious allegiances will lead you nowhere. Everything is in flux. Views are changing. Three of the aristocratic women here have either fathers or husbands who are active Royalists located close to the court of Charles Stuart. Are they immediately suspect?"

"None of those women—and I suppose you mean Lady Sophia, Lady Evadne, and young Isadore Liffey—are above suspicion, but their Royalist connections are well-known and not denied—unlike a fourth aristocrat who has concealed her real identity."

Grace blushed, and Luke went in for the kill, "Why is Grace, Countess of Merrick, pretending to be the unmarried Grace Harrison? You are still married to the earl."

"My little sister is a blabbermouth. My husband has been in exile for years. I have learned to live without him and consider myself Grace Harrison rather than the Countess of Merrick."

Luke decided to exaggerate.

"Not convincing, Countess! We have information that proves you and your husband are in constant contact and that he regularly sends generous funds to you and your family. The earl wishes you to join him on the continent, but for some reason, at the moment, you prefer to stay here in relative poverty with a most annoying sister."

"Yes, my husband and I remain close, but given his political views, he cannot return to England."

"Then what is he up to?"

"In what sense?"

"In blackmailing your father to send you here instead of your mother? You don't like Audley. You don't like your sister. Why are you here, and why did a Royalist courtier peer want you here?"

Grace tried to answer, but Luke cut her short, "I will answer for you. There is an obvious scenario that explains your situation and the problems that confront me. You are Belladonna. Your wealthy Royalist husband is funding the coup, and you are bribing or blackmailing one of Liffey's officers to defect. You are not sure that this officer will go through with the plot, so you are on the spot to ensure his compliance."

"A fairy tale! There not a single piece of evidence to support such a wild accusation," replied a somewhat-surprised Grace.

"It is circumstantial, but a number of small points add up. You have continued your husband's obsession with horse racing, you with the horses and he with the betting. You know Newmarket exceedingly well—an ideal place for your secret organization to meet. Secondly, you have a sister who is a keen herbalist. You could have picked up your code names from her botanical interests. If my story is so fanciful, why does the Earl of Merrick want you here?"

Grace became silent, clenched her fists, and gently drummed them on the table. She finally spoke, "I have a sealed letter from my husband for Mr. Thurloe's eyes only. He knew if I came here, I would have access to senior members of the Cromwellian administration that would make the delivery of the letter easier and conceal his role in the matter."

"Mr. Thurloe is the head of the Protector's intelligence agency, but I am head of military intelligence. I can take the letter."

"No, Colonel, my husband was adamant that it was for Mr. Thurloe's eyes only. Given your reputation, you would remove the seal and read the letter before you passed it on."

Luke could not respond to this accurate assessment of his approach, but he remained unconvinced with her explanation of Merrick's interest.

"You story does not make sense. Your future brother-in-law Viscount Audley will soon be the most senior political peer in the land. You could have given your husband's letter to him to pass on to Thurloe. Audley does not have my ruthless reputation."

"Audley will have nothing to do with Merrick. He blames Baldwin for his first wife's betrayal. The earl was very close to my aunt and defended her at the time. Anthony has never forgiven him."

"Do you know what is in the letter?"

"Yes! It contains nothing against the government and could provide a boost for Cromwell's fortunes."

Luke had reached a dead end.

He decided to facilitate the Countess of Merrick's agenda.

"Mr. Thurloe has a direct agent in the house: Captain Castle. And he is still young and green enough to be honest. And you can be sure he will not pass it on to me."

"Have you finished your interrogation?"

"Yes, but I do have some general questions to which your answers could help my investigation."

"As I said at the beginning, you don't have anything to investigate. Monitor the senior officers day and night, and there can be no coup."

"Even if I accept your assessment of the situation, I still have two murders and one attempted murder to investigate. Someone is slowly killing off Liffey's officer corps."

"To what end?"

"To replace them with men compliant to Weld's will—men determined to rise against the government."

"And have the murdered officers been replaced?"

"For the very reason outlined, no replacements have yet been made. The only new officer in camp is Castle, and he is Thurloe's man."

"Can you be sure? From gossip forwarded by my husband, Royalists are rejoicing that they are beating Thurloe at his own game—having their agents pretending to be his. Given what you have just told me regarding the timing of Castle's appointment, I will certainly not give him Baldwin's letter."

Luke did not want to admit the possible truth of her cautious approach and assessment of the situation.

He continued, "This delay in finding replacements cannot continue for long. Your future brother-in-law is about to retire before the army leaves for Flanders. There has to be a very senior appointment to oversee the artillery, which will play a major role in Flanders."

"Have we finished?"

"Not quite! If my view of the situation is correct, which of the women here are most likely to be Belladonna?"

"How can my answer be of any validity? I have only known most of them a few days."

"Most of my women friends give great weight to intuition. Do you have a feeling concerning any of them?"

"I have had only two overwhelming thoughts since I arrived. Evadne and Sophia are very powerful people who completely dominate those around them, and Penelope's attempt to play the scarlet woman within such an austere and Puritan environment made me uneasy."

"What do you mean uneasy?"

"I've since discovered that she had something of a lurid past, but why would she flaunt it here? She must have an ulterior motive."

"And what would that be?"

"By creating the impression she is little more than an adulterous slut, you would rule her out as a possible conspirator. Obvious, my man! If Penelope is Belladonna, Sir Peter is Weld."

"That's a link I had not thought of—a husband-and-wife combination."

"And it is relevant not only to the Marlowes but to Richard Grey and Evadne Rede."

"That is getting very far-fetched."

"Enough of your questions. Try some of that pheasant and sage in aspic!"

A servant refilled his glass several times over.

After this discussion with the countess, Luke was even more confused.

He had started the conversation convinced that Grace was Belladonna. Now he was unsure.

Was he losing his touch? He was initially sure that Belladonna was the Baroness Sophia. If it was neither the baroness nor the countess, who is it? He would discuss the state of affairs with his officers, but first, he must speak with Penelope Marlowe.

And before he could do that with confidence, he needed an update from Jane.

Jane explained that the women, except for herself and the Grants, largely ignored Penelope.

"And why do you think that is? Is it her reputation as a scarlet woman?"

"Only in part! It is status. The other women are aristocracy or about to enter its ranks. Penelope is the lowly wife of a penurious knight."

"So that is why the only three untitled women have befriended her? Has the group divided along class lines, the aristocrats and upper gentry opposed to the lower gentry many of whom like myself are untitled?" suggested Luke.

"Yes, Sophia and Evadne dominate any discussion and seem to determine any group decision, although Grace Harrison seems to be above herself—one of the few lesser lights who will argue against the two aristocrats."

"That is because Grace Harrison is an aristocrat. She is the Countess of Merrick."

Jane expressed surprise. "Doesn't that make you suspicious? Why the deception?"

Luke surprisingly found he had modified his views regarding Grace in such a way as to excuse her in front of Jane.

"She has her reasons that are not relevant to our case. Lady Penelope—has she gone out of her way to provoke the other women by her outrageous dressing? She leaves nothing to the imagination. Why does she do it? It only embarrasses her and her husband."

"Is this her way of getting back at Sir Peter for some personal offense?" asked Jane.

"There does not appear to be any overt antagonism between the couple. Another far more sinister reason has been put to me. Penelope is Belladonna, and she is overplaying the role of adulterous seductress to put us off the track. And that her husband, Sir Peter, is Weld."

Jane gasped. "Does Liffey have a similar view? Is that why Sir Peter is to lose to Grey the position of second in command?"

"The general has always had doubts about Marlowe's loyalty whereas Grey is resolutely a warrior of the protectorate, but there is not the slightest evidence of Marlowe's treachery."

22

True to her reputation, Penelope adopted another French fashion. She received Luke in her dressing room.

Having just completed her toiletries, the femme fatale revealed all the aids available to a maturing woman. Her box of creams, potions, and powders lay open on her small dressing table, which fronted an enormous mirror.

In spite of the artificial aids to beauty, the paleness of the face produced by an excess of white powder fixed by a combination of egg white and vinegar, and overpainted red cheeks, Penelope possessed a natural allure.

Her long shiny curly hair reached both shoulders while a fringe of curls dominated her face or rather competed with unusually large dark-brown eyes.

As she rose to greet Luke, her low-cut bodice revealed ample breasts only technically covered by see-through fabric.

Now in her midthirties, Penelope retained much of the beauty that in her late teens must have attracted many would-be lovers.

No wonder Peter Marlowe, twenty years her senior, courted the young girl.

Penelope opened the conversation, "Sir, I am surprised that given both our reputations, we have waited so long to meet. Those young innocents whose company I am forced to endure while at Austin Friars are all in love with you."

"Lady Penelope, you are a beautiful woman, and I can see how you have created your reputation. However, I am not here to seduce you or pass judgment on your behavior. Your fellow guests seem to have done that with unrelenting fervor. My mission appears known to all the women of the household—solve two murders and uncover two clandestine Royalists who are believed to be here. One line of inquiry is that the answer to these issues lies in what happened in the Caribbean. You are the only mature woman here who was there. Something trivial or unimportant in your eyes may give me untold assistance."

"It's a pity that our personal encounter has to be put on hold, but Christopher is so obsessed with this Royalist nonsense we will both be here for months."

"Why nonsense?"

"The Royalist could be anybody who was in the Indies. Attitudes to our former enemies modified rapidly in that environment. I had cordial relations with dozens of Royalist gentlemen exiled to the islands of the Caribbean—and with their wives. Except for Christopher and Dick Grey, the attitudes of all of us to the Spaniards, the Irish, and English Royalists were, if not friendly, certainly not governed by any fanatical hostility that pervades the current government."

"Why was this?"

"Familiarity and the limited number of Cromwellian supporters in the area."

"Expand!"

"The planters in those islands were Royalists when the civil wars began and have remained so since. In addition, hundreds, if not thousands, of Royalist officers were sent there technically as prisoners. The allegiance of Barbados to the Parliamentary cause was a result of astute diplomacy by the leading planters and the constant threat from Admiral Blake and his invincible fleet."

"Then any or all the officers associated with Liffey could be clandestine Royalists?"

"Yes, because all of them, probably on a monthly basis, were offered incentives to join the cause of Charles Stuart."

"How do you know this?"

"Living in the tropics may slow you down physically, but it does not turn you into an idiot. At every social event, these issues were discussed and offers openly made. If all the senior officers on Liffey's staff, except for Peter, were not so wealthy in their own right, they would have succumbed given the vast amount of money offered."

"Are you suggesting that the main incentive to become a Royalist is money rather than conviction?"

"No, but those of little wealth and little conviction would more readily jump at the funds offered and change sides. For the wealthy and those with strong ties to the current government, a change of heart would be necessary."

"Did any of Liffey's officers show such a change?"

"Luke, we were in the Caribbean for five years. When Peter first took up his position, England was run by a corrupt Parliament, and most were delighted when it was replaced. However, the replacement, an assembly of religious fanatics, divided the group. Dick was delighted, but the others expressed grave disquiet. And at that time, some were tempted to prefer the Stuarts to the fanatics."

"How did they react when Cromwell seized power in late 1653?"

"Overjoyed."

"Have you heard any rumbles against the Cromwellian regime in recent years by any of them?"

"Only regarding the delay in bringing them back to England when their term had expired."

"You know those officers better than I—"

"Naughty Luke! I have not slept with all of them."

"I was simply implying that you knew them for five years. I will get to any information you might have obtained in your other role later."

"Colonel, don't expect that I would divulge to you, a stranger and a government officer with a reputation of brutality if needed, any information that might adversely affect my friends. To me, none of the officers under suspicion is a Royalist, yet on the other hand, if one of them was proved to be so, it would not greatly surprise me."

Luke was beginning to realize that Penelope was not just a painted face but was revealing aspects that suggested that she would be capable of organizing the coup.

He changed tack.

"My lady, if you are unwilling to help me by talking about your friends, let me focus on you."

"You want me to prove that I am not this Belladonna that the rest of the women seem fascinated with?"

"Yes. At the moment, overplaying the role of the scarlet woman may be a deliberate ploy to hide your real abilities as the organizer and financier of the conspiracy."

"I have a simple answer that completely demolishes that fanciful suggestion."

"And that is?"

"Money! Years ago, I was the most beautiful girl in the county, daughter of an impoverished nontitled gentleman. I was successful in winning the heart of a much older but equally impoverished knight who had just inherited a small but unproductive estate. Our income is Peter's army's pay, and a posting in Barbados increased this substantially."

"Why did you not stay behind and try to build up the Marlowe estate as Lady Evadne did when Richard Grey took up a similar position."

"Neither Peter nor I had any interest in farming or managing a property, and the property was so run-down it was not worth investing any time and effort into it. Peter's army career is our future and our only income."

"Is there no heir for whom the property might be redeveloped?"

"Peter and I had no children. I am infertile."

"No one can be sure which party is at fault in such a situation," pontificated Luke.

"I can be. That is one reason I embarked on my many affairs, safe in the knowledge that I would not get pregnant. Peter had no trouble in his youth in getting several of the village girls with child. By the time he married me, he had lost interest in that side of a relationship, especially after the initial attempts to beget a child failed."

"Given that you could not give Peter an heir, why did he not divorce you? Your behavior would have given him ample justification."

"Despite the negative view of our marriage by outsiders, we are both happy with each other and accepting of Peter's obsession with his work and my many dalliances. He has no desire to maintain his family dynasty. He hated his father. It was an unhappy youth that propelled him into the army."

"Your lack of income is certainly a strong reason to reject you as Belladonna, but I can't."

"Why not?"

"Because of your many affairs with wealthy Royalist sympathizers. You may be organizing this conspiracy and funding it with the money one or more of your former lovers is providing."

"You do have a convoluted mind."

"Regarding those affairs, I appreciate the need to keep them secret, but I plead with you, however, to reveal anything you discovered in the Indies from your illicit partners that may help me preserve the current administration."

"I did not waste time discussing politics. Most Royalists I slept with were happy to ride out Cromwell's regime and hoped that on his death Charles Stuart would have enough support to return to England as king. They would not risk the loss of any further property and maybe their life by plotting against the government. Your friend Mr. Thurloe has such a network of agents across the Caribbean that it was far safer to be an adulterer than a plotter."

"Did you sleep with any of Thurloe's agents?" asked Luke unexpectedly.

For the first time during the whole discussion, Penelope hesitated.

Luke narrowed his question, "Did you sleep with Peebles or Blair, our two murder victims?"

Penelope remained thoughtful but mute.

Luke was patient.

"Colonel, as both men are dead, I will confirm that I slept with Robert Peebles and knew a lot about Blair, although I was not intimate with him."

"Tell me all you know about them."

"Blair was a clandestine Royalist who tempted many in the Caribbean to join the Stuart cause. He was organizing a small Irish and Royalist army made up of deserters and a fleet of vessels officially missing or wrecked."

"And Peebles?"

"A government agent who was following Blair."

"Did Peebles murder Blair?"

"I think so."

"Then who murdered Peebles?"

"We all know that as it occurred the first day we were here—a red-haired assassin everybody calls Yarrow."

"Acting under whose direct orders: Belladonna or Weld?"

"I have no idea, and does it matter?"

"One last question! You had a serious incident with Richard Grey while in the Indies that has led to a continuing estrangement. What was it about?"

"Richard Grey is a moralistic precisionist—an extreme Puritan of the most fanatical type. He was so appalled at my behavior on Barbados and my husband's refusal to discipline me, divorce me, or send me back to England that he tried to force Peter's hand. He followed me on one occasion. He created such a furor, demanding that my then-unfortunate partner write a letter confessing adultery, which he handed to Peter, in turn, demanding that he denounce me."

"What did Peter do?"

"He attacked Richard where given his lowly beginnings it hurt most. He told him that whatever happened between wife and husband was their affair only and that no gentlemen would have stooped so low as to follow the wife of a comrade in such a fashion. He challenged Richard to a duel."

"Did it happen?"

"No, Christopher intervened and threatened both Peter and Richard with court martial and immediate dismissal if either of them referred to the matter again."

"But Richard continues to badmouth you?"

"Yes, but he has another reason to detest me."

Luke's interest piqued.

"I discovered that this godly man whose wife had remained in England was showing an undue interest in young Ursula. With her father often away on the other islands, inspecting and erecting fortifications, Richard delighted in taking his place. He probably lusted after her in his godly way. Ursula told me of his unwelcomed attentions, so when I went to St. Kitts for one of my assignations, I took Ursula with me to get her away from Richard hopefully for the duration of Anthony's current absence."

"How was this good deed turned against you?"

"Richard followed us, abducted Ursula, returned to Barbados, and claimed he had rescued her from moral temptation and perversion, stemming from her association with me. Ursula informed her father of the truth, but he chose overtly to believe his fellow officer Richard Grey."

Luke liked Penelope—but she joined Evadne, Sophia, and Grace as a possible suspect.

23

Ursula Audley's appearance contrasted with that of her friend and mentor, Penelope Marlowe.

She wore no makeup.

Her long blonde hair was shiny clean and exuded a faint but distinctive scent of roses. It was uncurled except for a tiny fringe across her forehead.

She had a thin face with a high aristocratic forehead and a small pointed chin.

Her eyes were small and of a cold grayish-blue color.

These she used to stare effectively at persons whose comments and behavior displeased her. The Audley stare had already irritated several of her fellow guests.

Her mouth was small, and her lips did not have the benefit of any coloring, and her overall pale complexion resulted from her careful avoidance of the sun rather than the use of artificial whiteners.

Here was an attractive young woman whose still single state raised questions.

"Lady Ursula, one of the women with whom you have been forced to consort since your arrival here is a Royalist on the brink of effecting a coup against the government. Have you seen or heard anything that might help me identify the culprit?"

"Sir, I know you and Father are friends, so I will help you in any way I can, but as one of the youngest women here no one listens to or confides in me, except for Penny, who I have known for a long time."

"You suspect none of them?"

"I distrust my future stepaunt, Grace, the Countess Merrick."

"You are unhappy with your father's intended marriage?"

"On the contrary! Felicity and I get on well together. She will make Father very happy, and I see her as a sister rather than stepmother. However, when my mother deserted Father, her family blamed him rather than her. Grace is my mother's favorite niece— even more favored than I, her own daughter."

A tear rolled down Ursula's cheek.

"How do you and your father get on? There was an incident in the Indies involving Colonel Grey in which your father took his side rather than believe you."

Ursula began to sob with exclamations of distress.

Luke offered her a large handkerchief as she fell into his comforting arms.

As she calmed down, she smiled at Luke and asked, "May I call you Uncle Luke? With Father about to be married, I need someone to turn to in moments of distress."

Luke, caught unprepared by such a reaction, could only mutter, "Of course, Ursula. Why the sobbing?"

"It was the thought of that incident in which Colonel Grey spied on me and reported back to Father a pack of lies."

"If they were a pack of lies, why did your father believe them?"

More tears began to flow freely down Ursula's cheeks.

"Because I had earlier betrayed my father and given him good reasons to believe Grey's lies. Have you not wondered why an attractive young lady with a massive potential dowry is not betrothed by now? Most of my contemporaries are long married," confessed Ursula.

"What form did this betrayal take?"

"Not long after we arrived in the Indies, I was seduced by one of father's fellow officers. I was only fourteen. He was not married, and we both believed that our one night together would be the beginning of many. I told Father what happened and of my desire to marry my seducer. Father was livid. I refused to name the man as, until my recent return to England, I believed that he and I would marry. My desire to wait for my lover and the fact that an aristocratic bride who is not a virgin is not a highly marketable subject, have left me a spinster. It was this earlier episode that led Father initially to believe Colonel Grey's version of events."

"May your new uncle ask a very personal question? Is the man for whom you waited present at Austin Friars?"

"Even an understanding uncle cannot be given an answer to that question at the moment. He might put two and two together and come up with five. It is a very delicate situation."

"The incident involving Grey—did he pester you?"

"Yes, but he never touched me. When Father was away, he was always close to me, watching me, assisting me in whatever trivial task I was engaged in. It was unnerving. I felt he was attracted to me, but his religious convictions prevented him from taking things further."

"Did Penelope lead you into dens of moral iniquity?"

"No! Penny was not taking me into the brothels of the Caribbean. Her assignations were with wealthy gentlemen meeting in comfortable mansions on various islands. It was always a one-to-one relationship. I spent my time sitting on beaches or drawing, although I was always included in the lavish meal that followed such liaisons."

"There was more than one such adventure?"

"Yes. Grey did not catch on to what was happening until my sixth or seventh excursion with Penny."

"During these dinners, did the gentlemen attempt to conceal their identity? Did you recognize any of them on a different occasion?"

"All the men revealed their identity, or Penny told me who they were. Such affairs were part of the accepted culture of planter and military life on these islands. It was only the stuffy Puritans who objected or, occasionally, a wronged partner."

"Were any of your father's fellow officers among these men who availed themselves of Penelope's favors?"

"The man who was murdered on our first day here, Robert Peebles, was one of her regulars."

"So none of the other officers took advantage of Penelope's availability: Liffey, Grey, Halliburton, your father, Blair, or young Redmond?"

"We were a very close group. Penny would never reveal that destructive sort of information even to me, but she kept a diary in which she recorded her adventures in detail."

"Lady Penelope kept a diary of her affairs," repeated a jubilant Luke.

"Yes. I also remember her mentioning Timothy Redmond. She jokingly said that half the officer corps in the Caribbean preferred him to her."

"Were any of Liffey's group that way inclined?"

"What do you think? Soldiers, deprived of female company, resort to one another for satisfaction. Of all the officers on Liffey's staff, only Sir Peter had a wife in the colony."

Luke waited for Ursula to elaborate.

Instead, she suddenly decided to bring the chat to an end.

Had she revealed something she regretted?

Luke walked around the manicured garden. He was both delighted and concerned by the insights he had received from this still very young yet clearly troubled woman.

Many of the issues that could surface among the officers as they trained for Flanders may have had their origins in the sexual relationships that developed, or failed to develop, in the Indies. The motives behind the murders of Blair and Peebles could have had a similar origin. Ursula's seduction at the age of fourteen by an officer who may or may not be at Austin Friars supported a sexual interpretation of events.

But he was more interested in two other facts. Ursula Audley and Penelope Marlowe were very close—and the latter kept a diary.

Lydia Veldor was the next on Luke's list to be questioned.

She was thirty years old and about to marry Christopher Liffey who had never married and now at the age of fifty-five was to confront it for the first time.

The pressure came from his newfound status, given the imminent death of his father and elder brother. As Earl of Liffey, he must marry and produce an heir.

Lydia was the daughter of a baron and scarcely a suitable wife for the earl in waiting.

She was also typical of the worst of her class.

She kept Luke waiting for over an hour. After all, he was scarcely a gentleman.

She resented having to talk to people of low rank.

Luke sensed the antagonism as soon as he entered the antechamber that she had designated as their meeting place.

She was conservatively dressed with a deep-brown bodice and matching skirts and large silken collars and cuffs.

Her time in the convent rather than her brief interlude at the French and Royalist court determined her dress. She had not succumbed to the more outrageous Gallic fashions that would have angered many of the other women present.

Her unattractive and abrasive personality was matched by her appearance.

Her short mousy brown hair was heavily curled. She had a very long forehead, sparse eyebrows, a prominent nose, and large teeth that seemed even too big for an extremely large mouth.

Luke took a safe course with the aid of a few white lies.

"Lady Lydia, thank you for finding time to see me. I have been asked by your husband-to-be to uncover the Royalists among the gentry and aristocratic women present."

"I refuse to help you. Until my betrothal to Christopher, I lived with my father. He is a baron, exiled from his home by the murderers you support."

"I can only assume that by living in exile with your father in recent years and deserting your mother, you were proclaiming that you are indeed a Royalist. Your father hopes that your marriage will persuade Christopher to change sides?"

"We make no secret of it, although Mother continues to support your illegal government. I will never help you. You may take your leave, Colonel. We need not speak again as I have no intention of betraying those loyal to our king. In fact, I will do all I can to thwart your current investigation and assist any Royalists you uncover. You have been warned."

"Overt Royalists are not my problem, my lady. Mr. Thurloe has your every action monitored. It is those who pretend to be friends of the government—agents of deceit—who are my target."

He left the antechamber convinced that Liffey was making a terrible mistake.

To marry such a woman at his late stage in life was an unnecessary personal chore and a potential danger to the government.

Had Liffey investigated the credentials of his bride-to-be?

An obvious question: why was a thirty-year-old unmarried?

The marriage age for aristocratic women was normally in their mid-to-late teens.

Were there serious impediments to her betrothal?

Clearly, the marriage was for one purpose: produce an heir as quickly as possible. Sophia must know what was happening and the risks it involved.

There were three women that Luke had yet to question: Veronica and Rose Grant and Isadore Liffey with whom he had already had a brief discussion.

It was Isadore who next approached Luke.

"You have just interviewed that witch—the high-and-mighty Lydia. She is only the daughter of a mere baron. Do I, the daughter of an earl, behave so badly to the inferior classes?"

Luke had to smile. The younger generation of aristocratic women were much more concerned about status than their mothers.

Isadore continued, "Brother should be betrothed to the mother. Lydia is completely insensitive to the feelings of others. She openly denounces Cromwell as a regicide and all those that support him as enemies not only of England but of God Almighty."

"Have you raised these concerns with your brother?"

"He simply adopts the typical male position that when they are married, Lydia will obey him and conform to his views on the relevant merits of Oliver Cromwell and Charles Stuart."

Luke suddenly had a worrying thought, which he immediately communicated to Isadore.

"Could she be a deliberate plant by the conspirators to put us off the track and that she and her mother are working together to bring down the government? As they could be openly Royalist, the responses of the other women to her position would enable them to assess whether they would have any allies when she reveals herself as Belladonna or Belladonna's assistant?"

"There is no way that Lydia is Belladonna. She couldn't organize her dolls into a straight line, let alone a coup against the government. And her servants would probably have to do that. But her mother is a different proposition."

"Since we spoke last, have you seen signs that might help my inquiry?"

"None of the younger women seem capable of organizing anything. I wouldn't waste time on Lydia, Ursula, Felicity, Rose, or Veronica. Jane is a fellow government agent, and I am a loyal supporter of the government. Any of the older women could be Belladonna: Penelope, Evadne, Sophia, or Grace."

Luke, half in jest, replied, "Thank you, Isadore, for your advice. Contrary to your assertion, there is one younger woman who might be Belladonna."

"Who could that be?"

"You."

Isadore smiled. "I am too busy scuttling my brother's marriage to have time to organize an insurrection."

Luke delivered a gentle warning, "In carrying out your mission. Do not complicate mine! Although I think you are right, I will speak to the Grants."

24

Luke was awakened in the middle of the night.

Two horsemen, who had ridden posthaste from London, were shown into Luke's apartment.

He was astounded. The smaller of the two men was Thurloe's chief agent, William Acton; and the second man, easily recognized by the blondness of his hair, was Luke's former deputy Simon Cobb.

"Good grief, man. Are you not the deputy governor of Jamaica?"

"I am, but given the crisis, I was sent back to England by the governor to warn Whitehall."

Acton intervened, "Colonel Cobb has confirmed the existence of a small Royalist-Irish fleet and army gathered together in the Indies, which sailed for Europe weeks ago."

"One of our frigates sighted the fleet just off Santa Domingo, and its captain recognized some of the ships as those that had been listed as wrecked. Some were flying the flag of Saint Patrick and others that of the Stuarts. I boarded our fastest ship, hoping to outrun the enemy ships and get here before them. The governor of Jamaica sent another ship to find Admiral Blake so that his fleet, somewhere off Spain, might intercept the invasion flotilla before it entered English waters," explained Cobb.

"Since Cobb's arrival yesterday, Mr. Thurloe has sent ships to inform our other fleets," added Acton.

"Where is it headed?" asked Luke.

"No real evidence, but given the information from various agents and the well-known deployment of our own fleets and armies and the assumed intention of our opponents, expecting an uprising on English soil to coincide with their arrival, their destination is probably one of two areas within striking distance of London: here, in the Medway and Thames estuaries and the Orwell and Stour estuaries on the Suffolk-Essex border," answered Acton.

"Such an enterprise has major logistical problems, the solving of which would be difficult for the Irish. To get the timing right would be impossible for professionals like ourselves even over a short distance. There must be a staging port in western Ireland or on the continent where they will wait until news of the coup is received," said Luke.

"To be blunt, if there is no rising against Cromwell and if the small Irish army aboard the fleet is not reinforced by local and Spanish or Dutch soldiers, it could be wiped out by a single company of the Protector's veterans. If the invasion fleet meets any one of the English republic's fleets, it will be annihilated. Our enemies, unless Providence suddenly favors them at every turn, are on a suicide mission," declared Cobb.

"This scheme must have been hatched and led by a complete fanatic."

"It was and is. It is led by my twin brother who is now General David Doyle."

Luke suddenly took in a deep breath.

Cobb was immediately apologetic. "I am sorry, Luke. I know my brother murdered a woman with whom you were deeply in love."

"It was a long time ago, Simon, but speaking of him does bring back painful memories. This is serious, but why the drama of waking me in the middle of the night?"

"A frigate will leave London early this morning with a company of troops drawn from the capital's garrison. It will collect Audley,

Cobb, and you and sail for Harwich, where the three of you will ensure that the port can be defended. Cobb will take over as military governor of the town for the duration of the emergency. Audley will inspect and modify the defenses. Tremayne, you planned to visit this part of the world as part of your general inquiries. Two ships will move to a station just off Harwich as the first line of defense. Our North Sea fleet will sail up the coast to the tip of Scotland, hoping to engage the enemy fleet, which we suspect will take the northerly route rather than risk the channel," elaborated Acton.

Luke was not happy. Only Castle could have informed Thurloe of his planned visit to Harwich and Newmarket. If you cannot trust the husband, can you trust the wife?

Acton continued, "Liffey is to put together a company of the more advanced recruits to be battle ready, and I will send some veterans from the London garrison to combine with them. There is no time for chatting. You must leave here before the tide comes in and be at Chatham at high tide to join the frigate for Harwich."

An hour later, Luke, Simon, and Anthony rode across the rapidly submerging causeway and headed for the naval base and dockyard westward along the Medway estuary.

As they trotted in the moonlit early morning, Luke raised the issue of Peebles with Cobb.

"You know about Peebles?"

"Yes. Acton told me last night. I am sure with your experience, you will quickly bring his murderer to justice."

"To do that, I need answers. Did you ever suspect that Peebles might be a Royalist double agent?"

"No, why would you ask such a question?"

"My evidence on Peebles is scanty, but two direct observers of his behavior in Jamaica suggest that he was often absent without reasonable excuse."

"My missing major, as the ranks called him had a habit of disappearing, satisfying his lust with a range of frustrated army wives. It was with my approval. He obtained more information from his bed mates than from any other source."

"Did he ever go to Barbados?"

"No, why do you ask?"

"I am sure that he was murdered because he saw or heard or met someone from the Barbados establishment that he was surprised to find at Austin Friars."

"Peebles met women from the larger islands on the smaller and more remote islets. It was common practice for persons of both genders to take a break away from routine by spending time on semi-isolated isles—as isolated as you can be when you take dozens of servants with you."

"If he had an affair with any women from the Barbados military establishment, he only had two choices," suggested Luke.

"One, not two," interrupted Anthony. "My daughter did get into trouble from which she was saved by Dick Grey, but it did not involve men. Peebles's partner could only have been Penny Marlowe."

Luke did not comment and asked Cobb, "What was Peebles's last message to you?"

"It was simple. He said the rumors concerning a hidden army and fleet were true, and he had commandeered a ship and was sailing in the direction of the Lesser San Pedros. I did not wait for any further communications from him as one of our ships had already sighted the fleet sailing up the American coast, clearly hoping to pick up the right winds to push them across the Atlantic. I guessed they would sail much farther to the north before turning east to avoid other shipping. Reports said the ships were overloaded and not making good time. I set out to get here before them and warn the authorities."

"Why come yourself? The captain of the frigate could have delivered the warning."

"My murderous brother must be brought to justice."

"Your concept of justice where your brother is concerned does not involve the magistrates," remarked Luke.

"True! He murdered my, and his, family. He murdered the love of your life, as well as dozens of other innocent victims. You and I have a moral right to remove this animal. I want him to land where I am so that I can exterminate him."

"The ocean might beat you to it. An overloaded boat in the North Atlantic is not likely to survive," remarked Anthony, anxious to lessen the developing tension that Simon's obsession was fomenting.

The three officers met their scheduled transport at Chatham and after an uneventful trip arrived in Harwich.

Cobb and Audley immediately set about their designated jobs while Luke headed for Veldor Lodge with his letter of introduction from the baroness.

Veldor Lodge was a large manor whose core had been the hunting lodge of a medieval baron. It had undergone extensive additions over two centuries and was now a hodgepodge of architectural styles.

A servant ushered Luke into the entrance hall where the steward, a tall thin man who introduced himself as Barnaby Brett, received him.

Brett opened Sophia's sealed letter.

It was clearly an overwhelming endorsement of Luke and his mission.

"Her ladyship says you want to become involved in the horse-racing fraternity of the area and says she has given you some advice on where to wager your money. She adds that this is only an excuse because given your reputation and friendship with Cromwell, you are on a mission for the Protector himself."

"The baroness is very perceptive," Luke remarked.

"Do not fear, Colonel. Under her leadership, Veldor Lodge has been the focus of pro-Parliamentary and pro-Cromwellian sentiment in the whole of the area, even though her fascination with racing brings her into contact with a rump of unrelenting Royalists."

"And what about yourself, Mr. Brett? Did you serve during the late wars?"

"Yes, I was a trooper in the first group of cavalry that Oliver Cromwell raised as part of the Earl of Manchester's Eastern

Association. My loyalty cost me my position here as Baron Veldor fought for the king."

"I belonged to the same unit. Our paths may have crossed fifteen years ago."

"I did not last long in that illustrious and elite regiment. I was badly wounded in late 1642 and spent the rest of war on garrison duty until the baroness, on her husband's desertion, appointed me here."

"He fled to the continent long before the king's forces were finally defeated?"

"Yes, Baron Veldor is a coward, a charlatan, a ne'er-do-well, and an adulterer. Lady Sophia is well rid of him. She completely reversed the fortunes of the Veldor estates. If you look around this house, it now reflects the austere yet pragmatic furnishings of a Puritan household. The Parliament passed legislation, depriving Baron Veldor of his estates and bestowing them on his wife. The baron can never return, except on conditions approved by her."

"The marriage of Lydia and Christopher Liffey would unite the families of two extremely Royalist aristocrats, both desperate for an heir. Lydia spent her formative years in France. How is she reacting to her proposed marriage?"

Brett put his head in his hands and proclaimed, "The whole enterprise is a disaster. Lydia is not right in the head. Before I came here, there was a tragic accident. The young Lydia killed her even younger brother, heir to the title and family fortune. The girl was so disturbed by the incident that she was sent to a convent school on the continent involving confinement under strict supervision. Her doting father in recent years without any evidence that the girl's condition had improved released her from the convent and had her stay with him at the Royal and French courts. Ever since she returned from France, she has been critical of her mother and constantly demands more and more money so she can live as a daughter of a peer should. She sees her mother as a penny pincher. She has a cruel and vindictive streak, evident in her treatment of the servants and the animals. After meeting the girl, I pleaded with Sophia to veto her husband's plans to marry their dangerous daughter to Lord Liffey."

"Does Lydia depend entirely on her mother for funds?"

"Yes, as does her father. There is no money in the Veldor family other than that accumulated and controlled by Lady Sophia."

"So Sophia is financing Lydia's return and any costs caused by the betrothal?"

"Yes."

"I can understand why Baron Veldor wants this marriage, but I cannot fathom why Sophia supports it."

"Sophia told me that her errant husband was strongly in favor of the match because he believed that when Christopher acceded to the earldom he would become a Royalist. Sophia is convinced of the opposite result. On marriage, Lydia will obey her husband and become a loyal supporter of the Protector. Sophia is being misled by both husband and daughter. Liffey has invited into his household an open Royalist with a dangerous personality."

"These dynastic machinations could have serious implications if not repercussions for national security, let alone family harmony," Luke observed.

"That is why, Colonel, you must save the baroness from herself and prevent this betrothal. She seems taken with you. Talk to her!"

A small slightly plumpish young man with a crop of curly brown hair, or an atrocious fitting wig, entered the room.

When he saw that Barnaby had a visitor, he scuttled away.

"Who was that?" asked Luke rudely.

"Alphonse Dupont, valet and dog's body to the Lady Lydia, sent by her father to ensure the marriage went ahead."

"Then why is he here and not at Austin Friars?" asked Luke.

"A good question, Colonel!"

25

Over dinner, the two former Ironsides discussed the early days of the Parliamentary cavalry and the role that the now Protector played in turning gentry and yeoman horsemen into an effective fighting force.

Luke trusted Barnaby.

He confessed that the baroness was correct. He was not interested in Newmarket because he wanted to wager large sums of money on the races.

He was anxious to uncover a covert group of Royalists called the Garden, who met in the area, hiding among the transient racing fraternity. Its leader was a wealthy woman who called herself Belladonna and who currently was at Austin Friars in Kent.

"You thought the baroness could be this Belladonna?" asked Barnaby.

"Initially yes! She is wealthy. She is obsessed with horse racing. She is married to an extreme Royalist peer, who is openly proud to be a courtier to Charles Stuart. She has inserted into the tense situation at Austin Friars, a young woman who is an even more fanatical Royalist than her father."

"You no longer suspect Sophia?"

"I may be wrong, but from what I have discovered, and especially from what you have told me, the only common factor I can prove between Belladonna and Baroness Veldor is her wealth. She detests gardens and is most unlikely she would give herself a horticultural code name."

"Exactly! Sophia would not know the name of single herb. In truth, the only plant that she would recognize is the rose because it is part of the Veldor crest."

"Is there any local gentlewoman who might meet the profile of Belladonna?"

"No, although as steward, the habits of neighboring landed gentry, especially in regard to their interest in gardening, are not an issue that I have ever confronted. Sophia's head gardener is a better source for that type of information."

The two men drank well into the early hours of the morning.

Luke arose late and was treated to a meal of local bacon and the freshest of eggs.

There was little point in going onto Newmarket, and he would best serve his inquiry by an immediate return to Austin Friars.

Would he go overland through London where he could speak to Thurloe or return to Harwich or any of the ports on the Stour or Orwell and find a vessel sailing south?

Barnaby forced his hand.

"Luke, I am to visit Harwich today. If you are returning there, we could ride together."

On arriving on the outskirts of Harwich, Luke was not surprised to find armed musketeers blocking the road.

Cobb had put the town on alert and was monitoring every arrival and departure.

Those who had no acceptable reason to enter the town were refused admittance.

Luke found a coastal transport that was sailing for the Medway midafternoon.

With several hours to fill in, he visited Cobb.

"You've got things moving quickly," Luke remarked.

"And just in time," replied Simon.

"What do you mean?"

"A boat, fishing off the northern Netherlands, reported a small fleet of ships flying no distinguishing flags. One of the trawler men who had been with Penn in the Indies claimed that one of the ships was the vessel he served on in the early months of that enterprise, the *Falcon*. The *Falcon* was reported lost at sea at the same time as Penn and Venables abandoned the attempt to capture Santa Domingo. It's probable that this is my brother's fleet. I have alerted Whitehall."

"It's arrived too early. Plans to take over the new army and assassinate Cromwell cannot yet be that far advanced," said Luke.

"Or the conspirators have outsmarted you and are much more organized and closer to acting than you have assessed. Get thee to Austin Friars as fast as you can!" advised Simon only half jokingly.

Luke did.

It was dark as he rode across the causeway, which the incoming tide had already submerged to a depth of almost a foot.

He asked John Martin for an update on developments during his absence.

"A half company of musketeers has been sent from London. I did hear a couple of the soldiers complaining that they would have to act as nursemaids to a lot of callow youth."

Next morning, Luke asked Liffey how he would utilize the reinforcements.

"Mix the veterans with the more advanced trainees at the platoon level. There will be two veterans to every six or more recruits. This will provide a regiment of musketeers ready to defend our installations across the area. I have appointed Richard to command this composite unit. Peter will continue to train and command the newer recruits."

Luke smiled.

"Tremayne, I see nothing to be amused by," remarked an irritated general.

"I can see a major positive in this new situation. Our conspirators were hoping to subvert a small army of new recruits who had no loyalty to Cromwell. The men you have mixed with these green skins are Cromwellian veterans from the London garrison. They are not likely to be subverted. This will stymie the Belladonna and Weld conspiracy."

Liffey seemed taken aback by these comments and momentarily was lost for words.

Finally, he responded, "Not necessarily! The most likely change of plan is that they will act sooner rather than later. Good god! Luke, you must find these deviants now."

Luke agreed.

He called a meeting of his officers and Jane Castle to review the situation.

His summary was simple.

"We have three conspirators in our midst: Belladonna, Weld, and Yarrow. Yarrow is hiding among the servants and has probably dyed his hair. Belladonna is either Sophia Veldor, Evadne Rede, Grace Merrick, or Penelope Marlowe. But none of them fit the picture perfectly. Weld could be Liffey, Grey, Marlowe, Halliburton, or Audley. I would exclude Grey because he is so vehemently anti-Royalist and Audley because he has a great future as a politician and local magnate under Cromwell. Liffey and Halliburton are unlikely. The former has sacrificed so much to serve Cromwell and has now reached the pinnacle of his career to command an army abroad. The latter is a competent professional soldier who would serve any government, but I cannot see him risking his future by participating in any dangerous uprising in which the winning side was not already known."

"So that only leaves Marlowe?" commented Evan.

"Yes, but there is no evidence against him. I have a feeling that Weld and Belladonna might be close personally—such as husband and wife.

In that case, we have two possibilities: Peter and Penelope Marlowe or Richard Grey and Lady Evadne."

"Not necessarily! Spouses-to-be may be as powerful a combination. Liffey and the openly Royalist prig Lydia, Audley and the bookish Felicity, and Halliburton and the nervous Rose Grant," said the ever-practical Strad.

"Immediate plan of action?" asked Evan, tired of the theorizing.

"Jane, monitor the conversations of the women and try to unearth if any of them have hidden links with Liffey and his officers or unknown sources of great wealth! Strad, list and interview every servant currently on the estate. Ask each servant whether he or she knows those retainers that surround their master or mistress! John, maintain security on the estate and control who comes in and out! I will interview the Grants."

Jane intervened, "Colonel, don't dismiss the younger women. Felicity Harrison is a bright, intelligent, and capable woman who may hide political passion and cunning behind her intellectual and scientific persona. Ursula Audley seems to harbor secrets that may motivate her to take part in a political plot. And if I were asked to name my prime suspect among the younger women, it would be Isadore Liffey."

Luke was surprised.

"Why Isadore?" he asked.

"She has the weakest reason for being here. The marriage of Liffey and Lydia is being pushed by the respective families—by the absent Royalist patriarchs of each—the Earl of Liffey and Baron Veldor. What role is there for a sister of the bridegroom, particularly one who is estranged from the rest of the family because of her alleged devotion to the Protector and his cause?"

"She claims she is here to protect her brother from an ill-advised marriage," replied Luke.

"Unless she has an incredible hold over her much older brother, her influence in such high-powered marriage arrangements would be zero," Jane responded.

"Luke has a blind spot. He likes Isadore," commented Evan.

Luke was not pleased.

The group dispersed.

Luke met with Rose Grant, and they strolled around the estate.

"How are you finding your stay at Austin Friars?" he asked.

"To be honest, we feel completely out of place. David is rarely here, and the aristocratic women look down on us as hardly human. That Lydia is monstrous, and she is openly a Royalist. She should be sent away. If you really are looking for a Royalist plotter, you don't need to look farther than that abominable woman."

"Rose, open enemies are rarely my target. I have the responsibility of unearthing from among our pretended friends, two very dangerous Royalists who if successful could bring down the government. Tell me about yourself!"

"I am the daughter of a gentleman farmer with several estates in Cambridge shire and southern Suffolk. During the war, he was a captain in the cavalry attached to the Eastern Association but was badly wounded in 1644 at Edgehill. My brother has managed the estates since then and provides me with a small allowance."

"These properties are near Newmarket?"

"Yes, they are."

"Are any of them used to breed horses?"

"No, but those that belong to my uncle, Veronica's father, breed some of the best horses in England."

"What type of horses: palfreys, cavalry mounts, or racehorses?"

"During the war, Uncle James concentrated on cavalry mounts as they were in great demand and brought a good price. For the last six or seven years, he has moved over almost exclusively to the breeding of racehorses."

"Does he race any of these regularly at Newmarket?"

"No, Uncle James believes the sport is being ruined by the amount of betting that takes place at Newmarket and solely concentrates on the breeding of the animals. He does not even get involved in their training. He leaves this to his daughter Veronica. She not only supervises the stud and stables for her father, but she has horses of her own that she does race on a regular basis."

Luke was getting excited.

"Would you say that your uncle is a wealthy man?"

"Yes, and so is Veronica in her own right."

"How can that be?"

"When her mother, my aunt, died, by some quirk of the legal system, she was left the properties brought to the marriage by her mother. These will not revert to her father until she marries. That is why such a wealthy woman remains a spinster."

"Under what circumstances did Veronica obtain an invitation to attend Austin Friars?"

"When David told me his commanding officer had ordered him to have a wife, actual or potential, to come here, I was terrified. I discussed it some time ago with Veronica who knew one of the other guests through her racing."

"Let me guess! Baroness Veldor."

Rose expressed surprise.

"How did you know that? It came as a complete surprise to me as we Grants do not move in the same circles as the Veldors. I have often heard Veronica complain that she cannot get her horses in a race against the best in the surrounding counties because the aristocratic owners will only race against animals owned by fellow peers."

"How long have you known David?" Luke suddenly asked.

"Since childhood."

"What happened five years ago that propelled him to take a position in the Indies?"

"It was my fault. We had been close friends for years, and every time David returned from his military duties, we came closer to announcing our betrothal. Five years ago, he asked me to marry him."

"What went wrong?"

"My father was in very poor health. His mind had gone, and he needed nursing every hour of the day. My mother had done this for years, but she died. My brother—who, given father's incapacity, was head of family—rejected David's request for my hand, declaring that I must do my duty as a loving daughter and take my mother's place. Marriage was out of the question. David was heartbroken, and when a position in the Caribbean came up, he jumped at it."

"You resumed your relationship on his return?"

"Almost accidentally. He was visiting the Veldors on army business, and my cousin Veronica happened to be there, selling a horse. She indicated that Father had died, and I was still unmarried."

Luke's mind was swirling.

David Halliburton had visited the Veldors as had Veronica Grant.

"Austin Friars has a very extensive herbal garden for both medicinal and culinary use. Did any of your estates have a similar garden?"

"No, none of our family's estates were former monastic possessions."

"What about your uncle's estates? Did they contain herbal gardens?"

"Yes, his father bought up a considerable amount of monastic land."

"Did your cousin take a particular interest in their gardens?"

"Only so far as they contributed to potions that she could administer to her horses. She made great use of the local cunning woman who was expert in the application of herbs to animals."

Luke could hardly contain himself.

He could not wait to ask Veronica Grant some direct questions.

She could be Belladonna.

26

Veronica Grant had no time for the pale face and red lips that were the pinnacle of contemporary fashion. She spent too much time outdoors—or had Mediterranean ancestors. Her olive skin was in complete contrast to the other women.

She had black hair that was cut short and fringed across her forehead. Deep green eyes and dark eyebrows, a small nose and mouth, and a long neck set off by an emerald and gold pendant provided a colorful contrast with her bodice and skirts in various shades of gray, with tiny linen cuffs and collar.

Luke met her in the kitchen garden where he hoped to use the presence of herbs to elicit more information from a woman who had suddenly risen into the position of prime suspect.

Veronica opened the conversation, "Rose had told you more than you need to know. Even as a young child, she was eager to confide in strangers."

"You and your father have been very kind to her."

"She has had a sad life. Her father was ill for a long time, and her mother died when she was about to escape her conditions by marrying David. Her brother has been very cruel, forcing her to eke out a living on a pittance and giving her very little help when she was nursing their father."

"You know horses?"

"Yes, Father breeds them, and I train, race, and sell them."

"Is that how you met Baroness Veldor?"

"Only indirectly. We lower orders are not admitted to races organized by the high aristocracy. I have learned to keep my place. One of Veldor's servants attended the races confined to the lesser gentry and was so impressed by one of my horses that he told Veldor's steward about it."

"Barnaby Brett?"

"You are well informed. The end of this story is that the baroness bought the horse. I only met her once just recently when I went to Veldor Lodge to receive payment, where incidentally I was surprised to meet David Halliburton, my sister's long-lost love."

"Does your role with horses extend to keeping them healthy?"

"Stupid question! Every horse owner strives to keep his animals well."

"Do you personally have the expertise to administer potions and powders to assist an animal?"

"I don't personally administer any medication, but I supervise its preparation. I engage a variety of farriers and wise women to advise me and then dispense any necessary remedies."

"If I led you through the herb garden, could you tell me how a particular herb might help an animal?"

"Enough, Colonel! I know what you are trying to do. The woman you seek allegedly calls herself Belladonna. You falsely assume that only those with an herb garden or knowledge of herbs would give themselves such a name. Logically, it does not follow. I know the herbs and how to mix them into powders, potions, and drenches to keep my horses happy. I can see that this garden is overrun with elecampane or horse heal. You feed it to your horses if they have a lessened appetite. It's a pity that your suspect does not call her self Elecampane. Then you could arrest a horse trainer such as myself."

Luke's attempted reply was stifled by several voices calling his name.

He responded and confronted Evan who had run into the garden.

"What's the problem?" Luke asked.

"Another death. Lady Penelope has been brutally murdered."

"How do you know it is murder?"

"You don't sever your own head accidentally or even deliberately."

Luke ran to the scene of the crime.

Evan had already cordoned off the area.

"Has anyone told Sir Peter?" asked Luke.

"No, according to John Martin, he is in London for the day. He left before dawn to catch the low tide."

"When did it happen?" Luke asked.

"Within the hour."

"Do the rest of the household know?"

"Only young Ursula. She found the body. She staggered out of Lady Penelope's bedchamber just as I passed by. She was in shock and could not speak. She pointed into the room. I entered, saw the body, cordoned off the room, and put Ursula under the care of Jane Castle. They are in your room, which was the nearest."

"So Jane also knows what happened?"

"Only if Ursula has regained her voice. I simply told Jane that Ursula had received a massive shock."

Luke went to his room.

Ursula was lying on his bed. She was asleep.

Jane told him she had forced a small glass of Luke's whiskey down the girl's throat before she passed out.

"Did she speak at all?"

"No! Her eyes were filled with terror as if she had seen the devil himself. What happened?"

"For the moment, keep this to yourself. Penelope Marlowe has been decapitated."

Jane paled and looked as if she was about to vomit.

"We both need a glass of the Irish. Stay with Ursula! I will place two of my men here—one in the room with you and the other outside the door. I'll inform Liffey and her father."

Luke sent a message ahead of his arrival, requiring an immediate meeting with Liffey in the presence of Major Audley.

When Luke arrived, an irritated general did not hold back.

"Just because you operate under the direct authority of the Lord Protector, it does not give you the right to demand my attention on the slightest whim."

"This, my lord, is no whim. The wife of one of your officers has been brutally murdered in her own bedchamber."

At this point, Audley entered the room.

Luke recounted the details of the murder.

Liffey was visibly shaken.

Audley commented, "Has Peter been told?"

Liffey remarked, "He is in London. I will send a messenger to inform him and seek his immediate return."

Audley continued, "Then why am I here?"

Luke explained Ursula's role in the discovery of the body and its traumatic effect on her.

"I will go to her at once," said the anxious father.

"Anthony, with the general's permission, you should both leave Austin Friars."

"Why?"

"Ursula may be the murderer's next victim. All the persons who were in the Indies but not part the general's senior officers, except for Ursula, have been murdered: Blair, Peebles, and now Lady Penelope. The murderer—and I think it is the same person for all three—believes rightly or wrongly that one or all these victims saw or heard something that would be detrimental to his current activities."

"Is the murderer Weld?" asked Liffey.

"He may have given the order, but Yarrow would have carried it out."

Liffey responded as if partially traumatized, "This Yarrow is a professional killer. The brutality of Penelope's murder indicates a personal hatred rather than a mercenary execution. This may not have been part of Weld's plan."

Liffey seemed disoriented and muttered, "You must find this monster."

"My best man is working on it as we speak. I had hoped Yarrow had escaped our net and was long gone, but this ghastly murder suggests otherwise."

Liffey turned to Audley. "Anthony, please feel free to leave and take your daughter to a safe haven. My idea of bringing the families together is proving a calamity. Perhaps I should send everybody home?"

Luke's response was brutal.

"No, my lord. This environment is forcing the conspirators to show their hand prematurely. If you send everybody home, Lady Penelope's death would have been in vain."

Anthony's response surprised both Luke and the general.

"My daughter and I will stay. Ursula may be the next target, but she will be safer here surrounded by Luke's men than home on my estate."

Two loud explosions interrupted the conversation.

One of the windows of the general's room shattered, and all three men could see smoke arising from a tent in the training area.

A soldier ran down the slope toward them. He confronted the guards at Liffey's door, who speedily admitted him.

"What happened, Sergeant?" asked Liffey.

"A terrible accident! The men were training to lob grenades. They were not primed."

"At least two of them were primed," said Luke cynically and largely to himself.

"Yes, sir."

"Was there anybody in the tent?"

"Lieutenant Colonel Halliburton."

"Is he all right?" asked Audley.

"No! I ran here to inform you. My corporal is sealing off the area, awaiting your arrival."

"What was Halliburton doing in the tent?" queried Luke.

"For the last week, the officer supervising the training used that tent. This week Marlowe was supposed to be on duty, but Halliburton arrived in his stead."

"My god! Both Peter and Penelope could have been murdered within hours of each other," exclaimed Luke.

The officers made it up the hill to what was left of the tent—and David Halliburton. Body fragments were scattered far and wide. The first blast killed David, and second spread his remains across the landscape.

Luke moved a troop of his dragoons into the area as Evan and Strad began interviewing the trainees.

None of the recruits in the training detail were responsible. They had no facilities for priming their grenades, and the sergeant affirmed that the material needed was under lock and key in one of the outbuildings.

Audley, the expert in explosions, confirmed this by concluding that the primed grenades were lobbed into the tent from behind other tents in the same row.

No one saw any strangers in the area.

Liffey gathered the household together on the lawns of Austin Friars. He announced to the assembled group that David Halliburton and Penelope Marlowe had been murdered and that Ursula Audley was in a traumatic state. He had initially decided that for their own safety, the wives, partners, and friends should depart for their own homes. However, Colonel Tremayne deemed it safer for them to stay where they were, with an increased guard mounted to protect them all.

Before the group gathered on the lawn, Luke informed Rose and Veronica of David's death and suggested that, contrary to his advice to Liffey, they were free to leave.

Rose cried constantly, but Veronica revealed a steely determination.

"We will stay. I will do everything I can to assist you in finding David's murderer. Why would anyone kill him? He was not political, kept to himself, and was devoted to his life as a cavalry commander."

Luke responded, "It may have been a mistake. Sir Peter Marlowe was supposed to on duty using that tent as his headquarters. The murderer may not have known that David replaced Peter at the last minute."

That night Evan and Luke had a quiet drink in the former's room.

Luke reviewed the situation.

"It is black humor to suggest at this rate, the only woman and senior officer left standing will be Belladonna and Weld. Weld can only be Liffey, Grey, or Audley—the three most unlikely."

"Or Marlowe? His absence may have been deliberate to avoid suspicion," added Evan.

"The women who may be Belladonna have been reduced considerably. I trust Jane Castle implicitly, Felicity Harrison in no way approximates to our villainess, Rose and Veronica Grant following David's death seem irrelevant, and Ursula Audrey is so traumatized by events she is incapable of action, and Penelope is dead. That leaves five possible suspects: Evadne, Lydia, Sophia, Grace, and possibly Isadore."

"Luke it was a major mistake to ask Liffey to keep everybody here. If he had sent them home, those who had to stay to complete their mission would have needed to find an excuse to remain. They would have been forced to reveal themselves and implement their coup immediately."

"They are already rattled. I expect them to act prematurely."

27

Next morning, John Martin reported, "Sir Peter has left Austin Friars under cover of darkness for the last three Wednesdays, including yesterday, returning very early the next morning. On all three occasions, he said he was to meet at Liffey House with men considering enlistment."

At first, Luke was not greatly interested.

"Peter's role is to recruit junior officers to serve in this army. It would be convenient to summon those interested to London for interview, and Liffey House is a convenient location."

"Sir Peter made a comment to one of my men this morning that he had met a man he long admired and, until recently, deputy and heir apparent to Oliver Cromwell, General John Lambert."

Luke whistled.

"Where did Peter meet Lambert?" he asked. "If it were a casual meeting or a social engagement, there would be no problem, but if he was at this meeting of junior officers destined for our Flanders army, it is a major worry. John Lambert is against the hereditary protectorate and is refusing to take the oath of loyalty to His Highness the Lord Protector. He is also against the current war with Spain and our alliance with France, which this very army is designed to cement. Cromwell will have no alternative but to stand him down. It is rumored that since the offer of the Crown to

Cromwell, Lambert is encouraging many veterans to oppose it. If Marlowe is stacking this new army with pro-Lambert junior officers who are not absolutely loyal to Cromwell, we are in deep trouble."

"If that is the case, then there is a good chance that Marlowe is Weld, and with a solid corps of junior officers supporting him, taking over this army would be relatively easy," commented Evan who had joined the conversation.

"But Lambert would not work with the Royalists. He may dislike what Cromwell is currently doing, but he would never replace the current government with Charles Stuart," concluded Luke.

"If Marlowe is regularly absent on a Wednesday, that must be known by some of the officers and men here. Therefore, yesterday's explosion that killed Halliburton might have been aimed at him after all rather than Marlowe," said Evan complicating the issue.

"If the murderer knew Marlowe was absent, it frees him from any link to his wife's murder. The murderer with Peter away knew that he would not be disturbed as he butchered Penelope," John Martin soberly remarked.

"Don't be naive, John! For most other women, your assumption might hold true, but there was a good chance that Penelope would have had company in her bedchamber—especially with Peter away," Luke riposted.

"Nevertheless, John's assumption concerning the virtue of married women may have been shared by the murderer," suggested Evan.

"And which one of our suspects would hold such a view especially given Penelope's reputation?" Luke asked.

"You are now being naive. Genteel society has not seen the depraved side of human nature as we have. The younger women here would not have any idea, and the older aristocratic matrons have had a limited experience of real life," declaimed a surprisingly animated Evan.

"I will ask Liffey about Marlowe's recruitment strategy. I won't talk to Peter himself this morning, given the tragic loss of his wife."

"Luke, you are being too soft in your old age. Given the state the man is in considering the nature of his wife's murder, he will be especially vulnerable to some intimidating bullying. If you are reluctant to be ruthless, I am quite happy to interrogate the grieving widower," announced Evan.

"Maybe later! Strad, did you discover anything of interest in your questioning of the servants? It would be too much to expect that you have isolated Yarrow?"

"I am close. I asked three questions. Was the servant known to his fellows from the same estate before they came here? Did he dye his hair, and was he aged somewhere between thirty and forty? Unfortunately, the aristocrats brought servants from more than one of their estates, and where there was only one servant from a particular household, there was no one to verify his or her credentials. On this basis, there was one servant each of Lady Evadne, Lady Sophia, the Countess of Merrick, and Lord Audley whose authenticity could not be vouched for. On the second question, there were at least five male servants who dye their hair and one who wears a wig. Most servants were too young. If I combine my three lists, the suspects are reduced to three. I will take steps to examine the hair issue more thoroughly. Dyeing needs to be repeated. There is little place to hide in the cramped conditions under which these servants live."

"Unless they are given access to the facilities available to their master or mistress," explained Evan.

"Would any of our aristocratic ladies keep a maniacal killer hidden in their wardrobe?" teased Strad.

Luke was pleased.

"Great work, Strad. You isolate Yarrow, which at the same time may pinpoint Weld or Belladonna."

Evan was critical.

"You cannot assume, Luke, that just because Yarrow is found to be masquerading as a servant for the Baroness Veldor that she would be aware of this and is therefore Belladonna."

"Did you have a bad night, Evan?" said Luke testily, tired of Evan's carping.

Before Evan could reply Luke continued.

"Strad, continue your work on the servants, but be ready at a moment's notice to follow Sir Peter to London and take the part of an officer interested in joining the army here. John, let Strad know immediately Peter leaves the premises. Evan, I want you to take over the investigation of both the Peebles and Halliburton murders. I will concentrate on Marlowe."

Luke later discussed the overall situation with Liffey.

"How is Peter taking the death of his wife?" Luke asked.

"The death in itself does not worry him. They led very separate lives. But he is distraught over the manner of her death. Its brutality has left him devastated. He is almost equally distressed by the death of David Halliburton. I gave Marlowe and Halliburton responsibility for the training of the newest recruits while Grey and Audley supervised the more advanced units, strengthened by veterans from the London garrisons."

"Why was he particularly upset about young David's death?"

"He believes that Halliburton was an innocent victim—that he was the target. The murder of his wife and the attempted murder of himself would pose a major new problem for all of us. He supervised the training of the recruits from the tent that was bombed, usually taking it in turns with Halliburton."

"I originally thought that was a possibility until I discovered that the senior personnel on the base would have known that Peter was regularly absent in London every Wednesday to recruit his junior officers."

Liffey looked surprised.

"Not true! I, as his commanding officer, knew of the occasional trip to London to interview a few interested and experienced men to serve as captains in our army, but I did not know it was a regular commitment."

"If you as general did not know, was there anybody here that he would need to inform of his absence."

"On this occasion, only Halliburton."

"So the deceased Halliburton is the only person at Austin Friars that definitely knew of Marlowe's regular commitment?"

"Yes, but you can scarcely consider a few visits a regular commitment."

"Maybe not! Did he give you the names of the men he had selected or recommended for the positions?"

"No."

"Why not? You have often suggested that of all your officers Marlowe was the man you suspected most of being the hidden Royalist."

"We are all under pressure to have an army ready to take the field in Flanders in weeks let alone months. Each of my officers has a special talent in selecting the men they want for their particular regiment or company. I have no expertise in testing a junior officer's loyalty. I have delegated all authority regarding recruitment to Marlowe and Grey for the infantry, Halliburton for the cavalry, and Audley for the artillery."

"Have any of these junior officers yet arrived at Austin Friars?"

"No, we have not been funded to employ them until four weeks hence. Also, according to Audley, these men want no part in the training unless they are paid more than we can offer."

"Well, that is a relief. From now on, the names all junior officers being considered for this army must be given to me and that no final commitment be made to them without my approval. Thurloe and I will check their credentials."

"You will have to answer to His Highness for any delays in meeting our deadline. Cromwell has promised the French we will be in Flanders within eight weeks."

"I am sure that Cromwell would prefer to break his word to the French than have the army he is carefully training, turn against him, having been taken over by disloyal officers."

Luke returned to his quarters.

As he sipped Irish whiskey from his favorite ceramic mug, he wondered aloud, "Why were Penelope and David murdered? If the target was Peter, was there a plan to murder husband and wife within hours of each other? If so, why?"

As Luke drank more and more, his mind slipped into the simplest explanation for all the murders: someone who feared his or her plotting was in danger of unraveling believed it imperative that all those that had spent time in the Indies had to be silenced.

What had happened in the Indies that made it necessary to exterminate so many people? What did these victims know that could undermine Weld and Belladonna's current enterprise?

Luke suddenly rose to his feet, gulped down the last of his drink, summoned three of his men, and headed for the apartment of the late Penny Marlowe.

She had kept a diary. Perhaps it contained material the murderer was trying to obliterate.

They searched the apartment for over an hour.

No diary was found.

He then headed for the Audleys.

Felicity Harrison opened the door and explained that Anthony was supervising grenade training.

Luke asked whether Ursula had recovered her senses.

"No."

Luke then asked, "Is she here?"

"No, my sister Grace has taken her for a walk around the grounds."

"Great, my men and I must search her chamber. Lady Penelope may have given her a book that will help us solve these murders. We cannot yet ask her ourselves."

Felicity looked ill at ease and asked, "Do you know what you are looking for?"

"It is a diary that Penelope kept during her time in the Indies. It would have had to survive quite humid conditions."

The scientist in Felicity immediately responded, "Colonel, you may not be aware of it but a stationer in London has for some years been producing a special quality of paper that withstands mold and other natural dangers caused by heat and moisture. If Lady Penelope intended to keep a diary from the beginning of her time in the Caribbean, she might have purchased this special paper."

Luke was taken with this young woman's knowledge.

"His name? He probably keeps records of his sales, especially special items such as this."

Felicity gave Luke the information he needed.

Luke and his men searched every inch of Ursula's apartment.

No diary was found.

28

Later that day, Peter accosted Luke in the reception hall.

Luke expressed his condolences.

"I won't pretend that our marriage was a traditional relationship, but Penny and I remained good friends throughout the various crisis of our lives. I hope you find the animal who did this."

"We will, but at the moment, there are doubts concerning the actual executioner but even more as to who ordered it," answered Luke truthfully.

"I did not seek you out to discuss my wife's murder but to refute any lies that Liffey may have told you this morning. He suspects me of being the secret Royalist, and I am sure he took the opportunity to blacken my name further."

"He did raise questions in my mind concerning the loyalty of the junior officers you are recruiting," commented Luke honestly.

"The devious bastard! He is angry with me for selecting men of my own rather than relying on the contacts that Richard Grey and he gave me. If anyone wants to stack the army with men of their own kind, it is those two. I now suspect that in giving me sole responsibility for raising the infantry officers for this last batch of recruits, he was setting me up for some final fall."

"How did he know that you had not followed his advice?"

"Each time I return from London, I give him a summary of whom I have talked to and to which of them I would offer a commission."

"You give him a list?"

"No, I speak to the notes I have made."

"I am inclined to repeat your words *devious bastard*. When I asked Liffey whether you presented him with a list of possible officers, he correctly answered no but in the process implied he had no knowledge of whom you had talked to. In what way did he and Richard try to fill this new army with young officers who held similar views to themselves?"

"Dick Grey was at least open. He suggested I visit Blackfriars Parish in London and seek out a particular gentleman who could gather together a dozen or more experienced young men who would meet my requirements. I may have been in the Indies for years, but I know that from before I left for the Caribbean, Blackfriars was a hotbed of religious fanatics."

"Did you go to Blackfriars?"

"Yes, and I interviewed about a dozen men who, true to my assumptions, revealed a strong religious commitment. Some saw Oliver Cromwell as God's agent, but others openly viewed him as the new Antichrist. If Oliver accepts the Crown, more will fall into the latter camp. I decided not to take the risk and in the end selected none of them."

"Well done! My information, when I was in Wales and dealing with this same problem, was that Blackfriars was largely dominated by the anti- Cromwell group."

"That was my sense of the situation. I then took up Liffey's suggestion. I contacted Viscount Broke at his townhouse in Wimbledon. Broke is an Irish peer who grew up with Liffey. He fought for the king in the First Civil War but surrendered on the battlefield and in order to retain his estates promised not to take up arms against the Parliament again."

"And the men he offered you were all former redeemed Royalists?"

"No, I could not claim that. Some probably were, but others had fought on Parliament's side. But they were all Irish."

"I can understand your hesitation. The Irish, Catholic or Protestant, are duplicitous. How did you come up with a recruitment network of your own?"

"By sheer good fortune. I was walking back through Wimbledon when an old comrade accosted me. I explained my situation and asked if he would be interested. He was not, but he had just left a group of officers who had been meeting with General Lambert in his Wimbledon premises. He said there were dozens of Yorkshire men who had fought under Lambert who would be anxious to take up arms again. He promised to spread the word through the northern towns. That is why I set up a regular meeting place and time to enable possible recruits from the north to meet me."

"So most of the men you have met over the last three Wednesdays have been northerners who fought under Lambert?"

"And before him under Lord Fairfax."

"There was no better general after Cromwell than John Lambert. He has been Cromwell's real deputy for years. He drew up the first protectorate constitution, and he was behind the creation of the major generals," said Luke with a tinge of admiration.

Luke continued with less enthusiasm, "But the two of them have fallen out. Lambert opposes the war with Spain and the increase in civilian influence on Cromwell. The last straw for Lambert was dismantling the rule of the major generals and the offer of the Crown to Cromwell. He has made it clear that in these circumstances he will not take the oath of loyalty."

"That does not mean all of Lambert's veterans are of the same mind. If Cromwell does accept the Crown, some of the most loyal Cromwellians such as yourself may reconsider your position. At least, we can be sure that men recruited from this background will not be Royalists."

"True, but if it came to a clash between troops remaining loyal to Oliver Cromwell and those remaining true to the good old cause and objecting to Oliver taking the Crown, the current government would be in so much trouble that the Royalists would strike immediately to take advantage of the chaos."

"Luke, you have an insurmountable problem. The murders that have plagued us and the rumors of a conspirator or two in our camp that could be Royalists will keep you busy. On the other hand, they could equally be religious fanatics or simply veteran soldiers, askance at the civilians taking over the government and depriving us of hard-fought gains."

"Truly said, Peter! On a related matter, do you know anything about a diary that your wife kept? It may help explain her murder."

"I am sure it could. Penny kept a very detailed account of her adventures from the moment she arrived in the Caribbean."

"Did she purchase special paper for that enterprise that would stand the humid conditions?"

"She did. It was so expensive that I insisted she buy it from her own funds."

"Have you seen that diary lately?"

"There is not just one book. The diary was written on small loose sheets, and at the end of each year, the loose leaves were sent back to England to be bound. Penny always said the diaries would protect our future. Last year's book was collected only a week or so ago just before we moved from Liffey House."

"So there are several volumes to be found."

"All bound in expensive red Moroccan leather."

"Who was the binder?

"The stationer who supplied the expensive paper. I have his address."

"Thanks, Peter. I already have it. During your meeting with the northerners, did General Lambert ever attend in person?"

"No, but he did arrive in his coach to take some of the men to his house where I imagine they stayed until their return to Yorkshire."

"I will come with you on your next recruiting trip to London, and at the same time, we will visit this stationer bookbinder."

"None of the diaries are here at Austin Friars?" asked Peter.

"No, I have thoroughly searched her apartment and yours and that of Ursula Audley. When in London, I will search the rooms she occupied at Liffey House. Do you know of any possible information contained in the diaries that would lead to her brutal murder?"

"Not specifically, but I imagine that she could have recorded the follies and alleged follies of all of us. Given her friendliness with so many people, she undoubtedly picked up every piece of gossip available. But nobody really knew what Penny recorded."

"That is precisely what led to her death. The murderer could not risk any information that he thought Blair, Peebles, or Penelope possessed. He may also think this information is also known by Ursula and yourself. The killing of Halliburton may have been a mistake, and you were to die on the same day as your wife."

"Have you additional guards protecting young Ursula?"

"Yes! Do you recall the slightest piece of gossip that Penelope may have hinted at that would be relevant to my inquiries?"

Marlowe remained quiet for some time, racking his brain for any possible tidbit of information he could offer Luke.

"Sorry, Luke, Penny did not discuss her life with me and certainly not any secrets that she was privy to. Only once did she make a comment that could have implied she knew more than she was saying."

"And what incident was that?"

"The appointment of that quean Richmond to Liffey's staff. Amid the widespread incredulity at the appointment, Penny simply commented that she was not surprised."

"Suggesting that Richmond was Liffey's lover?"

"It's a reasonable deduction."

Luke added another chore to his imminent visit to London. He would look up Timothy Richmond, and hopefully, the young man had recovered sufficiently to be interviewed.

"Given your unusual relationship with your wife, I imagine her death will not lead to you resigning as Liffey's deputy for the army training for Flanders."

"Liffey has already replaced me as his deputy with Richard. Richard has command of the battle-ready regiment while I have been given the raw recruits. I have little in life now except my army career. Flanders gives me a chance to be part of an army engaged in battle."

"Sadly, you will have no pitched battles such as you saw in our civil war. The Spaniards are holed up in well-defended towns. They will send out raiding parties to harass your encampments but avoid all direct conflict. Unless the artillery can weaken their defenses, your infantry will largely be involved in siege warfare—a soul destroying activity."

"Thanks for that positive assessment of my future," remarked Peter with a trace of a smile.

"One final question! Did Penelope's extramarital adventures include any of your close associates?"

"I know nothing for sure, but I had a feeling at one stage in Barbados that something had happened not only with Richard Grey, which was not an affair but with Liffey himself. It does not conform with what I said earlier regarding Liffey and Richmond, but for several weeks, I was convinced that Penny was sleeping with Liffey."

Luke was troubled.

Was Marlowe's intense dislike of Liffey beginning to cloud not only his judgment but also his memory?

29

Four days later, Luke and Peter were in London.

They arrived the day before Peter's scheduled interviews to provide time for a thorough search of the rooms that the Marlowes had occupied at Liffey House.

Some of the lighter furniture and the moveable furnishings had been taken to Austin Friars, but the heavy cabinets and showcases remained.

The two men looked into every drawer, lifted rugs looking for hidden trapdoors, and tested the walls for hidden passages or rooms. There had been rumors of priest holes and escape routes, but if they existed, they did not start in the Marlowes' former rooms.

Luke was disappointed.

Peter was more positive.

"I am trying to remember where else in this house Penny may have spent more time than expected. The only other woman here at the time was Ursula. Her room was just through this door."

The initial burst of optimism was soon dashed.

Nothing was found in Ursula's room.

Peter and Luke adjourned to the nearest inn where they engaged in a hearty meal of boiled mutton, parsnips, and peas, washed down with blackish syrupy beer.

Luke gazed vacantly into his flagon.

Without warning, he jumped to his feet. "I have an idea. Where are books usually found?"

"In a library."

"The last place to look for a hidden diary would be where it is on open display in a book shelf. Let's go back to Liffey House and search the general's library."

"Did he take many volumes to Austin Friars? It will reduce the time we have to spend searching, if he did," commented an unimpressed Peter.

Armed with three large candles, which the housekeeper was loath to provide, the two soldiers carefully searched nine ceiling-high bookcases.

The shelves were crammed.

As midnight approached, weariness set in.

"Leave the rest until tomorrow!" declared a tiring Luke.

Peter punched the air with his fist. "No need! I have found four volumes."

"Where? I have already checked those shelves."

"Yes, but you only skimmed the shelves looking for small possibly untitled red Moroccan-covered volumes. I removed the books. These and other small books were shelved behind the larger volumes. The general has so many books he was forced to double shelve. You missed them."

Peter handed the books to Luke.

Jubilation immediately turned to frustration.

"Damnation, they are unreadable."

"In a foreign language? Penny was fluent in Spanish."

"No, they are coded—a mixture of numbers and a few symbols."

"Get them up to Whitehall in the morning. Thurloe's experts will quickly decode them," suggested Peter.

"No, until we know what they contain, Thurloe does not need to be bothered. Anthony Audley's betrothed is reputably a wizard in mathematics. It would be better all round for both Penny's reputation and your peace of mind that few people know the contents of these diaries."

Next morning, Luke sat beside Peter as he interviewed a number of northerners who sought junior commissions in the new army.

He was very impressed with the experience of these men. The older veterans had references from Sir Thomas Fairfax and the younger from John Lambert, two of Parliament's ablest and respected generals, who between them had held the north of England against the Royalists for the previous fifteen years.

Luke explained his presence, emphasizing the need for discipline and loyalty.

He had intended to elaborate the delicate situation in detail but stopped suddenly when he realized he would have to present the men with contradictory messages.

On the one hand, the loyalty of junior officers to their senior commanders was a major reason for Parliament's success against the king.

On the other hand, these men may need to refuse to follow their leaders should these try to turn the army against Cromwell.

Luke was personally acutely aware of the imminent dilemma that might face them all.

In the afternoon, another small group of men arrived accompanied, as Peter whispered to Luke, by army's most popular general, Cromwell's longtime deputy, John Lambert.

Luke rose to his feet.

"Pray be seated, Colonel Tremayne! I have never had the pleasure of serving with you, but your exploits are well-known to me. Whenever I had a major security problem and brought it to Cromwell, he would tell me not to worry. He would refer it to Luke Tremayne for solution. You saved Oliver's life on a number of occasions, and according to my comrade John Desborough, you made a major contribution to the defeat of the recent uprising of Welsh fanatics. Your presence at Austin Friars and here today suggests to me that the government is terrified that this new army could be turned against it."

"That is exactly the situation, General," Luke replied.

"A problem of its own making! Most generals opposed the idea of a new army. Desborough and I believed enough troops could have been raised from the existing army by bringing the necessary men from our tried-and-tested troops in Ireland and Scotland and from the major garrisons spread across England. Monk has Scotland so cowed that a few companies of cavalry would keep it contained. Listening to civilians has led Oliver astray. Whenever he ignores the army's advice, things go downhill. Abolishing the major generals, wasting money on the war with Spain, and now thinking of the offer of the Crown reflect the growing influence of clandestine Royalists and antiarmy Parliamentarians with the Protector."

"The offer of the Crown has made my task difficult. Some of Oliver's most loyal supporters are disturbed by this development," Luke admitted.

"Colonel, I expect you personally face that dilemma. Tomorrow John Desborough, Charles Fleetwood, and I, Oliver's three most senior generals, are informing him that fifteen of the seventeen generals in England oppose him taking the Crown, and fifteen of them insist that he reinstate the rule of the major generals."

"I am personally against Cromwell accepting the Crown and have told him so, and I am even more alarmed at the declining influence of our army on the affairs of England. If Oliver gives way to the civilian demands formulated by John Thurloe, how do you think the army will act, General?" Luke asked pointedly.

"The primary enemy are still the Royalists, and a secondary problem are the religious fanatics. Both, I imagine, wish to take over the new army and replace Cromwell with Charles Stuart or Jesus Christ. The veterans of the New Model Army will not act to advance either of those scenarios, but let's be blunt. It cannot stand by and allow the return of monarchy even if the king is Oliver."

Luke thought it better not to comment.

Lambert continued, "My advice is to fill your army with as many of my former officers as you can. When the crisis comes, they will fight to the death to prevent the rule of the Stuarts or the religious fanatics. They will fight to retain the good old cause and army dominance even if that involves withdrawing support from Oliver. I hope that you can reinforce what the generals will be telling Oliver by showing that middle-ranking officers are also united in opposing his acceptance of the Crown."

Lambert raised his fist in a symbolic gesture of a united army response against the creeping takeover of their government by civilians.

Luke was suddenly aware of the stark alternatives.

Cromwell had to decide whether he was with his old comrades in defense of what they had fought for or move with the civilians into an entirely new world in which the most loyal of past friends could be his new enemies.

Luke was depressed.

He had been increasingly aware of the growing conflict between the military and civilian supporters of the protectorate.

His relations with Thurloe with regard to intelligence was a microcosm of the conflict.

But he had not previously known how determined the senior army officers were in reversing the trend, even to the point of removing Cromwell.

On reflection, his realization of the urgency of the situation led Luke to adopt a position that was the opposite of his original intention. To fill the army with Cromwell's veterans, men who had a political agenda and knew what they were fighting for, and who were absolutely loyal to Cromwell at the moment, could, if Cromwell accepted the Crown, turn into his most bitter and experienced opponents. Officers of a Royalist inclination or of no political agenda would more likely obey their superiors. Cromwell might be in less danger from an army whose junior officers were made up of former Royalists, whose weak political agenda could be suppressed entirely by army discipline.

To knowingly stack the army with potential Royalists was not ideal, but it might be the best option available.

Suddenly, Luke had a flash of enlightenment.

There was a more simple solution that would avoid this dangerous outcome.

Luke turned to Peter. "To reduce the chances of the army's subversion, balance out the men you recruit with a third Lambert Loyalists, a third religious fanatics, and the remainder potential Royalists. As we both know, an army divided cannot agree to any concerted action. A treacherous commander would have great difficulty in convincing the majority of his junior officers to follow him into attempting a coup if they have strongly conflicting views among themselves."

Luke left Peter to complete his interviews while he visited the mansion of Timothy Richmond's uncle.

He was not able to see Richmond.

His uncle explained that he was paralyzed from the neck down and, in addition, had no memory at all of the past.

Later, Luke met up with Peter outside Penny's stationer.

Peter introduced himself as the husband of the woman who had imported some of his special paper to the Indies and whose diaries he had bound.

The stationer looked alarmed and called for assistance.

Four or five men gathered around the two soldiers, who were both confused.

"Sir, we are here on government business. I am directly employed by the Lord Protector who is vitally interested in this case."

"How do I know who you are?" asked the affrighted stationer.

Luke, after much fruitless searching, found the license that gave him authority to act in the Protector's name and presented it to the stationer.

Luke then asked him, "Do you always act like this when customers seek information?"

"Only when I am told a deliberate lie."

"And what lie would that be?"

"That your companion is my client's husband."

"But that is true."

"How can it be? My customer is a man, Anthony Viscount Audley, and the most recent diary was collected by his daughter the Lady Ursula."

Luke and Peter were dumbfounded.

The stationer presented his evidence in the form of his accounts—clearly signed by Audley.

"Did you ever meet Viscount Audley?"

"No, but he certainly paid for the paper and the red Moroccan leather and my services over the time he was in the Indies. I had hoped that on his return, I might meet him, but he sent his daughter to pick up the last volume."

The two men thanked the stationer for his assistance, and as they left his shop, Luke casually asked, "Can you describe Lady Ursula for us?"

The answer stopped the two soldiers in their tracks.

The description was not that of Lady Ursula.

Nor was it Penelope Marlowe.

It was Felicity Harrison.

30

Luke returned alone to Austin Friars.

Peter accepted Luke's advice to recruit widely and remained in London. He would revisit the contacts suggested by Liffey and Grey.

This action might also improve his standing with his senior comrades.

Luke could hardly wait to interview Felicity Harrison and then his friend Anthony Audley.

What were they up to?

Felicity enthusiastically welcomed Luke into her room.

She was sitting at her table covered in sheets of paper on which Luke could see rows of letters and numbers.

Luke went for the kill, "Have you decoded the latest volume of Penelope's diary?"

Felicity showed no signs of embarrassment or guilt and replied, "Not yet! I need a day or so more."

Luke waited for her to explain her devious behavior, but no apology was forthcoming.

He pressed home on another issue, "Why did you impersonate Ursula Audley to obtain that diary?"

"Because Ursula and Anthony asked me to."

"Why did they do that?"

"Penny did not want it known that she kept a diary. By pretending I was Ursula, any troublemakers at the bookbinders would think that Ursula, not Penny, was the writer, and as Anthony paid the account, the bookbinder did not quibble when I arrived with the payment."

"Why were Ursula and her father involved in this personal enterprise of Penelope's? Anthony paid for the yearly supply of paper and the annual binding of the loose sheets."

"Anthony believed that what Penny recorded would provide evidence to justify actions he took in the Indies and might take in the future. Above all, he saw it as a guarantee that Ursula would be protected. Don't ask me for the details. I was never told. Since we have been at Austin Friars, Penelope not only asked the Audleys to obtain the latest volume but made it clear in my presence that she would give all her volumes to Ursula for safekeeping."

"Did she?" asked Luke, trying to trick the erudite Felicity.

"No, she said that when she returned to London, she would retrieve them and bring them to Austin Friars. She died before she could do so."

Luke asked for Felicity to wait a few minutes.

He returned, satisfied with Felicity's explanation, but eager to find out why Anthony was so involved.

"Here are the missing volumes. Peter and I found them in Liffey's library, hidden behind other books."

Luke sought out Anthony.

At the far end of Austin Friars, bordered by an unusually deep part of the shallow Medway estuary, Anthony had created three gun emplacements and moored a number small boats at various distances offshore.

Intermittent salvos of artillery fire dominated the environment.

The trainee artillerymen were being put through their paces. For every real shot they were allowed to fire, they had to go through the protocol nine other times.

Their training had reached the point where Anthony had asked the corporal in charge of each battery to estimate the distance of the boats, change the elevation of the cannon, and fire.

Batteries One and Two missed their target by a dozen yards or more. Battery Two did not even reach the water's edge.

Battery Three amazed Anthony.

The cannonball hit the target boat and sank it.

Anthony immediately congratulated the corporal in charge and asked him if he had had previous experience.

"Yes, sir, but that was many years ago. It was a lucky shot."

Luke observed the corporal as Anthony addressed him.

Luke felt uneasy.

The trickles of perspiration that ran down the gunner's face were brown.

This was either a very dirty corporal, or he dyed his hair.

Luke sent one of the recruits to find Strad and have him report to the artillery range immediately.

Anthony turned to Luke.

"You did not walk across the island to watch our newly recruited artillerymen. What is it?"

"A simple question! Why finance Penelope Marlowe's diary keeping?"

"Penny never charged for or received many gifts as a result of her activities, although such activities cost her a considerable amount of money for clothing and toiletries. The Marlowes had no income other than Peter's army pay, and you could not expect him to assist his wife in her dubious activities."

"That does not quite answer my question. Why did you help?"

"Just after Ursula arrived in the Indies in her early teens, she was seduced by an officer. She refused to name him then and still does. However, she did confide in Penny who assured me that the details had been recorded in case Ursula or I wanted to act further down the track. Over the five years working together on Barbados, I often confided in Penny and asked that these confidences be recorded. She also noted information she gleaned from her lovers, including their views on third parties. These diaries are Ursula's and my protective shield. In essence, while on Barbados, Penny was a surrogate mother for Ursula. That is why she is so traumatized by the brutal murder."

"These diaries are potential poison for others. Thus her murder. If you and Penny were close, why did you not believe her story regarding Ursula's problem with Richard Grey? I understand you accepted Richard's version and punished Ursula."

"Living and working in close proximity to the same people year after year can create tensions. I fully accepted Penny's and Ursula's views of the situation, but in the interests of group harmony among the senior officers of the Barbados administration, I pretended to support Richard. It kept him on side, and he tended to vent his moralistic spleen against Peter Marlowe."

"So, Richard, despite all the initial praise of the man from you and others was, in reality, a difficult colleague?"

"You have interviewed him. Did you not reach the same conclusion?"

"No, my only concern with Richard was the level of his religious radicalism."

"And you are right to be so. In recent weeks, this obsession has intensified. I work with him every day, training the more advanced troops. He has expressed great delight that the troops from the London garrison sent to reinforce our group in the face of possible attack include many noncommissioned officers who are of his religious persuasion. He also hoped that Marlowe would listen to him and not Liffey and recruit more junior officers from among his friends in the Fifth Monarchy community."

At that point, a breathless Strad arrived.

Luke pointed out the gunner with the striped face and asked Strad to follow him and find out all he could. Yarrow may have given up his disguise as a servant and taken on a new role as one of the recruits.

As Luke entered the reception hall of the main house, Jane Castle greeted him, "London trip useful? You may have forgotten, but you passed on to me the letters of Lady Isadore from her brother. I have read them all twice over and can find only two snippets of information that might interest you. In one place, he moves into Spanish which Lady Felicity translated as 'Whatever

I do in the future, it will be for family honor and the future of England.'"

"That is not surprising. Although Liffey does not claim to speak Spanish, his five years in an area where a lot of Spanish was spoken must have left him with a smattering of the language."

"The second snippet may be more serious. On a certain date, which Liffey gives, he says he made a trip to the Ile de Marie."

"How does visiting a French island raise suspicion? The French are our allies—at least for the moment."

"For a month before and three months after the date that Liffey lists, the island was occupied by the Spaniards."

Luke whistled.

"And there is more. Around the time of Liffey's visit, the island provided a harbor for the Spanish squadron, allocated the task of protecting their treasure fleet."

"And a squadron with some of the fastest ships on the high seas that kept constant communications with Spain," uttered Luke as he gave Jane a big hug.

His deprivation of female company for so long proved too much.

Luke and Jane were not seen for the rest of the day, reappearing at the formal supper at which Liffey expected total attendance.

Ursula, given her condition, was the only person absent.

Liffey was in a bad mood and could not help exerting his status-given right as the senior aristocrat to dictate the lives of lesser mortals.

He addressed the gathered throng as the domineering patriarch of a recalcitrant household.

"I am very disappointed that my generosity in inviting the womenfolk of my officers has not been blessed by convivial interaction and pleasant leisure-time pursuits. Most of you spend time alone in your rooms and scarcely converse with one another. Tomorrow, should the weather be fine, we will all have an outdoor banquet on a more salubrious part of the Kentish coast—a neighboring estate, which contains its own forest and much wildlife. We will indulge in a little hunting. Some of you ladies are experts in using the small bow to hunt conies, small game animals, and birds. Everybody, except Colonel Grey and Major Audley, who will be needed to supervise the training, will attend. That includes you, Colonel Tremayne, and your officers. I have already ordered the kitchen to prepare a range of roasted meats that we will eat cold. I hope we can gather some mushrooms, nuts, and berries to add to the hares, swans, deer, and partridges you will catch. I have borrowed a number of barges from our neighbor that are ideal for moving around the quieter waters of the estuary. They will transfer you and the food to the banquet site."

Felicity Harrison, who was seated next to Luke, whispered, "Lucky Anthony! How many women outside the odd duchess would know how to hunt with a small bow? Liffey lives in the past. I am glad Anthony resigns his commission shortly. Next, we will hear that Liffey is reintroducing the long bow as England's most effective weapon. After all, he still has faith in the pike."

"How are you going with the decoding?" asked Luke, deliberately changing the topic.

"I know the role of the symbols. They are letters of the Hebraic alphabet, which determine the code being used. Penelope had hidden talents. She used six or seven different codes to encipher letters into numbers."

"When you are able to translate sections of the diary, I want you, as a matter of urgency, to concentrate on these dates."

He passed Felicity a one-page note.

Countess Merrick, who was on the other side of Luke, exclaimed, "Christopher is mad. The last time I had a bow in my hand as a girl, I nearly killed one of our servants. A rabbit ran behind me, and I just let fly. The arrow was miles off course."

Luke became alarmed.

"Countess, you are a marvel!" Luke exclaimed as he grasped her hand below the table level and gave it a big squeeze, which was aggressively reciprocated.

"Why are you so pleased with me?" She pouted.

"If I was planning another murder, an accidental shooting accident would be the perfect cover."

"You have authority from Cromwell to override Liffey. Use it! Stop this madness," suggested the now-alarmed countess.

"Yes, but only if I have evidence that Liffey himself is the danger to the government. If I act without justification, I could spend years in The Tower. Fortuitously, my senior officers and I have been invited to the banquet. I will bring most of my dragoons with me."

Felicity regained Luke's attention.

She whispered, "I was talking to Evadne just before supper. She is now convinced that her husband is Weld. She needs to talk to you urgently."

"I will seek her out as we leave here."

31

Luke walked Evadne back to her apartment where she provided each of them with a glass of mulled, overspiced, and oversweetened red wine.

Luke took one sip and hurriedly placed it back on the small table and grabbed the hand of his hostess. "Don't drink it! The excessive spicing and sweetening could hide the taste of a poison."

"Why would anybody want to poison me? I have no links with anyone except my husband, and murdering me is not going to affect him in anyway. I am the last person that Belladonna and Weld need to remove."

"My god, maybe I was the target. Did you tell anybody that you would be seeing me?" asked Luke.

"Yes, but you know that. I told Felicity. You can't believe that Felicity is out to prevent what I have to say being revealed, although she may think I know something detrimental about her betrothed."

"Where did you get this wine? Did some unknown servant bring it here?"

"No, Felicity gave it to me."

"This is Felicity's wine?"

"Yes. I stopped having wine brought to my room, but as I planned to see you, Felicity gave me half of the large flagon she had just received from the cellarer."

Luke jumped to his feet. "I will be back. Felicity either tried to kill us both, or she was the intended victim."

Luke ran to Felicity's apartment and banged on the door.

An agitated Anthony Audley answered with sword drawn.

"What are you up to, Luke? Knocking on the door of my betrothed at such a late hour. Are you drunk?"

"No, and more importantly, have you or Felicity drunk any of the mulled wine?"

"No. I took one sip and poured it out the window. It was revolting."

"Thank god! That wine tasted so bad because its excessive spices were designed to conceal the taste of poison. Someone is trying to kill Felicity."

Felicity, who had entered the room and heard Luke's comments, said quietly, "Weld and Belladonna must know I am translating Penny's diary."

Anthony commented undiplomatically, "How would Felicity's death help them? If they killed her, you would get Thurloe's experts to decipher it."

"True, Anthony, but the critical ingredient is time. Weld must act now. I am sure the recent murders at Austin Friars reflect this growing concern. There must be increasing pressure on him to act with or without any help from the fleet of Irish and Royalists, last known to be sheltering among the islands of the northern Netherlands. It awaits a signal from here to move south."

"That fleet is no threat. It is too small. The government has dozens of ships between the northern Netherlands and the Medway," commented the pragmatic Audley.

"True, but to sail after dark with no lights! The North Sea is larger than you think. They may have already transferred to small keel-less Dutch barges that apart from one small dash across the open sea can hug the coastline out of range of our ships and in places where we do not have shore batteries. They could be on our doorstep, and we would not have heard a thing," answered Luke.

He turned to Felicity. "You are in grave danger. With your permission, I will place guards outside and within these rooms. You must not be left alone day or night."

"But I still have to go on that stupid outdoor banquet—and hunt."

"I will have my men beside you the whole time you are there." Luke returned to Evadne.

To his surprise, she had partially disrobed and had sent her servants to their quarters at the far end of the house.

He explained that fortunately Anthony had thrown away the strange-tasting wine.

"Why did you want to see me?" he asked the mature but still attractive woman.

"It's not to seduce you, but we might come to that later. My husband and I do not have a perfect relationship, but I respect Richard and admire what he has achieved. I also respect the role of a wife in keeping the failings of her husband within the family."

"Evadne, what are you talking about?"

"Richard is Weld."

"Rubbish! Have you any evidence?"

"Some of it I have heard myself. The rest has come from one of my man-servants whom I transferred to Richard as his valet while he is at Austin Friars."

"I am listening."

"Richard has smuggled into Austin Friars a dozen or more men, officers and ranks and concealed them within the regiment that was augmented by men from the London garrison. He actually persuaded some serving officers to resign their current positions and come here."

"How can he get these men onto the estate? My men monitor both ends of the causeway and list who comes and goes, and they patrol the perimeter of the estate by boat at high tide to check that no one enters by sea."

"You have few men, and the perimeter is long. Richard's men wait until your patrol has passed by and then come ashore."

"But where is the boat or boats that they use? We are not idiots. We search the shoreline for any unattended boats all the time."

"But not at low tide. At high tide, the boat is either offshore, waiting for your men to pass, or hidden in a cave, whose entrance is completely below the water level. The cave is also at the bottom of a steep cliff, which would most likely only be picked up from a seaward inspection at low tide."

Luke was piqued.

"That information certainly destroys my claim to control movements on and off this estate. Does Richard go to London recruiting?"

"Not anymore, but he told me the other day that Marlowe might do the right thing and recruit a number of officers from his religious compatriots. A captain that was smuggled in and placed within Richard's regiment goes to London on a very regular basis to bring back more Fifth Monarchy men."

"All this is worrying, but it does not prove that Richard is Weld. Richard believes that Liffey or Marlowe is Weld and is stacking the officer corps with men who, while they may hate Cromwell, hate Charles Stuart even more. I cannot see Richard fighting with the Royalists under any circumstance."

"Richard is ready to strike. Last night, into the early hours of the morning, he entertained his religious comrades with a sermon, much Bible reading, and numerous exhortations praising the Lord Jesus. His apartment has an adjoining door with mine. It was locked, but Richard spoke from the end of his room adjacent to mine. I froze when I first heard his message. I will never forget it."

"What did he say?"

"I quote word for word: 'What we are about to do, we do in the name of the Lord Jesus and for His chosen land, England.' It was followed by loud and repeated cries of amen."

"Maybe what Richard has in mind is to remove Liffey rather than a coup against the government?"

"In either case, we must inform Christopher! To leave Richard on the estate tomorrow when the rest of us are chasing hares and picking mushrooms gives him a major opportunity to strike."

"No, Evadne, I take full responsibility for your husband's actions. Liffey must not know, assuming he is not already aware of Richard's possible defection."

Evadne took Luke in her arms, squeezed him tight, and gave him a long passionate kiss.

Luke did not resist.

"Don't misinterpret what I just did. I do want to proposition you but not for an immediate seduction. Through my relationship with the one true love of your life, Elizabeth Hanes, I feel I have known you since childhood. If you and Elizabeth do not come to an arrangement soon and if my husband is no longer around, I would wish to propose marriage to you. Now you better go."

Luke was stunned—and flattered.

Next morning, it poured with rain.

Liffey reluctantly postponed his outdoor banquet for the following day.

Luke was relieved.

Another day might enable Felicity to crack the codes and give him the information he needed before she risked the dangers of an outdoor excursion.

The Grant cousins waylaid him as he walked to Felicity's rooms for an update.

They wanted to talk to him in private as a matter of urgency.

The chapel of the old priory, which they approached, proved a suitable venue.

As Luke and the two women sat in the same pew, Rose began to cry.

Obviously, the death of her betrothed was still eating away at her.

Veronica spoke, "Rose and I have thought constantly of David's death. He was the target, not Sir Peter, and we know who murdered him."

"Serious charges! What has led you to these conclusions?"

"When David spoke to Rose about coming here, he pleaded with her to find a major reason not to attend. I became suspicious of this request when I realized that two women from his time in the

Indies would also be here. I never trusted him. I confronted him and asked if he had had an affair with either Penelope or Ursula."

Rose, whose sobbing had stopped, intervened, "At first, he lied, denying anything, except a casual but repeated liaison with Penelope. I could have no objection to a man having sexual dealings with another woman, especially before we became betrothed. After a few days here, it was obvious that David was sorely troubled."

"He slept in the adjoining room to Rose and me. My presence was to guarantee that nothing happened between Rose and David that was not acceptable to my family," remarked Veronica.

"A few nights before his death, he obviously had a dream, and we both heard him shouting and crying and begging forgiveness, and one word sent a chill through me: Ursula," announced Rose through her renewed sobs.

Veronica took up the story, "Next morning, I confronted David. He was in a shocking state. He asked me not to tell Rose. On his arrival in the Indies, he succumbed to the obsessions of a young teenage girl, whom he claimed he thought was much older. When her father discovered the affair, he ensured that there could be no more meetings between the two. David nevertheless continued to leave messages for Ursula, claiming his undying love for her. He promised that once they left Barbados and were back in England, he would openly court her to the point of marriage."

"And Ursula remained loyal, refusing to divulge the name of her seducer?" commented Luke.

"She maintained a static picture of her ultimate future for more than five years. She must have been devastated when she arrived here and found Rose as David's betrothed."

Veronica continued, "This discovery turned her mind. She told her father, who, being an expert in explosives, organized David's execution. If Audley could do this, he might also be your missing Weld."

"Audley could have organized the explosion that killed David, but he did not execute the act himself. He was with Liffey and me at the time of the explosion."

The Grant cousins appeared disappointed.

Luke tried to raise their spirits. "You may be right. David's death could have been a personal act of revenge and have nothing to do with Weld and his conspiracy."

"One last matter, if Ursula remains traumatized, is it not possible that the next two persons killed at Austin Friars will be my cousin and I? After all, Rose supplanted Ursula in David's affections. We need your protection," pleaded Veronica.

Luke needed a drink.

There was evidence pointing the finger at Liffey, Grey, and Audley. If Halliburton and not Marlowe was the intended victim of the latest explosion, then Marlowe himself might still be Weld.

Perhaps Liffey's excursion onto the mainland for an outdoor banquet and hunt might clarify the issues—or create further problems.

Luke's intention to follow up the insinuations against his friend Anthony Audley and to monitor Felicity's progress with Penelope's diaries had to be put on hold given the security implications of Liffey's outdoor folly.

It was a nightmare.

It was not a simple question of dealing with a dozen or so nobles, gentry, and their womenfolk. They all insisted on bringing servants.

As they boarded the barges that Liffey had hired, Luke counted over fifty persons.

And there was no time to record names or check credentials.

Liffey sent soldiers across to the site much earlier to erect tents and to light a number of fires for cooking.

There was no chance of verifying the identity of these men either.

Luke feared that Yarrow would cross to the site of the banquet in the guise of one of the soldiers and hide somewhere in the woodlands to effect another murder.

Luke noted the constant transfer of food and utensils by servants of the house.

Goodness knows what else had been spirited across the channel!

The new environment created an ideal opportunity for a mass abduction or, even worse, a wholesale massacre.

On landing at the site, Luke was surprised to find more of Liffey's men than his own protective detail of dragoons.

Luke was decidedly uneasy as his limited numbers forced him to confine his activities to the protection of Felicity.

He was further alarmed to find the officer directing activities was not Liffey.

It was Richard Grey.

Were the religious extremists about to make their move?

And where was Liffey?

32

"What are you doing here, Richard? Anthony and you were to stay behind and continue training."

"Christopher woke me before dawn to say he had been called away, and I was to organize and supervise this entertainment."

"That leaves Anthony alone in charge of the camp?" queried Luke.

"He won't have much to do. The men will be limited today to musket drill. There will be no artillery or cavalry training. When we resume full-time training tomorrow, can you help us with the cavalry? Since David's death, we have no experienced cavalry officer to direct proceedings."

"Solving existing and preventing further deaths will keep me too busy to assist," Luke quickly declared.

Luke saw the opportunity to follow up on the accusations made by Evadne against her husband but decided to wait until proceedings got under way and both men had some free time.

"What is about to happen?" asked Luke.

"Each of the ladies has been given a short bow and accompanied by one of their male servants or one of my men. They will proceed to hunt, hopefully providing us with part of a meal."

"Is there much edible game available?" asked Luke.

"There is but most of it not suitable for this Liffey feast. There are plenty of hares, but no one eats them within a week of killing, and the deer will only be slightly maimed by the pitiful bow strength that the women will exercise. They will be limited—and their guides have been told this—to rabbits and swans."

Luke replaced the soldier who was to accompany Felicity with two of his men.

The women and their guides moved into the forest, after which Richard sent some of his men to follow them to obtain berries, nuts, and, above all, mushrooms to put into a much-anticipated rabbit stew.

Luke and Richard relaxed, sitting on a fallen log, drinking a Kentish beer, which clearly contained more hops than Luke was used to.

Luke noticed there were fires and cooking pots, but he could see little food.

"Liffey is surely out of touch if he expects these amateur hunters to provide our meal."

"No, at this very moment, the many cooks at Austin Friars are roasting various birds and sides of Kentish lamb. We will send back for the main dishes around midday. Have you solved any of the murders or discovered the identity of Weld and Belladonna?"

"No."

"And Yarrow is still at large?"

"Yes, but we do know he has dyed his giveaway red hair, left the service of whomever he worked for, and has now hidden himself among your troops."

"How can that be? You and we senior officers monitor the personnel under our command."

"Come, Richard, you have been undermining my attempt to know who leaves and who enters the camp."

"What do you mean?"

"You are subverting the rank structure of this army by secretly filling the junior-officer ranks with religious enthusiasts such as yourself."

"That is true, but I am compelled to act. You have failed miserably in identifying the officer about to subvert this army in the interests of Charles Stuart."

"But you, Richard, are doing exactly the same."

"No, I am not acting in the interests of the Stuarts but in those of a much higher power, the Lord Jesus. I had to move quickly as Liffey told Marlowe to fill the junior-officer ranks, the critical line of discipline and loyalty in any army, with his aristocratic friends most of whom are probably clandestine Royalists."

"Why have you decided to act now?"

"At the last meeting of the godly in London, I received a vision that gave me clear orders that I renounce the authority of all earthly governments."

"So you have renounced your loyalty to Cromwell and the present government."

"Not for the moment. I am still seeking the guidance of the Lord as to whether Cromwell is to be treated as his agent or as his enemy."

Luke signaled for Evan and Strad to join them.

In the presence of his officers, Luke formally announced, "Richard, in the light of your statement, I am placing you under arrest. When the barges are ready to return to Austin Friars to collect the food, I will accompany you and Sergeant Stradling back to camp. You will come quietly. If you attempt to escape or raise the alarm, my dagger will find your vitals. I am sorry about this, but you leave me no choice. Evan, you will be the most senior officer left here. Take command and await our return! Tell Richard's officers that he and I had to return urgently to camp."

The soldiers boarded the next barge returning to Austin Friars. It was propelled by a couple of pole-pushing servants designated to collect and transport more food for the banquet.

The barge landed the men at the causeway entrance to the camp just as a deafening explosion was heard.

Smoke and fire rose from the manor.

As all three men ran toward the building, they saw Anthony Audley running down the hill toward the house from the training camp.

Luke surveyed the damage and realized that Ursula's room was the target of the bomber.

Luke was about to offer his sympathy and engage in the hard task of recovering what remained of her body when Anthony, who had joined him, uttered a cry of jubilation, "Heaven be praised. This morning, as the house was largely deserted, I thought it would be safer for Ursula to be with me in the tent up the slope. Her two guards came with me."

"Clearly, the would-be murderer did not know that. It would have been easy for him to saunter past and hurl a couple of grenades through the window. Yarrow is an expert in that style of attack. I know from bitter experience."

Strad commented, "This attack is in line with my follow up of the hair-dyeing artilleryman. None of his companions knew him. He arrived the morning of the murder, claiming he was an expert, having been seconded to the unit by Lord Liffey himself. Since the killing of Halliburton, he has not been seen."

Audley confronted Richard, "Where did you get to this morning? You were supposed to be helping me supervise musket drill. I am no expert in that area."

"I am sorry, Anthony. I had assumed that Christopher had told you that I had to take his place supervising his outdoor banquet. He was called away unexpectedly."

Audley looked quizzically at Luke and continued, "Well, you are here now. Let's get back to work while Luke and his sergeant examine Yarrow's latest work in detail."

"I am afraid that is impossible. Richard is under arrest. He has admitted to filling the junior-officer army with religious radicals whose allegiance to Cromwell is tenuous at the best."

"Is it wise to remove Richard now when we expect a Royalist coup at any minute. When the time comes and we have to fight, Richard and his fellow Fifth Monarchy men will fight with us rather than the Stuarts."

Luke could not deny the logic of Anthony's remarks.

"Richard, you did say that the Lord had not yet guided you as to whether you would treat Cromwell as a leader of God's people or as the great betrayer. Give me your word as an officer and gentleman that you will not take up arms against the Lord Protector while stationed at Austin Friars!"

"If God moves and gives me an instruction, I cannot resist his will, but what I can promise is that over the next week or so, I will unearth for you the Royalist conspirators, or rather I will prove that either Marlowe or Liffey is your man."

Luke finally agreed, "I know, Richard, that you would never risk eternal damnation by siding with the known forces of evil: the Royalists. And if I eliminate you from my list of suspects, then Weld must be one of the men you just named."

Strad commented, "Sir, I will check with our men at the causeway as to where Liffey has gone."

Half an hour later, he returned.

"Liffey told the guards that he was going to Rochester on urgent army business."

"That does not help us!"

"But maybe this does? The sergeant commanding the group added that one of our men who had to go down the London-Dover road about the same time was passed by Liffey heading not for Rochester but for Canterbury."

"Now that is useful."

"But there is more. He was not alone."

Luke interrupted, "He was accompanied by a red-haired assistant?"

"Much more interesting. He was accompanied by a woman."

"Who?"

"She was hooded, and our man did not recognize her."

"Strad, look through the rubble here and see if there is anything that will help our inquiry! Richard and Anthony, go back to your training duties! I will return to our outdoor banquet to see which woman is missing."

Luke landed at the banquet site to be greeted by Evan, "The servants returning with the food said there had been a loud explosion in part of the house, and a couple of rooms had been demolished. Anybody killed?"

"No, it appears to have been Yarrow's attempt to kill Ursula Audley who luckily was with her father on the training ground. What's happened here?"

"We have been on the edge of disaster all morning. I canceled the hunting. The Grant women nearly sent an arrow through each other, and as expected, an arrow or two narrowly missed Lady Felicity. It could have been an accident. Our men could not locate its exact source in the chaos. What did you do with Richard?"

"I released him."

"Why?"

"We need him and his fanatics to fight the Royalist traitors. Audley has vouched for him."

"Have you not thought that either Richard or Anthony could be Weld and the other his assistant? Blair, as a double agent, may have given Thurloe only half the story. There could be more than one Royalist officer at Austin Friars."

"And equally, there may be more than one woman involved," replied an excited Luke.

He smiled at Evan and asked, "Are all the women of the household present?"

"I am not sure. I did not count them. The aristocratic three are here—the Countess of Merrick, Baroness Veldor, and Lady Evadne—the Grant cousins, and Felicity Harrison. I have not seen Lady Lydia Veldor."

Luke sought out her mother, Sophia.

"Sophia, where is your daughter? It is a very poor example that the one woman of the household that disobeys Lord Liffey is his betrothed."

"Not so, Colonel. I was awakened before dawn by one of Lydia's servants who told me that she would not be coming but had already left with Christopher for Canterbury. Surely, a man and his betrothed can seek time together without causing a security uproar?"

"It does seem strange that Christopher should choose a day that clashed with his much-flaunted social gathering of the whole household for a private tryst with his beloved."

"This gathering was planned for yesterday. Perhaps Christopher could not change what he and Lydia intended to do in Canterbury?"

Sir Evan ended the open banquet early without any further trouble, except three of the women claimed they had been poisoned after eating some of the mushroom stew.

One of the servants claimed he had seen a poisonous fly agaric variety of fungi added to the pot.

By the following morning, all alleged victims had fully recovered.

Luke had had a sleepless night.

He could hardly wait to interview Liffey.

He convinced himself that the general had absented himself from his position without due authority and for such a breach of protocol could and probably should be removed from his position.

Luke arrived at Liffey's office early next morning, but the general could not be found.

Why had Liffey not returned?

He groaned, *My god, surely not another murder?*

33

Around midday, Liffey finally arrived. After gaining admission to his presence, Luke let fly without any of the deference he should had shown to a superior officer.

Liffey was taken aback.

"Tremayne, you forget yourself! You may have a special license to invoke the Protector's overriding authority in critical situations, but I am a major general and you are a colonel. And I am about to inherit an earldom almost as large as the whole of England. Treat your social and military superior with respect, or I will shackle you, pending a decision from Cromwell himself concerning your future. What is your problem?"

"You deserted your post and lied about your illicit destination."

"I did neither of those things."

"Come on, sir, you left Austin Friars early in the morning and returned this morning. You told my men that you were going to Rochester when you headed off toward Dover."

"It's a pity you are not so good in discovering Weld and Belladonna as you are in tracking my movements. To take a day trip away with my betrothed is not against military protocol. The training on this camp continued in my absence. I did tell your men I was going to Rochester. That is where I thought I was going. Lady Lydia was negotiating with the clergy there regarding our wedding.

When I caught up with Lady Lydia, she told me the location had been changed to Canterbury."

Christopher continued, "In one sense, I am acting illegally. Lydia and I wanted to be married by the suspended Bishop of Rochester—or, failing that, by the suspended Archbishop of Canterbury—and according to the traditional Book of Common Prayer. Cromwell himself has turned a blind eye to such breaches of the current religious settlement. The bishop was unavailable, although I was not aware of this until yesterday, but the archbishop had arranged with Lydia to come to Canterbury yesterday to discuss the arrangements. We wish the marriage to take place before I leave for Flanders, which, given the current state of the army, will have to be within six or seven weeks."

Luke was deflated—and humiliated.

Several Weeks Earlier

Yarrow and his two accomplices reached the causeway leading to Austin Friars as the tide was about to recede.

A number of loaded wagons and two coaches were waiting patiently in line.

Yarrow briefed his men to wait at the mainland edge of the causeway, and if he did not return in an hour, they should turn back to an inn that they had passed half an hour earlier and take up lodgings there until he contacted them.

He then walked alongside the waiting vehicles until he stood with other pedestrians at the head of the queue.

Eventually, a liveried servant approached him.

He was led to an ornate coach whose occupant opened its door and signaled for him to enter.

He saw a woman, sitting alone, whom he did not recognize but whom, on her speaking, he knew was Belladonna.

"These are exciting times. Our enterprise will progress in leaps and bounds now that we are all at Austin Friars. You are one of my few male servants, ready to carry out any chores that my other retainers are not capable of achieving. The other servants know one another and are all drawn from the estate on which I currently abide. You have come from my nonexistent London townhouse. Dye your hair immediately before you alert that prying Tremayne to your presence."

"Have I an immediate task?"

"Yes, you are to execute our enemies one by one."

Yarrow took in a deep breath just as the coach began to cross the causeway.

Belladonna continued, "Our enterprise is under threat if some of those gathered here talk to one another or more seriously if they talk to Tremayne. There is evidence hidden in the memories of some of those who were in the Indies that might unravel our mission before it is completed."

"My first target?"

"Your first victim deserves to die for two reasons. He murdered Woad, John Blair. John was a brilliant Royalist agent who infiltrated Thurloe's inner sanctum. As a double agent, he kept us informed of what Thurloe knew or thought he knew about Royalist conspiracies. As Thurloe's agent in the Indies, he was able to build up a small army and fleet, unknown to government, that is at this moment already in European waters, awaiting our signal to sail here."

"Who killed Blair?" asked Yarrow, not unhappy about that particular death.

"At first, I suspected it was Tremayne, but now I have evidence that it was Peebles. He tracked Blair in the Indies. He probably discovered our man's double dealing. He could know a great deal more that may compromise our activities."

"Surely, he has told all he knows to Tremayne by now."

"No! He wants the glory of unmasking us for himself. He probably does not trust Tremayne who humiliated him in front of two seamen. But there is no certainty that he will not change his mind and inform Tremayne or Thurloe of all he knows."

"Do you have a timetable? I need to work out a plan that maximizes my chances of success and safe escape."

"As soon as possible," replied Belladonna.

"I have recruited two expert marksmen to assist me. They may have trouble getting onto the island."

Belladonna was furious.

She did not hide her displeasure.

"Was that wise? The fewer people aware of our activity, the better. Get rid of them."

It was Yarrow's turn to be angry. He would not be told by a female amateur plotter how he should carry out his mission.

He would deal with his men in his own time.

For the next few days, a black-haired Yarrow traveled over the island estate, concentrating on the area where musketeer training was taking place and the location of various tents and their proximity to where the officers took up their station to supervise the training.

There was only one problem.

Peebles never appeared.

Yarrow took his complaint to Belladonna.

Next day she told him that given Liffey's suspicions of the man, he had not been allocated any training duties.

She, in turn, asked Weld if he could solve the problem.

He did.

In two days' time, Peebles would join the other officers on the training ground.

Yarrow's strengths as a soldier had been as a grenadier and mortar expert.

For the task that lay ahead, he would need the assistance of the two marksmen he had employed.

Yarrow left the island and returned with his men just before dawn using a small barge to avoid Luke's patrols.

Belladonna had had Weld transfer muskets, ammunition, and grenades to a small room in her apartment for Yarrow's use.

Yarrow had carefully planned his assassination.

He had seen the servants of the house push rubbish in small two-wheeled trolleys to the far end of the island where it was dumped into a chalk pit.

The path used by the servants went right through the middle of the tents erected on the training field.

As the time for Peebles's appearance approached, Yarrow confiscated three garbage barrows, placed a musket in each, covered the weapons with leaves, and he and his expert marksmen wheeled them along the path through the training area.

They stopped when their presence was hidden by rows of tents, which conveniently were empty.

They hid themselves and the barrows in the tent that gave them the best sight of the position taken up by the officers commanding the musketeer training.

Yarrow was in luck.

Within minutes, Peebles came into view.

He was accompanied by Tremayne.

What an opportunity!

Kill them both and make Belladonna very happy!

Slits were made in the side of the tent and muskets positioned.

Yarrow and one marksmen would take out Peebles while the second would shoot Tremayne.

Yarrow got his shot off without any trouble, and its sound was hidden by the fusillade of the trainees. The shot of his assistant also found Peebles's head.

The victim fell to the ground.

The third assassin missed Luke's heart, only grazing his upper arm.

There was no time for reloading.

The slightly wounded Tremayne was already organizing men to search the area.

The three assassins moved beyond the tents, took the long way around, and returned along the coast to the manor.

Belladonna was delighted, even gleeful.

Late that same night, Yarrow rewarded his assistants with a gold coin—and a shot behind the ear.

Two days later, a hysterical Belladonna called him into her bedchamber, "You must execute another guest immediately. She kept a diary of her time in the Indies. It contains much that could destroy us."

"Who is the diary keeper?"

"Penelope Marlowe."

"I need time to study her habits and become familiar with her routine."

"You don't have time. I will help. Tomorrow morning, we shall visit her in her bedchamber. She will admit me, and you will follow as my dutiful servant. You will close the door and kill her."

Belladonna's plan worked perfectly.

As soon as the door was shut, Yarrow stabbed Penelope with one clean thrust; and she fell to the floor, mortally wounded.

He was astounded at what happened next.

Instead of searching the room for the diary, Belladonna picked up a heavy ceramic vase and repeatedly bashed the head and face of the dead victim until it was unrecognizable.

The butchery did not cease.

Belladonna removed a sword from the wall and with one movement decapitated the corpse.

Only then did Belladonna search the room but was almost immediately interrupted when Penelope's servant knocked on the door, asking if she was ready to be dressed.

Belladonna mumbled, "Not yet."

The servant replied, "I will return in a few minutes with embers to light your fire. It is very cold."

The two conspirators looked at each other meaningfully, waited a minute, and left the room.

They had moved only a few yards down the corridor when Ursula Audley passed them.

Later, they discussed the possibility that she had seen them leave Penelope's room.

The next day they were relieved that the discovery of the mutilated and decapitated body of her friend had provoked some sort of a trauma, and Ursula had been rendered comatose.

Belladonna was not sympathetic.

"She is your next victim. Do it before she recovers her senses! I will search Marlowe's room again. We must find that diary."

Next day Belladonna was enthusiastic.

"The view that Penelope was murdered in order to retrieve her diary has spread through the household. The ladies believe if the diary is not in Marlowe's room, Ursula would have it. We will repeat the performance of yesterday. I will gain you entry to Ursula's room, and you will dispatch her."

Yarrow, as a hired assassin, raised a salient point, "My lady, you hired me originally to assassinate Oliver Cromwell. It has now degenerated into the progressive murder of this entire household. I was paid for the Peebles killing but not for Marlowe's. A further advance would be timely before I consider Lady Ursula."

Belladonna was not impressed.

"You forget, Yarrow, that you were paid a fortune to kill the Protector, and you did not deliver."

Yarrow sensed that his request had created tension.

He knew he had the upper hand in any confrontation with Belladonna.

He alone of all the inhabitants of Austin Friars, except possibly Weld, knew her real identity.

It was a pity he hated Cromwell and his officers so much. Thurloe and Tremayne would pay him a fortune for this information.

Unknown to Yarrow, Belladonna had a similar fear. She would discuss with Weld how to deal with Yarrow. He could become a nuisance.

Weld came up with a temporary solution.

Yarrow would be transferred out of her service and attached to the artillery section of the army in training. This would put him into a better position to act on their behalf when the takeover of the army was under way.

34

On their deadly mission, Belladonna and Yarrow approached Ursula's room.

Belladonna uttered an oath that even surprised the worldly wise Yarrow.

Three dragoons blocked their path.

Belladonna muttered, "Tremayne is a devil. He thinks like us. Ursula must have that diary."

One of the dragoons made it clear that no one could enter the room without the permission of either Colonel Tremayne or Major Audley.

As she and Yarrow walked away, Belladonna recovered her equilibrium. "When an opportunity occurs, strike!"

Over the next few days, Yarrow blended in with the trainee artillerymen and took part in their daily sessions, changing batteries at the last minute.

He enjoyed this activity, and his old competiveness came to the fore. The trainees were divided into three teams and given three chances to sink some derelict boats on the Medway.

Yarrow could not resist showing off.

He sank the targeted boat.

The officers were impressed, Tremayne included.

The activity had made him perspire profusely.

When he brushed his face to remove the sweat, it was brown.

The dye in his hair had run.

Had Tremayne noticed?

He must disappear. The whole camp knew that Tremayne's men were looking for individuals who dyed their hair.

He could curse his red-haired parents.

Weld and Belladonna must solve this problem for him as a matter of urgency.

But it would be a dangerous confession of guilt if he suddenly left the artillery group.

The next day he turned up for training to find that none of the explosive experts were on duty. Their training was being monitored by a cavalry officer, David Halliburton.

Halliburton hardly left the officer's tent.

As the artillery corporals were going through the drill movements for yet another time, an explosion close to hand deafened them all.

Yarrow and his comrades witnessed the tent in which Halliburton was located rise in the air and its various fragments fly in all directions.

A rogue mortar had hit the tent, yet there were no mortars on the range that morning.

Yarrow was deeply troubled.

Was this murder of Halliburton using methods in which Yarrow was an expert an attempt by Tremayne to set him up? Tremayne may have already laid false clues so that he could be unjustly accused and then summarily executed.

Then a second more worrying thought entered his head. What if Belladonna had more than one agent working at Austin Friars? Was this an attempt to frighten him? Obey her, or the other agent would take over his role or, more dramatically, take him out?

A third possible explanation relieved the tension.

If Tremayne believed a coup was imminent and the identity of Weld not uncovered, to arrest or eradicate suspect senior officers would be a pragmatic solution. They were all expendable in the greater cause—the preservation of the Cromwellian regime.

Yarrow's enforced transformation was monumental. Hidden within the rooms allocated to Belladonna, he cut his hair very short, and he was fitted with a wig of closely cropped light-brown hair.

He was given a complete change of clothes and a new role as a special messenger for Weld and appointed to his staff as a lieutenant. He insisted that in this new role, he use his real name: Miles Thornton.

Belladonna's mood during this transformation also underwent a monumental change.

She was very relaxed when Yarrow began his conversion into Thornton.

She left for her usual morning chat with the other women halfway through his rebirth as Weld's assistant.

She returned highly agitated.

"Tremayne has found Marlowe's diary. It's in code or some foreign tongue. Our bookish Felicity is decoding it."

"That explains the presence of dragoons around her rooms as well as Ursula's. They are there in numbers. There are soldiers twenty yards from the doors and windows of her room, there are others outside every door and window, and I expect several within the rooms," Thornton revealed.

"You know what this means? You must eradicate the Harrison woman as well as Ursula."

"Given what I have just said, getting to Felicity Harrison will be difficult, if not impossible."

"Not impossible! Liffey's outdoor banquet will provide you with an opportunity to get both women. Felicity must attend, and Tremayne's protection of her will be more difficult, and Ursula, given her condition, may have to stay in her room in an otherwise largely deserted house and with much-reduced protection."

Thornton took to his new position with enthusiasm.

He was very surprised at the identity of Weld.

He had thought that two of the other officers were more likely candidates as archtraitor and conspirator.

Yarrow's task was made easier by his new position.

He could cover the whole camp on the pretext of delivering messages from Weld.

The day's delay because of the weather gave him time to plan his attack on both women.

He even took the opportunity to visit the location of the banquet on the mainland with a team of servants sent to erect tents and transport some of the basic cooking items.

He also discovered in his position close to Weld that Tremayne was furious that he would have to reduce his protective details on the estate to give certain women additional protection on this foolhardy excursion.

Thornton discussed the matter with Belladonna on the eve of the banquet.

She had heard that Ursula would be left behind with a minimum of protection. A grenade lobbed through the window from a considerable distance would do the job.

Felicity would be vulnerable as she and others moved through the woodland. It would be difficult for a marksman to shoot her from a sufficient distance away because of the intervening trees. This distant killing would have made escape easy.

He would have to be very close to the victim and make his escape in the ensuing chaos that he would have to create.

Thornton was not contemplating losing his own life in either operation.

Belladonna had a suggestion regarding Felicity.

"The women will be given small bows and a few arrows to try to hunt a few rabbits and birds. Become one of the guides, overtly carrying the spare bows, and take Felicity down! A tragic accident because of the misdirection of someone else's arrow. To make sure, I will give you some poisonous fungi, which you can put into the rabbit and mushroom stew that a cook said would be part of the victuals. In that situation, ensure that Felicity receives a very large helping."

Thornton was for the first time impressed by Belladonna.

He was glad she was an ally.

Then he shivered: what if, when he completed his tasks, he was deemed expendable?

He vividly remembered how she had defiled the body of Penelope Marlowe.

On the morning of the excursion, Thornton ascertained that Ursula would not be participating in the event.

He would deal with Felicity first.

Lieutenant Thornton had no difficulty in being accepted as a volunteer to guide the genteel women in the use of the small bow.

The guides, who gave the women instruction and practice, readily came to the conclusion that the Grant cousins were a danger to themselves and their neighbors.

Thornton magnanimously offered to accept responsibility for these two incompetents—a task the others were very anxious to avoid.

He introduced himself to the women and delayed their departure.

His comrades thought this was a wise move, allowing the other groups to move out first and be out of range of the wayward Grant arrows.

This was not Thornton's plan.

He waited until he ascertained where Felicity and her guide had entered the woods.

He quickly positioned his protégés adjacent to Felicity and moved forward quickly to catch up to her.

It was easy.

With Grant arrows going in all directions, Thornton was able to fire the spare bow directly at Felicity.

He had not allowed for the flimsy nature of these largely ornamental weapons. He snapped the string, and the arrow, with less power, fell away from its target.

Within seconds, Felicity was surrounded by dragoons and escorted out of the forest.

Thornton also took the Grant women back to the cooking area, explaining to Captain Williams, who appeared in charge, that the cousins were a little too dangerous to continue.

He noticed a large pot already beginning to boil.

The cook was seen putting in mushrooms that he had just gathered and a rabbit, which some soldiers had killed while the women pursued their fruitless frolic.

The pot would be added to progressively—if any more kills were achieved.

Thornton added to it the dried mushroom as he diverted the cook's attention.

Barges were moving constantly between Austin Friars and the excursion site.

Thornton headed back to the largely deserted manor.

He would now kill Ursula.

Back at Austin Friars, Thornton was delighted at the relative quietness.

The household, apart from the kitchen area, was largely deserted.

The trainee troops were limited to drill, with no live fire of muskets, cannons, or mortars being undertaken.

As he approached the outside of the Audley rooms, he was surprised to find the windows open and only one guard who seemed to have responsibility for the whole wing of the house.

He waited until the sentry had moved out of sight, primed two grenades, and lobbed both through the open windows.

He quickly moved to the kitchen where he claimed he was waiting to supervise the transport of more food to the banquet.

The explosion demolished the central portion of the house.

As he reached the embarkation point to return to the excursion site, he saw Major Audley running back to the house.

He spoke to the bargemen that had just brought Tremayne and Grey back to the island.

They had heard the explosion and were anxious for details.

Thornton described to them with some self-satisfaction the demolition of much of the building.

He even joked that luckily the kitchen and the servants' quarters had not been affected.

He hoped that on returning to the banquet, he would hear the calamitous news that many of the ladies had taken ill and some had died.

Some ladies had fallen ill, but no one had died.

Most blamed the cook, a Londoner, who, unlike the genteel experts, did not know an edible mushroom from the poisonous variety. Felicity had even picked a fly agaric to show the others what to avoid.

Thornton was annoyed that he had failed—yet again.

Annoyance turned to fury when he discovered on return to Austin Friars that Ursula had also survived. She had been with her father in his tent on the training fields and not in her rooms.

Weld and Belladonna were not pleased.

Two Nights Later

Luke had gone to bed quite deflated by Liffey's explanation of his absence.

It was hardly a matter for military discipline, and it did not in any way provide any evidence to clear or condemn him as Weld.

Several large whiskeys did not assist his attempt to sleep.

It was a restless night, and during one moment of sleeplessness, he heard heavy boots heading for his door.

His first thought was that Yarrow, with the assistance of some of Weld's men, was coming to murder him.

In the dark, he searched for his sword, which he had placed somewhere near his bed.

Instead of the forceful entry of Yarrow and his assassins, there was a gentle knock and voice of one of his men whom he recognized, "Colonel, open up! An urgent message from Colonel Cobb."

Luke opened the door to find one of his dragoons carrying a candle and another soldier who was dripping water and smelling of mud.

Luke's man used his candle to light several tapers that were on Luke's wall.

In the growing light, Luke recognized the stranger.

It was Cromwell's redeemed potential assassin: the lifeguard Tom Archer.

35

Tom unbuttoned his sodden clothing and withdrew an oilskin container.

From it, he pulled out a single sheet of paper.

Luke read it.

"The Lord be praised! Simon Cobb has done my work for me. He reveals the identity of Weld and informs us that the attempted takeover of the army is imminent."

Luke turned to Archer.

"How did you come to get this message?"

"Mr. Thurloe woke me and said he had just received serious news from Harwich, and I was to take this letter from Colonel Cobb to you immediately. I took a boat down the Thames, taking advantage of the receding tide, and then galloped here from my landing near Chatham."

"Why did Thurloe choose you?"

"Recognition! I was to deliver it to you alone. I knew what you looked like, and conversely, if I delivered it, you would know that it was a genuine message from Whitehall. And my horse is known for its speed."

"How come you are so wet?"

"My orders were to deliver that message to you as quickly as I could and before, as Mr. Thurloe said, hostilities actually commenced on the Medway. I arrived when the tide covered the causeway. So I swam myself and my horse across the channel. If I had waited on the tide, you would not have got the message for at least another two hours. Mr. Thurloe said every minute could make all the difference."

"An excellent job! Remove your wet clothes. Use some of mine, and I will send for food."

Luke turned to his own trooper.

"Take a few of your men and have them arouse the senior officers whose names I have written down. Tell them to report here immediately but do so quietly and, if possible, without being seen."

Within half an hour, all the senior officers except Weld were present.

"Gentlemen, I know the identity of Weld," Luke announced gently.

They all looked around the room, and all came to the same conclusion. Their missing comrade was the traitor.

Luke put their doubts to rest.

"Yes, gentlemen, the absent officer is Weld, the clandestine Royalist."

"Great work, Luke. How did you uncover the traitor?" asked one of the officers.

"No credit to me. The identity was uncovered by Colonel Cobb who was recently appointed governor of Harwich.

"His men intercepted messengers who carried letters from General Doyle sent from the rebel fleet last sighted off the northern Netherlands."

"How did that help your identification of Weld?"

"Cobb allowed the messages to be carried to their destination. Two messages were to be delivered here to Weld and Belladonna— but to their real identities."

"And what was the message?" asked Evan.

"Two words—'Now! Doyle.'"

"How did we receive the information before Weld?" continued Evan.

"Cobb delayed the delivery of this message for two days. Weld and Belladonna will get the message tomorrow. We will be prepared."

"What about the fleet?"

"The conspirators sail only at night and by day have been sheltered by the nefarious Dutch. Doyle aims to sail into the Medway under cover of darkness and unload his troops to join Weld's battle-ready troops. They will then move on either to London or the naval dockyard at Chatham."

"We can't stop them," Evan pessimistically concluded.

"We don't have to. Our navy will intercept the fleet. Whitehall and the London garrisons are ready to defend the capital. Our task is to prevent this army being taken over."

John Martin, normally quiet in the presence of superiors, asked, "If we all now know the identity of Weld, why not arrest him immediately, and the army here will be neutralized?"

The other officers mumbled in agreement.

Richard Grey jumped to his feet. "Let me deal with the traitor now."

Luke raised his hand. "No! It is necessary to catch Weld in the act of treason. At the moment, we only possess a one-word message from a known conspirator addressed to Weld's real identity. He could claim he was being framed. Royalists were out to remove this loyal officer from command of the Flanders army. Now that we are aware of the situation, you will simply refuse to pass on Weld's orders to the men and use your men to contain his unwitting accomplices."

"If everything else fails, I will kill him," exclaimed a highly incensed Grey.

He then asked," We have identified Weld, but what about Belladonna?"

"Still a mystery, but knowing the identity of Weld should make our task easier. And we still need to deal with Yarrow. Gentlemen, let's prepare for the coming crisis."

The Loyalist officers were supremely confident that they had matters under control.

They would have the element of surprise.

This confidence was soon shattered—utterly shattered.

Their planning was interrupted before first light by the sudden transformation of the camp.

Lights appeared everywhere, and junior officers could be heard shouting orders across the encampment.

Luke asked Evan to find out what was happening.

His answer shocked the officers.

"The junior officers have orders to have both regiments combat ready to march westward at low tide."

"God save us! It appears that Weld received the critical information before we did despite Cobb's delaying tactics," commented Luke.

"That was probably the real purpose of Liffey's trip to Canterbury. He received information from the enemy fleet, which must be just across the channel, maybe at Dunkirk. A message from there to Dover and on to Canterbury would not take long," Anthony Audley suggested.

"Quicker than Harwich to London to Austin Friars?" asked Evan.

"By a day at least!" replied Audley.

"I cannot see how Liffey can consider he has an effective army. He hardly had any junior officers who are the basic cement of any army," said Luke.

"From what I saw in my brief excursion a few minutes ago, each company had junior officers, none of whom I recognized," Evan replied.

"Sacré bleu!" exclaimed Richard Grey.

"That explains the disappearance of my boats. Luke knows I have been smuggling a few godly officers into the camp. Two days ago, my boats went missing. Liffey has used them to bring in a dozen or more Royalist officers over the last few days."

"I expect one of Liffey's orderlies will soon be knocking on our doors to summon us to take up our posts. Return to your rooms before this gathering is discovered!" said Luke, hurriedly concluding the meeting.

Within minutes, there was a gentle knock on the door.

Isadore, still in her nightwear, burst into the room, crying profusely.

"What is wrong, my lady?"

"It's Christopher."

"What's the problem with Christopher?"

"Luke, I won my little battle, but I suspect I lost yours."

"What do you mean?"

"Christopher came to see me half an hour ago in what I thought was the middle of the night. He told me he had orders to put the regiment into battle mode immediately. He told me that whatever he was about to do was for a higher cause—for God and family honor. He then confessed that he had been appalled by the behavior of his betrothed, and if he survived the imminent crisis, he would break off his engagement and find a more suitable wife."

"I'm glad Christopher has seen sense regarding the obnoxious Lydia, but why did you say you had lost my battle?"

"While Christopher was with me, a new officer knocked urgently on my door and informed him that the fleet was due at any time as it had been seen sailing through the Swale. Is Christopher really Weld?"

"Isadore, that officer could have been talking about our fleet, which is being sent to protect us. It may not refer to the expected Irish/Royalist flotilla."

"But it does. My brother is a traitor."

Isadore burst into further tears.

Luke held her in his arms and tried to console her.

He was interrupted when Liffey's new special messenger, Lieutenant Thornton, knocked on Luke's door and announced, "Colonel, the general requires your presence in the officers' tent within the encampment at dawn."

"What's going on?" asked Luke, feigning ignorance.

"The general has received orders to have both regiments battle ready and on the mainland at the next low tide, which is midmorning."

Just before dawn, the loyal officers made their way up the slight incline toward the officers' tent.

As they approached it, Richard looked alarmed.

"What is it?" asked Luke.

"That group of men in shackles that just passed us under armed guard. They are my officers. Liffey has removed his opposition."

Luke was increasingly apprehensive.

"The tent is surrounded with dozens of armed men. That would not be necessary for a simple briefing of senior officers by the commanding general. I will slip away between these tents to organize our resistance."

The other officers entered the tent.

Armed men immediately surrounded them.

Liffey spoke, "Gentlemen, I am using my powers as general to revoke your commissions. My men will escort you to one of the cellars in the old house where you will remain imprisoned until the current situation clarifies."

"And what situation is that?" asked Audley.

"The army you hear mobilizing around you is to march toward London, aided by several companies of Irish and Royalist veterans soon to land near here—both in the service of Charles Stuart. God save the king!"

A flash of concern spread across Liffey's face.

"Where is that devil Tremayne?"

Audley, Marlowe, Grey, and Williams remained silent.

"I have no time to waste."

Liffey turned to Thornton.

"Find the colonel and kill him."

Luke absconded from the group of officers as they were walking to the tent.

He made his way back to the house to round up his men who had been on guard duty.

He found none.

A servant said troops had arrived before dawn and taken them away.

He thought they were incarcerated in the cellar.

Luke knew that half of his men were on the mainland across the causeway.

He went to his room to arm himself with every weapon he could find.

Suddenly, the door burst open.

It was Strad.

Luke explained the situation, "We won't have to swim across the causeway. One of the barges that transported people and goods to the outdoor banquet is on the beach just down from the causeway. It has a sizable leak, but I'll plug it while you use the pole to propel us across the water."

Just before they left the building, the early-riser Felicity accosted them. "What's going on?"

"Liffey is Weld and has taken control of the army to march on London on behalf of the king. Marlowe, Grey, your betrothed, and most of my men are prisoners in the cellar. I am escaping to organize some resistance, although Whitehall has the big picture under control," replied Luke optimistically.

"If Liffey is Weld, who is Belladonna?" Felicity asked.

"I still don't know but it is now likely to be one of the three women associated with him: Lydia Veldor, Sophia Veldor, or Isadore Liffey. Be careful!"

"They could all be in the plot," mused Felicity.

Strad called out, "There is a detachment of soldiers headed this way led by that new special messenger who I guess is Yarrow wearing a wig. Let's move."

"Quickly, come through my rooms! The far window overhangs the water."

As they scrambled out the window, Felicity gave Strad a heavy bag.

"The diaries will be safer away from here. The translations to date are included. You will find them fascinating reading, but I doubt that they prove Liffey's treachery."

Luke and Strad reached the mainland.

Luke was delighted to find that sixty of his men were there or within an hour's reach.

Luke, John Martin, and Strad discussed the situation. Strad was militant. "Our sixty dragoons could delay that army as they attempt to cross the narrow causeway."

"But only until Liffey brought his mortars into play. No, we let the army march. I am sure that in response to Cobb's message, the London regiments will already be deployed to encircle any enemy outbreak from here. We must concentrate on the people left at Austin Friars."

"To what end?" asked Strad.

"To save their lives."

John Martin was astonished. "Lord Liffey is a fine aristocrat, a general, and a gentleman. He may disagree with us concerning the rightful ruler of England, but he would not slaughter the innocents at Austin Friars."

"You are naive. I fear for the three officers who were in the Indies with him and for the two women, Ursula and Felicity. Some of his actions may have been to cover his identity as Weld, but some may be more concerned with destroying the evidence of some Indies outrage."

"So what is the plan?" asked Strad.

"As soon as the army crosses the causeway and marches away from Austin Friars, we will return there but not across the causeway. We will use the barges to row or pole our way to the far end of the island and approach the manor, hopefully undiscovered by the treacherous guards left behind."

"We must save the women," announced John, eager for some chivalric action.

36

"Let's hope we do not face that problem," said Evan.

"Hopefully, they have all been allowed to leave, although Lady Ursula and Lady Felicity have probably been detained," commented Strad.

"If they are all still there, it will give us another opportunity to uncover Belladonna, but I fear Ursula and Felicity could be dead," Luke gloomily announced.

"Surely, with Weld's identity revealed and the insurrection under way, there is no need for further killings. Ursula and Felicity should be safe," suggested an optimistic Evan.

"I am not so sure. Belladonna is irrational or worse. I cannot see Liffey or even Yarrow battering and then decapitating the head of Lady Penelope. That horrendous act displayed an irrational hatred—it could only be the hand of a very disturbed Belladonna."

It took Liffey's two regiments much longer than Luke anticipated to cross the causeway.

They immediately disappeared from sight as a heavy North Sea fog descended without warning.

Luke was delighted.

It would make it difficult for Doyle's fleet to enter the Medway estuary.

In addition, it could hinder Liffey's army from joining forces with the invaders.

It enabled Luke and his dragoons to reach the manor itself without being discovered.

Luke divided his sixty men into four equal patrols, which he would deploy specifically once he ascertained the opposition he faced.

The dragoons initially hid in the dairy a few yards away from one wing of the house.

Luke and Strad's reconnaissance of the house revealed several servants in the vicinity of the kitchen, twenty men guarding the cellar, and six or seven men patrolling the corridors in the rest of the house.

Ursula's and Felicity's rooms were empty.

Luke took the risk that there were no guards stationed inside the rooms of the other guests.

He found Evadne's room.

He did not knock.

The door was not locked.

He entered quietly.

Just in time, he avoided the blow of a heavy candlestick by grabbing the assailant's hand.

"Evadne, you could have killed me," he announced with relief.

"I thought you were a rogue come to rape me. The aristocracy is not popular with either side at the moment. So Liffey revealed himself as Weld before you could definitely identify him! Who is Belladonna?"

"I thought you might be able to tell me. Chatter among the women now must be very revealing. Are they all still here?"

"Yes, but as prisoners. We have been ordered to stay in the house for two days, then all of us, except for Ursula and Felicity, are free to leave for good."

"Ursula and Felicity are imprisoned with the soldiers?"

"Yes. And I fear for Felicity. The new man with the short light-brown hair is determined to obtain the diaries with their translation. He made it clear that if she did not hand them over by noon tomorrow, she would be tortured and one of her companions shot."

"She cannot comply. I have the diaries, and they are safely housed a long way from here."

"Then you have to rescue her."

"I intend to."

"Can I help?"

"Not really. If all the women were on our side, I would use you to get the soldiers drunk. Fine aristocratic wine could not be resisted. As it is, if I raised that aspect with the women now, Belladonna, whoever she is, could negate it immediately. No, I will ask the female servants that remain in the kitchen to offer the men surrounding the cellar as much refreshment as they can take."

Luke returned to his men.

One unit would ensure no one crossed the causeway.

The second went up the hill to the ordnance tent to obtain any grenades and mortars that the army had left behind.

The third briefed the servants on how to distract as many of the cellar guards as possible.

As these guards left their post for a drink or cuddle in a dark corner with one of the willing wenches, Luke's men dispatched them.

The last group of dragoons, led by Luke himself, would storm the cellar.

Before this assault, it was critical to establish the whereabouts of Yarrow.

As Luke moved through the kitchen, the very old retainer rose from his seat within the large fireplace and stuck out his walking stick to gain the colonel's attention.

"What is it, old man?" asked Luke impatiently.

"The wenches have told me what has happened. I lost two sons and a grandson fighting against the old king. If the new king returns, they will have died in vain," he mumbled almost incoherently.

"Your family has made great sacrifices for our cause," said Luke as he began to move away.

"I can still serve the Lord Protector."

"How can that be?" said Luke, becoming slightly irritated.

"No need to storm the cellar through the external door. There is another entrance from here that has not been opened for years. It is behind that large plate dresser."

Six men moved the dresser to reveal a very thick oak door that was securely locked from inside the kitchen.

No one could have used it to break out of the cellar into the kitchen.

The old man could not remember where the key had gone, and the amount of rust in the lock suggested that it would not work anyhow.

The lock would have to be cut out of the door or wall, but there was no carpenter within immediate reach.

Luke sent his men to the wood heap where in an adjacent shed they found several very sharp axes.

As the men hacked away, Luke asked the old retainer, "What's on the other side of this door?"

"A large wine rack, which, seeing the house was unoccupied for some time before the army arrived, it is probably empty, but axes may be necessary there also."

The door finally moved, revealing a wine rack already pulled aside and Anthony, his daughter Ursula, and betrothed Felicity waiting to flee.

"Great work, Luke! Get the women out of here first," said Audley.

Luke had one of the serving girls lead the two women to Evadne's room with four of his men to stand guard.

The cellar was emptied of the prisoners.

Luke's imprisoned dragoons and Grey's Fifth Monarchist officers as well as Marlowe, Grey, and Audley were rearmed.

Luke led a group of them to confront the guards surrounding the cellar.

Marlowe took another troop back into the cellar in case the guards tried to escape into it.

Audley took a larger group to search the house for any Liffey men and, in particular, to find Yarrow.

Luke confronted the cellar guards with overwhelming force, and Marlowe emerged from the cellar, indicating that the rebel soldiers were completely surrounded.

Luke explained that the officers had misled them and the army had been subverted and was now marching toward London in the service of the king. If they supported such a cause, they were free to chase after Liffey's troops.

Those who took advantage of this would be arrested at the causeway, but it would help separate the duped from the duplicitous.

No one moved.

One of the soldiers exclaimed, "How do we know you are who you claim to be? You may be the Royalists."

Then surprisingly, one of the bedraggled troops spoke up, "No, these are really Cromwell's men. They arrested me several weeks ago."

Two other men supported what the speaker had just said.

They were the three London thieves.

"Why did you give up your lucrative life of petty crime to become a soldier?" asked Evan, attempting some lighthearted humor.

Wally was not amused. "The army has it in for us. We were having a drink and a noisy game of skittles in our local, the Bull and Bear, when the press gang arrived. They shackled us, put us on a barge, and after we berthed at Chatham naval dockyards, they marched us across the muddy foreshore to here. We had no sooner arrived than the officer told us the rest of the army was in battle readiness, but as we were untrained, we would stay behind to guard the traitors in the cellar and protect the rest of the house."

"If you wish to continue in the army into which you were press ganged, remain here. If not, disappear—now."

The three ran toward the causeway—and freedom.

The officers met Audley in Evadne's apartment to review the situation.

Felicity and Ursula were already there, protected by Luke's men.

Luke asked Evadne to describe what happened when Liffey and the troops left.

She revealed that she had gone to Audley's rooms and found a man there who claimed he was now in command.

He said he was Lieutenant Miles Thornton.

He was enjoying food and drink in excessive quantities and slowly sinking into a stupor.

He wore a close-fitting shorthaired wig.

Luke was delighted.

"Yarrow was still in the house a few hours ago," he exclaimed.

Luke took some of his men and headed for Audley's apartment.

Dragoons took up positions at all exits from the room as Luke entered it unannounced.

There were several empty flagons of wine and half-eaten carcasses of roast chicken.

And a discarded light-brown wig.

But the red-haired Yarrow was gone.

Luke's disappointment did not have long to fester when Strad came running to join them.

"Gentlemen, come with me. From the tower, we can see along the coast now that the fog has lifted. The enemy fleet has got through our defenses. It is unloading troops to join Liffey's army, which is patiently waiting for its allies to advance."

The officers climbed up the tower.

Luke was saddened that Liffey's treachery was receiving a boost from these reinforcements.

Then the unbelievable happened.

As soon as all the troops were unloaded, each ship ran down its Saint Patrick's flag and raised that of the protectorate.

Within minutes, the ships turned parallel to the shore, and a cannonade began.

Cromwell's men were bombarding Liffey's army, which was paralyzed by the unexpected turn of events.

As Liffey's subverted army endeavored to maintain some sort of order amid a relentless cannonade from the ships recaptured from Doyle, they were charged by a company of cavalry whose shining breastplates and red jackets and plumed helmets identified them as Cromwell's own lifeguard.

It was a massacre.

Those who survived were in full retreat.

Luke turned to Strad. "Watch the retreating troops! Some, including Liffey, may return here. We must be ready for them."

Luke need not have worried.

Most of the remnants, having faced their first battle experience, deserted.

A few surrendered to the cavalry.

Within half an hour, the government cavalry reached the causeway; and Luke greeted its commander, whom he had met at Whitehall: Captain Asa Glover.

Glover, promoted to colonel to lead the defense of the Medway, explained that he would answer Luke's questions; but first, he wished to contain the few prisoners that had surrendered and were now being escorted by Cromwell's infantry drawn from the London garrisons back to Austin Friars. They would be imprisoned on the island until decisions were made regarding their future.

Luke and his officers entertained Glover, a garrison colonel and a naval captain, at supper that evening.

Luke's first question was direct. "Liffey—dead or a prisoner?"

37

The visitors looked sheepishly at one another.

Glover replied, "Neither! He disappeared."

"You mean he escaped!" remarked Luke bluntly.

"He was last seen heading along the coast in this direction. I sent our ships' long boats along the shore, but they did not find him," said the naval captain.

"He probably has a few barges hidden along the shore and is hiding among the reeds," commented Evan.

"What happened to the enemy fleet?" asked Luke.

"It was allowed to leave Dunkirk, but as soon it reached the English coastline, it was attacked by a superior force of our fighting fleet and boarded by troops from the shore."

"And you replaced the enemy troops with our own men?"

"Yes, as soon as Whitehall received Cobb's message and our fleet reported the movement from Dunkirk, the London units were mobilized and urgent requests sent to major garrisons across the country to send men to London. His Highness even ordered General Monk to send a couple of regiments of infantry south from Scotland by fast frigates," answered Glover.

"You captured the Irish leader, Doyle?" Evan inquired.

"Yes and no," relied the naval captain.

"What does that mean?"

"Unfortunately, our men, remembering the Irish massacre of innocent English settlers a decade and a half ago, gave no quarter to anyone with an Irish accent. Casualties in the invasion force were almost total. A few jumped overboard, and the three that were permitted to surrender were taken to the Tower of London. All of them claim to be Doyle. One of them may be, but more likely, he is dead."

"There is no mistaking Doyle. He has the most blond hair I have seen on any male," said Luke.

"One of the men claiming to be Doyle is white haired," recalled the naval captain.

Richard suddenly announced, "I know where Liffey is headed."

"Where?" asked several officers in concert.

"Christopher is not a hotheaded fool. He is overcautious. He would have had a fallback position in case things went wrong. He is heading for the cave that he and I used to smuggle men onto the island. This would be a relatively safe temporary refuge until he can escape to the continent."

"And that is where Yarrow has probably gone as well," added Evan.

"They would not be able to access that cave yet. The tide is still well in. It's is a pity we can't be there waiting for them. They would spot anyone hidden along the shore and would be wary of any boats sailing in the area," bemoaned Luke.

"Do not despair, Luke!" replied Richard.

"When I knew I was coming to Austin Friars, I mentioned it to several of my congregation in London. One of them told me he had spent his boyhood stealing sheep from this estate. He was an impoverished child from Sheppey Island. They would come through the Chetney Marshes, swim across the various channels, hide in the cave he informed me of, come out at night, grab a sheep, and disappear. The shepherds never found a trace of the missing sheep. Nobody ever saw the thieves. Why? Because the cave had an exit inland, close to one of the outbuildings."

"So we can reach the cave by a land entrance and lie in wait for Liffey to arrive by sea," uttered Evan.

"Great! Richard, you and I and half a dozen men will leave for the cave immediately. Peter and Evan, you liaise with Colonel Glover and organize our so-called prisoners into those who want to remain as recruits for the army for Flanders and those who wish to disappear. There need be no reprisals, except for any captured Royalist officers who only appeared here over the last few days. They are to be shot. Anthony, take your ladies away from here! The library at Rochester Cathedral is holding Lady Penelope's diaries and the translations already done by Felicity. She may wish to continue her work. As we have yet to uncover Belladonna, it is safer for them and Lady Evadne to move to Rochester."

Anthony replied, "A great idea, Luke! I have relatives in Rochester. The ladies can stay there. I will return here tomorrow."

Luke discovered that the land entrance to the cave had not been used for years, perhaps decades. It was completely enclosed within a small shepherd's hut that had a raised slate floor.

After several failures, the relevant slates were lifted.

Tapers were lit, and Luke's group found that after an initial steep descent, their passage to a distant ray of light was easygoing.

Luke and Richard carefully examined the sea entrance to the cave and its surrounds, and they placed their men in appropriate positions.

This area of the cave needed no lights as the reflected daylight through the seaward entrance was sufficient.

As the water level lowered below the entrance to the cave, the waiting soldiers heard the noise of rowing. Just as a boat came into sight containing two men, there was a loud splash.

A third person had jumped in the water and waded into the cave beside the boat.

The wader was a redhead: the hired killer, Yarrow.

The two bargemen hauled their vessel farther into the cave.

Luke and Richard were astonished.

One man was, as expected, Lord Liffey.

The other stunned Luke.

It was Jared Castle.

Luke emerged from behind a large boulder of fallen chalk.

"Welcome, gentlemen! In the name of His Highness, the Lord Protector of the Commonwealth of England, Scotland, and Ireland, I arrest you all on the charge of high treason and for you, Yarrow, several additional charges of murder. Fetter and shackle, Yarrow, and disarm, Castle!"

Castle protested, "No need to include me among this Royalist filth. I am Mr. Thurloe's top agent. I have pretended to stand with Lord Liffey only to gather evidence to ensure his capture and conviction. His arrest now renders my role redundant. I will leave immediately and report the good news to Mr. Thurloe."

Luke was speechless.

His disgust at this critical betrayal almost overwhelmed him.

"You disgust me, Castle! A deceitful silver-tongued varlet to the end! I will not waste the time of our magistrates. As a military tribunal of one, I find you guilty as charged. You will be taken immediately to Sir Evan Williams on the training field. He is about to execute the Royalist officers that his lordship smuggled in through this cave over the last few days. You will join them and be shot within the hour."

"This is unjust. I am like you, a secret agent of the state. Take me to Mr. Thurloe!" demanded a blustering Castle.

"Boy, you are also an agent of our Lady Belladonna, in essence, a double agent with prime loyalty to the exiled so-called king."

"You have no proof."

"In looking over reports sent to me by Mr. Thurloe, I read up on your history. Mr. Thurloe's advisers recommended that you not become part of his organization for a lot of personal, political, and religious reasons. For one, you are a clandestine Papist. One man alone—and he happened to be John Thurloe's favorite agent at the time—pleaded for your appointment. That man has since been revealed as the Royalist spy par excellence John Blair. To assist him in his work, he planted you within the organization. Take him away!"

"Why not add Yarrow to your list for summary execution?" said Richard.

"Yarrow is not a gentleman or first and foremost a political traitor. He has probably been loyal to his revolutionary democratic principles. He fronts me as a criminal—as a cold-blooded, vicious murderer. Quick execution by an experienced firing squad is too easy a death for that creature," replied the vindictive Luke.

A disillusioned Richard turned to his longtime comrade and friend Lord Liffey.

"Why, Christopher? We worked together for five years, and I never once suspected that you would betray our cause. You sacrificed so much to serve Cromwell. I admired your dedication to your duties in the Indies."

"I am glad I could keep my real feelings secret for so long. I was double-crossed and humiliated by your high-and-mighty Protector. I was told in 1652 that I was to be appointed as lord deputy for Ireland. I was one of the few Irish aristocrats that had remained loyal to him through thick and thin."

"And at the last minute, he appointed his son-in-law Charles Fleetwood," added Richard.

"Yes."

"And you were persuaded to change your loyalty by John Blair while you were in the Indies. Apart from your disappointment at your treatment by Cromwell, what did Blair offer you?" asked Luke.

"That if as a second son I had no inheritance of my own, I would be made an earl and given the lands of those peers who had deserted the king. If I inherited my family estates through the premature death of my elder brother, I would be elevated to a dukedom. I would be made a lieutenant general and appointed as second in command to the Marquis of Ormond when the king regained control of Ireland."

Luke commented, "It is getting dark. Richard, escort his lordship back to the house! I will continue his interrogation later. I want a few words alone with Yarrow."

Everybody else left the cave.

Luke primed his pistol and his carbine.

He fired into each kneecap of the shackled Yarrow.

"That is for you several murders."

Although in excruciating agony, Yarrow spat out defiance, "Tremayne, enjoy your little victory. But like all agents of the tyrant, you are a complete failure. Yes, I killed Peebles and reluctantly Lady Marlowe. It was a quick and painless death—with one professional thrust of my dagger. I did not macerate her head. And I did not kill Halliburton. There is another killer at Austin Friars that you are clearly unable to find. And you have failed miserably to uncover the real identity of Belladonna."

Luke then took a heavy oar from the boat and walked up behind Yarrow, intending to strike his head several times.

At the last minute, he changed his mind.

"Your confession regarding Penelope, which intuitively I believe, has saved you from my Old Testament justice. I intended to leave your head in the same condition as I thought you had left hers, but I will show some mercy."

He then shot Yarrow behind the ear and dragged the body into the water.

Luke left the cave, confident that the incoming tide would pull the body out into the estuary, where it would eventually sink into the all-consuming mud.

Summary justice removed any chance that Yarrow and Castle would escape justice through the corruption of civilian magistrates.

And in Yarrow's case, it was very satisfying.

Yet Yarrow's comments niggled away at him.

Who had shown such barbarity toward Penelope?

It could have only been Belladonna, and given Isadore's comments about Liffey's plan to abort the marriage, Belladonna must be Lydia Veldor.

But who had killed Halliburton?

Richard, Anthony, and Peter, the remaining loyal officers of the new army, Luke, and his deputies Evan and John were joined for supper by Asa Glover and the naval captain from the force that had defeated the ineffectual Liffey insurrection.

Luke toasted the group.

"The future is already with us. Asa, your troops can return to their positions in London. Richard and Peter can begin to rebuild the army for Flanders. Anthony, you can retire a few weeks earlier than intended, and my officers and I still have an archtraitor to capture and a possible second murderer to find."

Asa interjected, "Unfortunately, Luke, that is not the future! Before leaving London, I was given various orders depending on what happened in the battle with Liffey."

"And given what happened, what are your orders?" replied Luke.

"I am to take Liffey to the Tower of London, the remaining loyal officers are all to be reassigned other responsibilities, and the recruits still willing and considered sufficiently loyal to form the bases of the Flanders army will be moved to a more convenient training ground at the other end of the Medway estuary. Austin Friars as an army base is no more."

38

"What about my investigation? The arch conspirator against His Highness is still with us and for all we know plotting further action against the government. I know who she is, but I need evidence to confirm my suspicions. I want to keep Liffey here for at least two days as a proper interrogation could give me what I need," asked a very displeased Luke.

"Luke, I fully understand. My men and I will take a day or two in reorganizing the remnants of the new army and escorting them to their new location. You can have at least tomorrow to question Liffey. But be careful! He is a peer of the realm and probably has friends in high places. I would not want him harmed while officially under my protection," replied Asa.

An agitated Richard asked, "What is to happen to Peter and me?"

"I am awaiting further instructions from Whitehall, but they will involve promotions for you both."

"Does that good news come from Thurloe or the army command?" asked Peter.

"Our three senior generals—Lambert, Desborough, and Fleetwood—are all currently in London. I am sure they have kept army interests to the fore."

Early next morning, Luke rode to Rochester. He wanted all the evidence he could obtain from Penelope's diaries before he again interviewed Liffey.

Felicity had completed the decoding.

Much to Luke's disappointment, they added little to the case against Liffey.

Felicity claimed there was nothing that incriminated Liffey as a Royalist agent apart from his frequent meetings with Blair, whom he could argue he believed to be a government agent under the control of Mr. Thurloe.

"But he had denied knowing the man before he was picked up by the *Defiance*," countered Luke.

"Maybe that is why Peebles had to die. Peebles had been following Blair and would have seen them meeting," added Felicity.

She continued, "The meeting with the Spanish admiral that appeared in the letters to his sister potentially damaging was not an act of treachery. Liffey was accompanied to that meeting by Lady Penelope, where, on orders from Whitehall, he negotiated an exchange of prisoners."

Luke thanked Felicity for her work and decided to spend time in the quiet of the cathedral's library to glance through the translations once more.

Felicity was right.

There was little evidence regarding Liffey's political allegiances but plenty concerning the personal life of the Barbados establishment.

Liffey was not the moralistic Puritan of his outward reputation. He liked young boys, and Richmond was clearly his lover. Yet at the same time, he frequently took advantage of Penelope's generosity. Given the warmth of this relationship, which permeated the five years of the diaries, it was unbelievable that Liffey would have ordered Penelope's death. This confirms that her brutal death was solely a Belladonna exercise.

Then Luke read a passage that proved to him Liffey's long-standing perfidy.

Penelope had noted that on a visit to St Kitts, she and Liffey had met the deputy governor of Jamaica whom she describes as having the whitest hair of any person she had seen.

Cobb, when he passed through Austin Friars a few weeks earlier, stated that he had never met Liffey.

As Luke explained to Evan on his return from Rochester, "Liffey not only planned to take over this army but was instrumental in the creation of the rebel forces in the Indies. He did not meet Cobb on St. Kitts. He met his twin brother, the notorious General Doyle. Peebles probably witnessed that meeting, as Blair, whom he was following, was also present. Peebles would have known that his commanding officer, Cobb, was still on Jamaica, and this man was the rebel leader."

Later that day, Luke questioned Liffey.

The general was supremely confident.

He refused to answer any of Luke's and Richard's questions.

He tried to provoke them by highlighting Luke's failure to discover that he was Weld before he showed his hand and Luke's continuing failure to uncover Belladonna.

He did not respond to Luke's references to his lies concerning his knowledge of Blair and his meeting with Doyle.

Luke had no alternative but to terminate the interview.

But Liffey had the last word that was to have fatal consequences.

"Colonel, I am a peer of the realm. The current regime, which is increasing its share of such people, will not permit my execution. I will sit out the next few years under comfortable house arrest and await the destruction of the Cromwellian regime—and then rejoice in the return of the Stuarts."

Richard froze and then screamed, "No, you won't!"

Before Luke could stop him, Richard had primed his pistol and aimed it directly into Liffey's chest, incanting, "In the name of the Lord Jesus, I send you to an eternity in hell."

Death was instantaneous.

Luke was in a dilemma.

"Why did you do that, Richard? Both us are now in serious trouble."

"This agent of the Great Satan would have used his status and corrupt friends to avoid punishment for his murderous and treacherous rampage."

"Richard, hold the body upright and turn it around. I will open the door. We must create the impression that he overpowered you and attempted to escape. I was forced to shoot him in the back as he ran out the door."

Richard maneuvered the corpse into the entrance, and Luke fired.

"To make our story more plausible, I will knock you about."

Before Richard could protest, Luke hit him on the back of the head with the handle of his carbine.

Richard fell to the floor unconscious.

Luke shouted out, calling for assistance.

One of his dragoons and two of Glover's cavalry entered the room.

After viewing the scene, Colonel Glover was not fooled. "I can see how you do the work you do. No loose ends!"

Luke could only manage a weak smile.

Glover called all the officers together.

"I have just received fresh orders from Whitehall. Colonel Grey, as a leading landowner in northern Essex, you have been appointed governor of Harwich and responsible for security in the ports of Suffolk and Essex. You replace Cobb, who should be here shortly to receive his new assignment. Sir Peter, years ago, you expressed a desire to serve under General Monk. He has recently had to dismiss senior officers for a religious fanaticism that threatened army discipline. You will go to Scotland and serve as his colonel in chief. Colonel Grey, you were Cromwell's first choice for that position, but Mr. Thurloe pointed out that your religious views would not be compatible with General Monk's eradication of sectarians from the army in Scotland."

Luke congratulated his two friends.

He volunteered to inform Liffey's sister and betrothed of the general's death.

With Evadne by his side to comfort the grieving women, Luke met Isadore, Sophia, and Lydia.

"Your ladyships, unfortunately, an hour ago Christopher attacked Colonel Grey and attempted to escape. He was shot dead as he ran."

Luke thought this brutal announcement might reveal a vulnerable Belladonna.

He was dramatically proved wrong.

No one shed a tear.

The only emotion that Luke sensed was anger, but was that directed at Liffey's death or at the peer's behavior that had provoked it?

Within two days, Austin Friars was deserted, except for a few servants attached to the house; the ladies Isadore, Lydia, and Sophia and their retinues; and Luke, his officers, and men—and Jane Castle.

The remnants of the army had gone and their tents taken down and transported to their new base somewhere to the east.

Colonel Grey and Lady Evadne returned to their Essex estate, pending Richard's move to Harwich.

Sir Peter Marlowe was tidying up his London affairs and about to depart for Scotland.

All the other guests had returned to their homes.

Luke attempted to keep life at Austin Friars normal for those that remained.

Evan, John, and he dined twice a day with the women, who, through Isadore, expressed their growing resentment at their obvious detention.

"Colonel, you cannot keep us here forever. When will we be free to return to home and to mourn our loss in private?" she asked.

Luke was well aware that he had only a few days at the most to prove that Lydia was Belladonna.

"You will all be home by the end of the week. One of you is a notorious conspirator and Royalist. If you were men and the situation dire, I would send all three of you to the Tower. Or you would all meet an unfortunate fatal accident. Someone murdered David Halliburton, someone smashed Lady Penelope's skull into oblivion and chopped off her head, and someone murdered John Blair and had Timothy Richmond beaten within an inch of his life. The confessed would-be assassin, murderer, and right-hand man to Liffey, Yarrow, claimed as he was about to die that he was not responsible for any of those acts."

"Why would you believe such a man?" asked Lydia.

"A man about to die has no reason to lie. Why confess to three attempts on the life of the Protector yet deny killing a cavalry officer?"

"What then do you intend to do over the next few days?" asked Sophia.

"I will talk to each of you once more with a string of new questions and hope that one of you will be caught out in your answers. I suppose no one wants to confess now. It would save us all a lot of trouble."

Luke waited and sighed. "I'm ever the optimist."

Next morning Simon Cobb arrived.

The two men greeted each other warmly.

Luke was anxious to find out the details of Cobb's operation in Harwich and his capture of Royalist agents acting as messengers between the Irish-Royalist fleet, Austin Friars, and the Royalist cell in the vicinity of Newmarket, which given recent developments was most likely to have been operating out of Veldor Lodge.

Luke asked a crucial question.

"Was the main agent you uncovered a tall man with a limp or a short younger plumpish male with a mop of unruly curly hair?"

"How did you know that that was the very issue I faced? It was the mop of curly hair—Alphonse Dupont. Why do the Royalists use people who are so easily remembered? Yarrow with his incredibly red hair, this Alphonse with his mass of curls, and my own snowy-haired brother."

"Talking of your brother, you are on your way to the Tower after leaving here to see if the one blond prisoner is indeed him?"

"I am, but it will be in vain. My brother is protected by the devil. He will be among the handful of men unaccounted for."

"On another matter, you never met with Christopher Liffey on St. Kitts?"

"No, I've never met the man face-to-face in Ireland, England, or the Indies."

"As I thought. He met with your brother in the very early days of this conspiracy."

Suddenly the relative quiet was destroyed by shouting and screaming women, the crash and breaking of household items, and the shattering of glass."

A female servant confronted Luke, "Colonel, come quickly! Their ladyships will kill one another."

39

A battle was being waged in Lydia's apartment.

Isadore had burst into the room and smashed up everything she could lay her hands on—including Lydia.

Isadore pulled her hair and punched her aggressively in the face.

She began to get the upper hand.

Lydia, struggling to withstand her younger and fitter attacker, withdrew a small ornate dagger from within her bodice and made several swipes at her opponent.

Luke's men dragged them apart.

Lydia was bleeding from the nose and mouth, had two blackening eyes, and, generally, a very puffy face.

Isadore had a small wound in her upper arm where Lydia's flashing blade had found its mark.

It bled profusely.

"This is not the behavior of two aristocratic women. What would your fathers say?" pontificated a moralistic Luke.

Lydia gave an unnecessary and surprising answer, "My father would be proud that I defended the family honor and proclaimed my loyalty to the king."

At the last comment, Isadore broke free of the soldier, picked up a curtain rod that had been dislodged during the brawl, and swung it into Lydia's stomach with such force that she fell to the ground, temporarily winded by the blow.

Isadore was again restrained.

Luke asked the obvious question.

"Isadore, why did you attack the woman who was to be your sister-in-law?"

"That is one big gain from Christopher's death. I do not have to welcome this serpent into our family. Christopher is dead because she used her feminine charms to persuade him to betray himself, his family, and the Lord Protector."

"Roundhead slut!" shouted the furious Lydia, who was just regaining her breath.

Sophia arrived.

Luke explained what had happened.

Sophia was very upset.

She led Luke aside and into the next room.

"Colonel, if only I had told you everything, much of this would not have happened. I told Christopher Liffey the truth just before he led that futile uprising. He passed the basic facts onto his sister who told me that he was about to call off his engagement. In addition, I just received a letter from Mr. Brett outlining the perfidy of a Lydia's servant at Veldor Lodge. There will be another murder here unless you can stop it."

Luke was astounded at what he heard, although it fitted the scenario that had slowly been emerging.

Luke admired Sophia Veldor.

She had been placed in an impossible situation.

Before he could act on the information he had just received, tragedy struck.

After supper, Sophia invited Luke to her room to expand on her earlier revelations and to advise him in planning an effective response.

Luke poured them both a glass of Bordeaux.

Too late, he knocked Sophia's glass to the floor.

He should have been prepared for this.

Belladonna had used the same method earlier: poisoned wine.

Sophia wriggled in agony.

Luke stuck his fingers down her throat and upended the writhing matron.

Miraculously, Sophia vomited and vomited and vomited.

Her eyes began to focus once more.

She whispered, "The monster within her has returned," and lapsed into unconsciousness.

Luke called for Evan to look after Sophia while he ran to Isadore's room to prevent her from succumbing to a similar attack.

A servant of Lydia's accosted him before he reached his destination and insisted he visit her mistress in the Audley's old apartment, where he would hear the truth about Belladonna.

Luke was on his guard.

Sophia's information had amazed, disgusted, and alarmed him.

He entered Ursula's old room to find Lydia sitting in one of the two large chairs with two glasses already full of deep-red Bordeaux placed on the table.

This was too obvious.

Luke sat in the remaining chair across the small wine-laden table.

Lydia did not waste time.

"Tremayne, you are the Satanic instrument that murdered my beloved. You did not tell us that you fired the fatal shot. It was completely unnecessary. Christopher, even if he escaped that room, was still surrounded by several concentric circles of your troops. It was cold-blooded murder, fitting your reputation for brutality. For that, you must pay!"

"And how, my lady Belladonna, are you going to accomplish that? I am a heavily armed soldier—and strongly built male. You are a weak woman with at the most a small dagger," replied the chauvinistic and overconfident Luke.

Belladonna smiled.

"Don't expect me to drink your poisoned wine," Luke continued.

"You are an arrogant fool, Tremayne, and you have only minutes to live."

Without warning, Belladonna put her hand into an open casket that lay on the table.

From it she threw into Luke's face a handful of fine powder, which he could not avoid inhaling.

Almost immediately, he felt the strength flowing from his body.

She threw another couple of handfuls in his direction.

He knew he should avoid breathing it in, but his body was not reacting to his commands.

Although he was completely conscious, he was now paralyzed, unable to move a muscle.

"Something a little stronger than Belladonna, my dear colonel! And now you must die—for Christopher and the king."

Belladonna rose from her chair and withdrew her fine dagger from somewhere in her clothing.

"I will cut your throat, and there is nothing you can do to stop me."

Luke had to agree.

It was not a fitting conclusion to his illustrious career that his life should end with the slash of a woman's dagger.

He had no resistance as Lydia pulled back his head by his hair to reveal more of his throat.

Suddenly, there was loud shouting; and a large cupboard against the wall disintegrated as three men shouting and waving their arms ran at Belladonna, knocking the dagger from her hand and her to the ground.

Belladonna outnumbered, rose, and ran from the room, unsure about what had just happened.

Luke's equally traumatized rescuers were in no state to follow her.

As Luke began to sense the feeling slowly returning to his body, his rescuers began to tremble.

Luke was overwhelmed. "You took a great risk. The witch could have stabbed one or all of you. I won't ask why three thieves are not already back in London. I saw you heading down the London road a day or so ago. Harry, Wally, and John, you saved my life."

Harry was so overcome with what they had just done that he grabbed for a glass of wine from the table.

Luke was still not strong enough to move.

He managed to shout, "Don't, Harry, it's poisoned."

He was too late.

Harry consumed the whole glass in one gulp.

Luke looked on unbelievingly.

Harry jovially commented, "Don't worry, Colonel. We saw the lady drink a glass or two before she refilled it when you came. If it is poisoned, then your would-be murderer would be long dead."

Within ten minutes, Luke had fully recovered and refrained from commenting on the stash of jewelry and silver plate that he saw among the wreck of the cupboard from which the London thieves had emerged.

"Thanks again, lads! I must follow that nefarious Belladonna, and you must leave for London immediately before the inhabitants here find their valuables have disappeared."

Luke found Evan, and both went to Isadore's room.

She was gone.

There was no body, but there were signs of a struggle and much damage to the infrastructure of the room.

"Hopefully, Lydia was just returning the favor for Isadore's demolition of her room," said Luke.

"Maybe, but where is Isadore?" asked an anxious Evan.

Luke ordered a complete search of the house and grounds.

Luck was with Luke, Strad, and their men.

The old retainer reported that he had pretended to be asleep when three women ran past his seat in the fireplace.

"Two of them were half dragging and half carrying the third," he explained.

"Three women?" repeated an incredulous Luke.

The old man nodded assent.

"Where did they go?"

"Up the narrow stairs that lead to the tower."

"Good, we have them!" said Strad. "They are trapped."

"Maybe, but let's reach them before they commit another murder."

"They would not harm Lady Isadore, would they?" commented Strad, still coming to terms with the extent of female vindictiveness.

"Strad, Belladonna came within an inch of killing me. Think how she might treat an innocent girl, but I am surprised there are three women," said Luke.

"Who is the third?" asked Strad.

"It must be a servant that Belladonna has forced to help her," replied Luke.

After a minute or two of contemplation, Luke continued, "Strad, we must prepare for the worst. Get all the mattresses, everything that is soft—dozens of cushions, wagons filled with hay bales. We must soften a fall should one of women tumble over the edge!"

"Pushed or thrown by the other two, you mean," retorted an incredulous Strad.

Luke, with two of his men, climbed the stairs up into the tower. As they reached a middle level, a door barred their farther ascent as it was locked from the inside.

Minutes were lost as the soldiers tried, eventually successfully, to force open the heavy door.

As they finally entered the upper reaches of the stairs, they heard Isadore screaming.

As Luke burst out onto the roof of the tower, a female voice shouted out, "If you come any farther, you are a dead man. We are both armed."

Luke was taken aback.

It was now his turn to misjudge the female conspirators.

He had not expected the quarry to be armed with pistols.

He did not stop.

He rushed at the women.

A shot hit his arm. Another grazed his earlobe.

He quickly withdrew.

He watched with horror through the half-open door of the stairwell as the women carried Isadore to the edge of the tower and attempted to lift her over the parapet.

It was now or never.

If they killed Luke, his men who followed would be successful.

The women would have no time to reload.

Luke flung the door open and rushed at the women, followed closely by two dragoons.

One of the women was on top of the parapet, trying to pull Isadore up, while the other was pushing from below.

Luke threw himself across the roof and grabbed Isadore around the waist.

A shot rang out from the ground, and Belladonna, who was standing on the parapet, fell back onto the tower roof.

She was wounded—but not fatally.

Strad was a brilliant shot.

Once again, his expert marksmanship had saved the day.

Luke looked down at the crowd gathering below. He wished to thank Strad on his effective marksmanship.

Strad had not fired the shot.

He was yards away from the crowd, just emerging from the house with a large mattress.

Standing to the side of the spectators, with a smoking musket at her feet, was Sophia Veldor.

40

On the top of the tower, Isadore sank into Luke's arms and sobbed uncontrollably as his men shackled her two assailants.

Lydia was bleeding profusely from a flesh wound and hysterically defiant, "You never discovered that I was Belladonna, and you were never aware that I had two other members of the Garden with me the whole time. Meet Foxglove!"

Jane Castle did not acknowledge her Garden pseudonym.

Luke could not help remarking, "Mr. Thurloe will be devastated—his organization infiltrated by three Royalist agents."

Lydia continued to rant, "What a lucky shot from your man. Otherwise, this Cromwellian slut would be dead."

"No, Lydia, it was not one of my men that shot you. It was your mother."

"That evil witch. She put me away as a child because I got rid of my little brother. He was a pest, so when no one was looking, I put him in the oven."

Even Jane looked shocked.

"You don't have the satisfaction that your identity remained a secret. Your servant Alphonse revealed all to Colonel Cobb who arrived here this morning, and your mother has told me of your horrific past. We were simply waiting for you to act. Why did you desecrate the body of Lady Penelope after Yarrow had killed her?"

"That whore could have destroyed too many lives—and she had slept with Christopher too many times. My honor demanded her complete obliteration."

Lydia began to wail, as if demented.

As she was.

Later that day, the remaining inhabitants of Austin Friars gathered for a final early supper.

Despite Sophia's pleas that her daughter, whose wound proved superficial, should stay under her care, Luke had Lydia heavily bound, hooded, and removed in an escorted covered wagon.

Her destination was Bedlam.

A distraught Sophia left for her estate, Veldor Lodge.

Isadore accepted Sophia's invitation to reside with her until matters of her inheritance and any possible marriage negotiations were sorted.

Luke was in two minds concerning Jane Castle: should she be executed as a traitor or persuaded to serve Cromwell as a double agent whose basic loyalty had been readjusted?

He had one last conversation with her.

"Jane, how did you become involved with the Garden?"

"It was all John Blair's idea—the Caribbean fleet and the Garden. He was the brains behind it all, although he received his orders from a leading courtier whom he refused to name. It was all an experiment. A group of inexperienced mavericks and a disgruntled general were manipulated into attempts at assassination and army subversion, which would cost mainstream Royalists very little but reveal how the government responded. John, Jared, and I quickly realized that Lydia was ill suited to her role as both betrothed and leader of the enterprise. I was surprised that Liffey did not discover her unsuitability earlier."

"Blair and then Jared and yourself fed Thurloe snippets of information about the Garden that, while true, did not reflect the whole picture?"

"Blair happily revealed to Thurloe that he was pretending to be a Royalist plant in the organization but kept our involvement secret. You were looking for one man and one woman when there were two men and two women active here at Austin Friars, not counting Yarrow."

"Thurloe will be shattered to discover that the three agents he used in this operation were, in fact, Royalist double agents. I don't know what to do with you, Jane. Should you be summarily executed, or could your undoubted talents be put to use in the service of the Protector?"

The decision was taken out of his hands.

As the tide receded, an ornate coach squished its way across the causeway.

Given that it had an escort of four lifeguards, Luke was prepared for its occupant. John Thurloe, closest adviser and chief minister to Oliver Cromwell and head of the government's huge and expensive intelligence network, stepped from the vehicle.

He met with the remaining officers.

"As a matter of urgency, I have orders for Colonel Cobb."

"What are they?" asked an anxious Simon.

"Will you accept command of the two regiments of troops that were being trained here at Austin Friars? In accepting this position, you are to move immediately to a new location farther along the coast, Medway Court. You will enter this new post with the rank of major general."

Luke was delighted for his one-time deputy.

Thurloe then turned to the rest of the group.

"A job well done, Luke! His Highness is delighted, so much so that he wishes you to undertake a very personal mission on his behalf. I will take Jane Castle back to Whitehall for interrogation and punishment. The Protector has sent you a separate note."

Luke opened the letter that bore the seal of the Lord Protector. It was simple.

Good friend, humor Thurloe regarding the Royalists who infiltrated his organization. Do not reveal this intelligence catastrophe to anybody. It is not in the interests of national security. But it does convince me that the last line of defense, which has never failed me, is the army. Consequently, I want you to undertake a special and personal mission on my behalf.

Report to the parish church, Chatham, noon three days hence.

Oliver

Luke smiled broadly.

It irritated Thurloe. "Don't be too pleased with yourself, Luke. You have once again effectively dealt with most aspects of this case, but the security problems remain, and there are still one or two criminal matters outstanding."

"What do you mean, John?" asked Luke, feigning innocence.

"The murder of Halliburton and Blair remain unresolved!"

"Peebles killed Blair, and despite his denial, Yarrow probably murdered Halliburton," lied Luke, whose emotionless face had won many a card game.

Privately, he was convinced that his good friend Anthony Audley had exacted revenge on Halliburton for the abuse of Ursula when she was little more than a child. Anthony could not have done it himself; but he knew many an explosives expert who, for a price, could have effected the execution.

Luke's conscience on this was clear. He lived increasingly by the Old Testament system of revenge. An eye for an eye was an uncomplicated and effective concept of justice.

The corruption and delays of the current legal system reinforced his tendency to exact summary justice.

Luke continued, "And what is the remaining security problem?"

"We have just crushed a half-baked attempted coup led by an inexperienced madwoman, a disgruntled rogue general leading a partly trained army, and an Irish fanatic whose tiny fleet was no match for even a small flotilla of our navy. The Royalists will try again. I am convinced that this episode was a pathetic trial to see how we would respond—a test of how many troops we could put against an invasion force and how quickly we could mobilize them."

Luke had a grudging admiration for Thurloe's acumen. His assessment of the situation was identical to Jane Castle's confession of Royalist intent.

Thurloe concluded, "A more dangerous invasion, which is imminent, will involve the professional navies of Spain and Holland and troops from Spain or experienced Royalist veterans currently fighting in European armies. Even the strategy of this group of no-hopers was wrong. They landed too far away from their objectives. To come ashore near the Chetney Marshes and then try to march on London was time-consuming and therefore self-defeating. It gave us the time we needed to organize our defenses. They should have landed at the other end of the Medway Estuary, captured our dockyard and its facilities at Chatham, and waited for reinforcements that would outnumber our depleted London reserves."

Luke, despite Cromwell's advice, could not resist a final jibe.

"Let's not denigrate our achievements totally. This bunch of no-hopers included three very skilled Royalist operators."

Thurloe, in return, delivered a telling blow, "By the way those letters from Lady Ashcroft, Liffey's sister, were not innocent family epistles. Acton discovered many concealed a coded message. For example, 'Regards from our dearest *Irish* friends. Your return *fleet* leaves when? *Must* you *sail Christmas* Day or later and confront the hurricanes?'"

"And what does it really tell us?" asked a cynical Luke.

"If you take the fifth word and then the following fourth and then the third and so on, it reads 'Irish fleet must sail Christmas.'"

Thurloe then adroitly changed the subject, "Where did this madwoman get her funds?"

"Not from her mother! Apparently, after the incident with her brother, Lydia was basically sent to France and imprisoned in a closed convent with the hope that the nuns might in time cure her of her problems. In recent years, her irresponsible father took her out of the protection of the nuns and groomed her for the role she was to play. As Baron Veldor has no funds of his own, he was obviously the conduit for funds from other wealthy Royalists on the continent."

"And why the elaborate secret code names of various plants? This is a sure sign of their lack of experience. Real spies don't have time for such games," scoffed Thurloe.

"Sophia told me that for over a decade, Lydia's condition was so severe that even within the closed convent, she was confined during daylight hours within a high-walled and locked herbal garden. Her only friends, which she talked to on a daily basis, were the herbs within the garden. It was one of the few things that she could translate back into the real world."

"Was Liffey aware of her condition?"

"Not until the eve of his insurrection. The Baroness Veldor told him of his betrothed's instability, and from what he told his sister, he must have realized that she was a killer and responsible for the desecration of his friend Penelope's body. Until almost the end, Liffey's ambition, and the brainwashing by his father and Baron Veldor, who were both determined to unite their families and produce an heir, blinded all three to the complete unsuitability of Lydia for any normal life. Blair and then the Castles tried to keep the enterprise on the rails."

In a moment of unexpected sympathy, Thurloe concluded, "From the beginning, this was an inane plan, concocted by out-of-touch Royalist extremists who manipulated the insane and disgruntled for the maintenance of family dynasties rather than the return of the Stuarts—a sad reflection on a father who sacrificed his disabled daughter for his selfish ends."

Printed in the United States
By Bookmasters